THE WOLVES
OF PARIS

THE WOLVES OF PARIS

A Novel

DANIEL P. MANNIX

ISBN: 979-8-3372-0038-5

This edition published in 2025 by Open Road Integrated Media, Inc.
180 Maiden Lane
New York, NY 10038
www.openroadmedia.com

In memory of my dear little wife, Jule.
Our last book together.

INTRODUCTION

There has never been an authenticated case of wolves in this hemisphere making an unprovoked attack on a human. The North American wolf and his European cousin are virtually identical, yet we have numerous stories of wolves attacking humans in Europe. As late as 1918, a woman was killed by wolves in France, and even today there are accounts of wolves killing villagers in Russia. Is the European wolf, then, more aggressive than the North American, or are these tales merely legends?

There is no doubt that there have been man-eating wolves. The most famous of these was La Bête du Gévaudan, who lived in France during the middle of the eighteenth century and certainly killed at least sixty people and possibly over a hundred. This wolf—or possibly wolves, as there may have been two of them—preyed on humans from 1764 to 1767. He then attacked a girl, who stabbed him in the neck with a homemade bayonet. The wolf ran off, but was followed and shot by a M. Antoine. The girl was able to identify the stab wound. This animal was five feet, seven inches long and weighed 130 pounds. The killings, however, continued, and another wolf was shot after it had devoured a child. The remains of the child were found in its stomach.

Some wolves that attacked humans were probably rabid. However, neither of these animals showed any signs of rabies. One was mated and had cubs. Both were well fed and healthy. Still, it may be that they were not pure wolves, but wolf-dog crosses. They were of an unusual color and the formation of their muzzles and heads was unlike that of ordinary wolves. Wolves have a natural fear of humans, while a wolf-dog hybrid is typically far more aggressive. Domestic dogs that have gone feral will often attack humans, especially children. For this-reason, I have made Courtaud a wolf-dog cross, although nothing is known of his background before he appeared at the gates of Paris in 1439.

During the Hundred Years War in France, conditions were ideal for producing man-eaters. The country was desolated, corpses were common, and mortally wounded men, women, and children who could offer no resistance lay in the ruins of the sacked villages. This is the classical pattern for producing man-eaters. The two lions that killed so many coolies working on the Mombasa-Uganda Railway in East Africa during 1898 that construction of the line had to be stopped for several weeks, became maneaters in much the same way. Many of the coolie laborers died and burial units were paid to inter them. While I was in Kenya, I was told by several men who remembered the lions (although J. H. Patterson, who finally succeeded in killing the man-eaters, does not say so in his famous *Man-Eaters of Tsavo*) that the burial teams often simply left the bodies in the bush to save themselves trouble. The lions found the corpses and, since lions, like wolves, are scavengers, learned to eat them. The lions would then run toward the burial teams expecting to be fed, which they promptly were, as the men dropped any body they were carrying and fled. Soon the lions would run toward any group of men and if the men did not feed them, the lions in a rage would attack them, apparently feeling that the men were withholding their food. These lions became so wedded to human flesh that they would ignore freshly killed zebras or live goats to seek out humans. They were finally lured in by using live humans as bait, protected by a cage made of railroad rails.

The bears in Yellowstone Park exhibit a similar pattern. They go to cars expecting to be fed. If no food is forthcoming, the angry bears often attack the people. This has become so common that now visitors are forbidden to feed the bears.

During the Middle Ages, wolves were so much dreaded that special shelters called "spittals" were built in Scotland where travelers could take refuge overnight in wolf-infected areas. In their outstanding work, *The Wolves of North America* (pp. 128–149), Stanley Young and Edward Goldman give a long list of apparently genuine cases of wolves attacking humans. Virtually all these cases occurred in Europe, and the few attacks recorded in North America are not well authenticated. Mr. J. Curran of Sault Sainte Marie, Ontario, Canada, offered a reward for any proven case of wolves attacking humans in this hemisphere. None was forthcoming. In 1940, Mr. Curran expressed the opinion, "Any man who says he's been et by a wolf is a liar."

It must be remembered that when Europeans arrived in North America, they had firearms. The medieval peasant was generally unarmed except for a staff and a knife. It is true that the American Indians had no better weapons than the serfs, but they were experienced woodsmen and, moreover, they had no domestic animals (except dogs) which served as bait to lure the wolves in. Also, there was plenty of game in this continent, so that the wolves were not tempted to attack humans. The great battues, or hunts, that swept the forests clear of game in the Middle Ages forced wolves in Europe to find other food, and the constant wars made human flesh readily available.

My information on Courtaud comes from two sources. One is Ernest Thompson Seton's *Great Historic Animals* (New York: Charles Scribner's Sons, 1937). The other is *Le Journal d'un bourgeois de Paris sous Charles VI et Charles VII, de 1405 à 1449,* Modern French text by Roger H. Guerrand (Paris: *Livre club du libraire,* no. 138, 1963). The bourgeois tells us that in one week of September 1439, Courtaud (or Courtaut as it is sometimes spelled) and his pack killed fourteen people. He was held in such dread that the usual farewell to anyone leaving the city was "Beware of Courtaud!" My account of his death comes from Seton.

The present efforts on the part of "sportsmen" to exterminate the few remaining wolf packs in this hemisphere are. of course, completely unjustified. They are apparently prompted by gunners who think this will leave them more caribou and deer to slaughter for their own purposes. Wolves are perhaps the most interesting and intelligent of all wild animals, and should be preserved.

D. P. M.

THE WOLVES
OF PARIS

ONE

The Fugitive

Even as the half-grown wolf cub made another desperate effort to force his way through the snowdrifts, he knew his strength was fading fast and soon his pursuer would be on him. Still he fought on through the quicksandlike snow. Make a two-foot jump. Bring the hind feet up beside the forefeet. Rest a few seconds. Jump again. His mouth was open now. His tongue hung out. Each burning breath he took sent puffs of white vapor into the cruel cold. No one could have guessed, watching the beaten, tortured animal, that a few years later he would be Courtaud, the Werewolf, who could drive a thousand men before him, hold Paris at siege for three months in the terrible winter of 1439, and every day devour a man as a dog might a bone.

A mile behind him came the *louvetier*, the professional wolf-hunter. The *louvetier* was a little man with high cheekbones, a flat nose, a short head, and skin the color of smoked beef. He was a Lapp, especially imported from Norrland for this hunt. For three months now, ever since this wolf had suddenly arrived from nowhere in the High Ardennes in northern France, he had been killing the peasants' sheep. Unlike ordinary wolves, who kill only what they need and devour their prey to the last shred, this strange wolf killed for pleasure. He had no fear of man. He would force his way into a fold, kill the guardian dog, and butcher twenty ewes, eating only the choicest portions from one or two. If the shepherd dared to challenge him, he would turn on the shepherd. At last the peasants living in this remote, inaccessible plateau sent for help to the Flemish merchants who purchased their wool, although it was well known that the Flemings had a purse for a heart and boasted, "We buy a sheep from the peasants for a groat and sell them back the tail for a guilder." Hard men of business the Flemings might be, but they had no wish to see the Ardennes flocks wiped out. So, through their connections with the all-powerful Hanseatic League, they had brought down this *louvetier* to eliminate the menace. The Lapps were experts at killing wolves. They had to be in order to preserve their vital reindeer herds.

Why did not the man sink in the soft snow when even the wolf's broad, furry feet could not support him? Strapped to the soles of the Lapp's boots were flat strips of wood, a palm's breadth wide and as long as the man was tall. These curious devices spread his weight over the snow and sustained him. By means of a pole held in either hand he propelled himself along, sliding over the snow as a skater might slide over ice. Although it was hard for him to go uphill, he could speed downhill faster than thought. People who saw him screamed and crossed themselves, calling on the saints to protect them from such witchcraft.

The little hunter seemed to carry no weapon except the skinning knife in his belt, but when he lifted his right-hand pole, the morning sun flashed on the tip. It was a spearhead, ground to such an edge that the man shaved with it. On the pole were three hundred notches, each for a wolf killed by the pole. Before noon, there would be three hundred and one and the *louvetier* would have the wolf's fell, or undressed skin, packed on his back and be able to claim the ten gold ecus, he had been promised for the *loup-garou's* head.

For three days the *louvetier* had tracked the wolf, taking up the trail by a fold full of slaughtered sheep. Now with victory only a bowshot away, the tough little man was still apprehensive. He hated this curious country. It was studded with weird-looking hills that seemed to have sprung up by themselves, cut by ridges, and crisscrossed by deeply eroded rivers and narrow ravines, which made it very unlike the safe, broad, tundralike plains of his home. He looked up nervously at the hanging masses of snow clinging to the cliffs above him and prayed to his gods to bring him safe back to the flat country of Norrland.

Also, this animal he was pursuing was different from any wolf he had ever seen. The beast was enormous. It must weigh more than he did and, standing on its hind legs, be four handsbreadths taller. He could put his whole hand in the creature's footprint and leave space around it. Such a brute would have been unusual enough in the far north. Here in France it was unbelievable. Also, it was a curious russet color with a white mark on the chest. In addition to their usual gray, wolves ranged in color from black to white, but he had never seen one like this. Lastly, the animal's head was all wrong. The muzzle was shorter than a wolf's should be and the skull looked rounder. Ah well, he would soon be up to it and then he would see if the *loup-garou,* bogged down in the two-foot snow, could withstand his spearhead. As he prepared for the last rush, the *louvetier* dropped his fur jacket, tossed away his cap made of wildcat hide, and discarded his heavy gloves. Now, stripped to his shirt, trousers, and tipped boots, he was as light and unencumbered as possible. On the way back, he could pick up his clothing.

Several times during the last three fearful days the young wolf had considered turning to meet his pursuer. If the hunter had retreated or shown any signs of fear, the wolf might well have attacked. Unlike other wolves, he had no innate fear of man, yet he knew well that men could be dangerous. He was convinced that this man would not dare to follow him so, unless the creature possessed some deadly weapon. So he had fled. Now he could flee no longer. The time had come to make a stand. Even as the young wolf sensed this, he topped a little rise and saw below him the surface of a frozen lake, swept clean of snow by the wind.

At the sight, the wolf felt returning confidence. Half rolling, half swimming, he plunged down the slope and reached the ice. Although he skidded badly on the slippery surface, now at last he could run. And run he did.

When the *louvetier* reached the crest of the rise and saw the wolf speeding across the lake, he cursed, then with a jab of his poles he sent himself flying down the slope. On the hard, frozen surface of the lake his skis could get no hold, but by pushing himself with his poles he made fair progress.

Ahead was a single peak draped with snow rising directly from the lake shore. The rising sun caught this peak, turning it into a silver arrowhead. Like a giant tombstone the peak overhung man and animal; to the Lapp it seemed like an ogre bending down to seize him or fling the mantle of snow that clung to its crest over him as he would throw a net on a mired-down hare. He shrank from it, yet it was toward this peak that the wolf ran. The *louvetier* could not understand why: the snow had drifted so heavily here that the animal was sure to be bogged in it. Wolves kept to a specific range which they knew by heart and always followed the same route, especially when pursued, because experience had taught them that this was the easiest way to travel. Yet there was no sign of a trail through the drifts ahead, nor up the mountainside.

The wolf reached the end of the lake and hesitated. He ran back and forth, seeking some way through the drifts, only to find himself trapped. Then at long last he turned at bay. His head went down and his ears were laid back. His tail rose and went rigid. The muzzle wrinkled and the long canine teeth were bared in a snarl. He crouched slightly, gauging the angle of his spring.

At the sight, the *louvetier* became jubilant. He dropped his left pole and seized the other with both hands, aiming the spearhead at the wolf's white breast. Taking care that his skis did not slip from under him, he came on slowly. The wolf watched him with its yellow slit eyes, taut as a bowstring as it prepared for the charge. So big was he and so obviously determined to go down fighting that the Lapp was somewhat perturbed. To give himself courage and also to daunt the wolf, he shouted his tribal war cry.

At the man's shrill cry, the great curtain of snow that hung from the side of the peak seemed for an instant to gather itself together. Then a crack zigzagged across its top where it joined the stone. Almost as fast as a jagged flash of lightning, the crack jumped along the smooth face of the snowbank. For a while nothing happened. Then slowly and majestically the snow curtain left the side of the peak and began to slide downward. For a few seconds it seemed to float like a giant feather. Then its fall became faster and faster as the avalanche gathered speed.

So intent were man and wolf on each other that they did not notice the menace above them until the light was suddenly obliterated by the falling mass. Both looked up. The wolf reacted first. He spun around and threw himself into the nearest drift. Wildly he fought his way in deeper and deeper, while behind him came the roar of hundreds of tons of snow plunging down the slope. For a long time the wolf lay trembling as crash followed crash. Even when all was still, he dared not move but lay in his cave, gasping at the air filtering through the snow.

At last he began to dig himself out. It was a long task and, tired as he was, he had to rest several times. Finally the dark wall around him grew translucent and he burst out into the light and, best of all, into fresh air. He bolted mouthfuls of it into his lungs. Then he floundered out toward the lake.

Before him lay the body of the Lapp. The edge of the avalanche had caught the little man and hurled him against an ice-covered rock. The wolf crouched down, watching carefully for some motion. He could smell the heavy, rancid odor of the man but there was no scent of blood and, for all he knew, the man might also be crouched motionless watching him. Gradually he realized the man's eyes did not focus and he was limp, not tense. Still suspicious, the wolf rose and circled the still figure. He came closer, grabbed the man's leg, dragged him a few inches, let go, and jumped back. Still no response. Again the wolf came in and this time satisfied himself by both nose and eyes that his enemy was dead.

For three days the young wolf had taken violent exercise and had not eaten. He was wild with hunger and, curiously, had no fear of man-smell. He came in for the third time and began to feed on the corpse. It was the first time he had ever eaten human flesh, but he found it sweet and tender.

The wolf pup was born in the kennels of the Count Raoul de Villeneuve in the *pays,* or region, of Champagne. The count was only moderately fond of hunting so he maintained no more than six hundred dogs of various breeds in his castle (a true hunting enthusiast like Count Gaston de Foix had a kennel of 1,600 hounds). Hunting was not only a sport, it was a necessity, for the castle depended on wild game as its main source of meat. The pup was born on a cold, windy evening in March, together with five brothers and sisters. His mother was a bitch wolf that had been dug out of a den three years before and kept for her urine, which was used as a bait to trap other wolves. She was chained to an iron ring in the wall and after giving birth went frantic with anxiety, for all around her were dogs fascinated by the newborn pups and she feared they intended to hurt the tiny creatures. In her hysterical efforts to save them, she would seize a pup in her jaws, run back and forth seeking some place to hide it, and by shoving the wretched, squirming little thing into some crack, wedge it securely by pushes with her long nose, and then hurry back to grab another. She kept this up all night and by morning, only one of the litter was left alive.

When the chief veneur, the master hunter, came at daylight, he was furious at having lost the bitch wolf's litter. He had had no idea that she was in whelp, for there was no male wolf in the castle. He was the only human who could go near her, and the bitch wolf allowed him to unsnap her chain and even to pick up the one remaining pup that had survived the ordeal. The man took her with her pup to a quiet room, provided her with food and water, and then left mother and pup alone. After hiding the pup under some straw, the mother quieted down. Although she would not eat, she lapped some water and then retrieved the pup only just in time to keep him from being suffocated. She licked all the human scent from him and then with her wonderful, all-purpose nose guided him to one of her dugs. The blind, toothless, hairless baby instinctively began to gum the hard teat and after a little managed to make the glorious warm milk flow. He nursed and nursed until he fell asleep.

The pup grew quickly, for he did not have to compete with littermates for his mother's supply of milk. When his eyes were open, in two weeks, the veneur took them back to the main kennels and the female was again chained to the ring. The pup was allowed to roam around as well as his clumsy baby feet could carry him and meet the dog pups that were about his age. Although the hounds were generally confined to the kennels, most of the other dogs were allowed the run of the castle and at meals fought over the bones the diners tossed among the rushes covering the floor.

At first the pup was almost pathetically eager to be friends with everything and everybody he met. He was so trusting and anxious to please that even the terriers with their hair-trigger tempers tolerated him. Utterly fearless, he several times wandered out of the kennels into the castle's bailey. This was a vast courtyard of almost constant activity. Women filled their buckets at the well, the count's men-at-arms—or gendarmes, as they were called—lounged about, squires in puffed sleeves and pointed shoes ran from the kitchen to the great hall bearing plates of food, and hawks screamed and shook their bells. Men galloped recklessly through the crowd on their way to the stables, and the pup would surely have been tramped to death or killed by an unfriendly cur if some well-disposed person had not carried him back to his overwrought mother. The pup accepted all this casually. To him, one place was as good as another.

This careless attitude began to change when he was a month old. By then, he was becoming suspicious of new places and strangers, either animal or human. His puppy innocence gradually left him and he came to realize that anything strange was potentially dangerous. At the same time, he began to react drastically to any sudden stimuli. A man's quick movement, a horn blown unexpectedly, the whiff of an unknown scent, caused him to recoil with incredible quickness. Even after he was satisfied that the alarm was needless, it took him some time to relax again. The dogs were puzzled and the men amused at his nervousness, but in a wild state either an animal reacts instantly to any strange event or it is dead.

Even though mother and pup were closely attached, each found the other's conduct confusing. Especially bewildering to the pup was his mother's attitude toward a certain great alaunt that strode grandly about the castle, the count's special favorite and the lord of all the other dogs. The alaunts were the biggest of all the dogs and were used on dangerous game such as wild boar and bears. They were also employed as watchdogs.

Whenever this particular alaunt went past, the pup's mother would put her tail between her legs, lower her haunches, hump her back, and put her ears down in token of abject submission. Often she would crouch down, whimpering, and try to crawl toward him. She always seemed astonished when he paid no attention to her. If the pup were nearby, his mother would pick him up in her mouth and hold him out to the alaunt as though she expected the haughty brute to be charmed by the little wiggling creature. When the pup was in the process of being weaned, his mother would regurgitate partly digested food for him, and the pup soon learned to encourage her to do this by nibbling and licking at the corners of her mouth. If the alaunt were there, the mother would stand back, holding her head high so the pup could not reach it, and watch the giant dog hopefully as though she expected him to join in the feeding of the pup, which, of course, he never did.

The pup was even more surprised by his mother's attitude toward fighting. When he was small, he and the other pups would tussle and roll about while his mother watched with pleasure. But by the time he was six months old and had his adult teeth, these squabbles ceased to be good-natured play and became serious combats. As soon as his mother realized that the roughhousing had turned to fighting, she became uneasy. She herself seldom fought, and for that reason preferred to be with the raches, the hounds worked in packs, who were more peaceful than the aggressive terriers or fierce alaunts. If a dog attacked her, rather than use her murderous fangs, she would turn sideways and knock him over with a blow of her shoulder. The pup had early learned to assert himself among the other pups. He had too much wolf in him—and wolves are also pack animals—to go about with a chip on his shoulder, but he had enough dog in him to be ready to fight. Once when he was in a fight and had managed to get his opponent down, he suddenly found himself treacherously attacked from the rear. He spun around with a snarl to find his worried mother pulling him off his victim by his tail!

Least understandable of all was his mother's attitude toward humans. She stood in perpetual awe of them, except for the veneur, the only man she trusted. The pup had no fear of humans whatsoever. This was not to say that he did not fully realize that humans, under certain conditions, could hurt him. He took good care to keep out of the way of a man armed with any kind of weapon, even a stick; but if the man was unarmed, the wolf-dog was indifferent to him. Women and children he openly despised. Early he discovered that if they had food and he charged them, growling, they would drop the food and run. He also enjoyed chasing livestock. His mother, even when she was allowed to run free, never bothered livestock as long as she was well fed. To her, there was no reason to attack an animal unless you wanted to eat it. She could not imagine doing it for sport. But all the half-grown young dogs liked to hunt for fun until they were broken of the habit by liberal use of the whip. However, the veneur quickly found that the wolf-dog furiously resented punishment, which the dogs accepted without question. To the wolf-dog, punishment meant that he was being attacked. It was also futile to punish his mother; it simply made her wild with fear and rage.

Wolves are not aggressive. Dogs are, but they are also man-oriented. Through centuries of domestication they have come to accept man as their master and to obey him. From his father, the alaunt, the wolf-dog inherited a dog's aggressiveness, but because of his wolf blood he did not have a dog's respect for man. By the same token, he had none of his mother's instinctive dread of humans. She was as apprehensive of a small child as she was of an armed man. If the pup could have expressed himself in such terms, he would have said that his mother had a superstitious dread of humans.

Only in one respect was his mother belligerent. If a bitch approached the big alaunt, his mother would attack her. If the alaunt showed any interest in the bitch, his mother was furious. She might take out her rage even on her beloved pup, so he learned to keep out of her way at such times.

Autumn had come. The hips burned red in the thickets, the haws were black in the hedgerows, and the leaves had turned russet. The wolf-dog that someday would be known as Courtaud was lying in the lists—the open space outside the castle walls—half asleep in the sun. Below him was the barbican that marked the castle's outermost defense, a fortified double gate in the palisade of sharply pointed logs that ringed the lists. The palisade was not intended to withstand a serious attack; only to hold back an enemy long enough for the alarm to be sounded, the drawbridge raised, and the portcullis dropped. But no danger threatened this peaceful fall day and only a token watch was kept.

A string of serfs, each bent almost double by the great load of faggots on his back, was coming through the barbican and starting up the hill on which stood the castle. Courtaud watched them idly. Even though he could not scent quite as well as the raches, and was completely outclassed by the marvelous limiers that were used only to start game or unravel a difficult spot in a trail, he had far better eyesight than either and he could see the oncoming serfs easily. Like most animals, especially wolves, he was able to notice minute differences in gait, bearing, and attitude. He could also tell a great deal about a man or an animal by the way the creature moved. Now, watching these serfs, he felt there was something strange about them.

For several days now, serfs from the village had been bringing wood to the castle against the cold days of winter, and this group appeared to be no different from the others. Neither the porter in the barbican nor the castle servants going about their tasks bothered to give the toiling villeins a second glance, but Courtaud rose to his feet, growling. These men did not move quite like serfs. They did not carry their loads in exactly the same way. And, most significant of all, as they came closer they did not smell like serfs. That last was decisive.

Courtaud barked. It was very seldom that he barked, in contrast to the dogs, who were always barking. This was an alarm bark. It was sharp, followed by a more drawn-out note ending in a number of softer, lower-pitched barks. No one paid any attention to him, so Courtaud barked again and, as his warning was still ignored, he raised his head and howled, the rallying cry that should have brought all his comrades racing to his side. Only his mother, chained far away in the kennels, answered him. The dogs did not know what the sound meant.

Rumbling deep down in his chest, Courtaud approached the line of serfs stiff-legged. He would dearly have loved to nip one of their calves, but hesitated. If only there were an older, more authoritative dog with him to take the initiative! Still growling, he followed the men across the drawbridge into the bailey. Here they stopped and their leader dropped his load and raised his head to look about him.

It was definitely not the motion of a serf and Courtaud barked again. This time one of the men-at-arms looked up, called to him, and then glanced at the serf. Instantly the gendarme stiffened. The serf had light hair and blue eyes! For a moment the two men stared at each other. Then the serf cried in a strange tongue, "Out swords!"

No one in the bailey could understand the foreign words, but there was no mistaking his actions, for as he shouted he reached into the bundle of faggots he was carrying and jerked out a sword. The other men also threw down their loads and produced various sorts of weapons, from battle-axes to great bows as long as themselves. Together they made a concentrated rush on the twin round towers that stood on either side of the castle's entrance and supported the ponderous portcullis.

In the bailey, there was the wildest confusion. Women screamed, men shouted, trumpets were blown. A group of men-at-arms led by a knight wearing only jerkin and hose, but carrying a sword and shield, rushed across the bailey in pursuit of the invaders. Two of the strangers turned at the entrance to the nearest tower and held the narrow passageway against them.

Now came a fresh diversion. From the direction of the woods that came within a bowshot of the outer palisade a trumpet sounded, and at once a stream of horsemen broke from the cover of the trees and raced toward the castle. These were men in full armor, although the armor was of all different shapes and designs. Before the porter could secure the barbican gates, the galloping horsemen had burst through and were tearing up the hill on which stood the castle. A few arrows pattered among them, discharged from the sentinels on the castle ramparts. Then the riders were across the drawbridge and into the bailey. The little group of men-at-arms were instantly ridden down, the others who were rushing out of the barracks were driven back, and the invaders were in possession of the castle.

Terrified, the young Courtaud fled to the only safe place he had ever known, the kennels, and crouched by his mother. Behind them came the tumult of the hounds and the barking of the alarmed, angry terriers. Outside, fighting was still going on. The cringing animals could hear the vicious hiss of arrows, the clash of steel, the war cries and the curses. Finally it died down. Now came a shout of "Break open the chests!" followed by shouts of delight. The looting had begun.

Soon the wolf-dog and his mother smelled smoke and the odor of cooking meat. They also smelled the sweet, tangy scent of wine as the casks were staved in. They heard shouts, laughter, and the screams and pleadings of women. All the dogs not locked in the kennels had run away, but Courtaud stayed with his chained mother.

An hour or so before sunset, some men came in. They were obviously very drunk. Courtaud could both smell it and tell by their voices and motions. They tried to grab him, but when he showed his teeth they let him go and drew their swords. Courtaud knew he had no chance against steel and allowed himself to be herded into the bailey. The men also tried to bring his mother, but she was plainly so terrified they let her go.

The bailey was strewn with bodies and the smell of blood and death was everywhere. They passed the corpse of Count Raoul, who had died sword in hand; beside him lay the body of the great alaunt, Courtaud's father, who had died fighting beside his master. A great fire had been lit and near it was a small herd of

frightened cattle. Some of their number had already been butchered and were cooking over the flames on the ends of long spits
held by weeping women. Not only cattle were roasting. Some of
the men had cooked a baby and were now forcing the mother
to eat parts of the burned little corpse while they howled with
mirth. Though it meant nothing to the wolf-dog, these men
were the *écorcheurs*—the "flayers"—one of the roving bands of
French, English, and German deserters from the armies who
lived off the land and spared nothing, often skinning their
captives alive.

Courtaud's capturers joined a group of men who had also
managed to obtain a few dogs. Others had tied a long rope
around the neck of a bull, fastening the other end to a ring in
the wall.

Now the dogs were brought up and encouraged by shouts
to attack the tethered animal. With their training against
molesting livestock, the dogs were at first uncertain what to do
and the bull was equally reluctant to open hostilities. To infu-
riate him, the men hissed, shouted, and waved their arms. Some
began prodding him with their spears and twisting his tail. The
bull roared with pain and fear as boiling water was flung on his
testicles.

Courtaud, pushed forward with lance heads, stared at the
tortured animal wonderingly. Unable to reach the men, the
bull charged the dogs. One turned to flee, but the bull's horn
caught him as he turned. He flew up in the air, yelping. Two of
the men sprang forward and tried to catch him to break his fall
but missed. The dog came down on the paving stones and lay
squirming with a broken back.

Now the bull turned on Courtaud. Warned by the dog's fate,
he kept as close to the ground as possible to prevent the bull
from getting his horns under him. Frustrated, the bull was

forced to try to impale the wolf-dog with his right horn, turning his head sideways. Instantly Courtaud seized him by the ear. The bull tossed his head and Courtaud in spite of his size and weight went flying through the air. He too would have come down on the stones, but two of the men used the butts of their lances to catch him in midair and ease his fall.

Shaken but unhurt, Courtaud faced his foe again. He would have liked to have gotten behind him. All his experience with cattle had taught him they are much easier to attack from the rear, but the bull's sweeping horns held him off. As the bull charged again with lowered head, Courtaud seized him by the nose.

The bull bellowed with pain and rage and tried to toss the dog, but Courtaud spread his feet and hung on. A bull's nose is one of the most sensitive parts of his anatomy, and the wolf's long canines were buried deep in the soft flesh. The bull could get no leverage to toss and Courtaud was holding him. The men were yelling with delight and making bets when the rope holding the bull broke. In an instant the animal was free.

"A lane!" shouted a dozen voices. The crowd opened as the bull by sheer strength forced the wolf back. Courtaud was forced to let go. Insane with pain, the bull charged blindly into the fire, scattering burning faggots in all directions. Flitches brought from the cellar took fire and their melting fat added to the flames. Tapestries brought from the looted castle flared up. The wine casks ignited and burst their bands. The hayricks by the stables went up.

Courtaud ran back to the kennels. His mother lay there dead with a dozen arrows sticking from her body. Some of the archers had amused themselves by using the helpless animal as a target.

Courtaud stood over the body uncertain what to do. Under

ordinary conditions the wolf pup would have refused to leave the body for some hours if not for some days. But these were not ordinary conditions. Panicked by the smoke, the shouting, and the strange men, Courtaud turned and ran. He dashed through the bailey and over the bridge. Now in the open, he ran as he had never run before, seeking only to put as much distance as possible between him and the horror.

These were terrible days in France. Not only the *écorcheurs* were devastating the land: Burgundy fought against Champagne, England fought against the unhappy young king Charles VII, and the powerful barons fought each other. Courtaud passed through district after district laid in waste. Sometimes he found half-rotten carrion to eat in the burned villages. Sometimes he was able to catch a vole or a rabbit. On and on he went northward, until the ground began to rise and he found himself on a tree-covered hogback called the Schnee Fifel in the Ardennes mountains. Here were many old castles and heavily fortified churches, with little towns clustered at crossroads or in a river valley. There were cloud-topped ridges, deep sinkholes, and great caverns. There were also vast coniferous forests where an army could hide.

The forests were rich with game, but none of it easy for the lone, inexperienced young wolf-dog to catch. Occasionally he was able to catch a marmot as the woodchuck-sized rodent was gathering food preparatory to its winter sleep. Once he had the great good fortune to capture a capercailzie nearly the size of a turkey, while the big black bird was busily eating red whortleberries. He chased varying hare, which were beginning to turn white, but these were too fast for him. The blue grouse that lived in the white birch groves seemed to have an eye in every feather, for he could not even get close to them. He had a little better luck with the hazel hens that ran through the elder thickets with wings drooping and tail partly extended, but even these could nearly always elude him.

Courtaud disliked having to catch small prey. The amount of food he obtained did not compensate him for the effort required. He needed to kill large quarry.

Large quarry meant deer. The most conspicuous were the red deer. Courtaud was careful to leave the stags, with their great antlers worn smooth digging for forage through the snow, strictly alone, but once he did dare to attack a herd of hinds and calves under the guidance of an old matriarch hind. They were eating the bark off a fallen tree when he approached them, hoping to cut out a calf. The old female turned to face him while the young mothers hastily gathered around their young to protect them. Circle as he would, Courtaud was always faced by a ring of lowered heads. At last, made reckless by hunger, he charged in. The old hind reared back and struck with her forefeet. Courtaud was knocked down, and luckily for him the ground was soft, or he would have been killed. He managed to escape with no worse damage than sore bones, but he did not attack red deer again.

Roe deer were safer. These were no bigger than large dogs and spent most of their time deep in the spruce forests, but one evening he surprised, a few eating willow shoots and rushed them instantly. The ear-splitting alarm scream of the nearest buck startled him and gave the herd a head start. Although expert at dodging, they were not especially fast, so he was able to overtake an old female and drag her down. Courtaud gorged, devouring half of the fifty-pound animal. He lay up a few yards away and returned the next morning to finish his meal, only to find that the foxes, ravens, and magpies had done it for him. After that, Courtaud always buried any surplus meat, adding a dab of urine to the spot to make it easier to find.

Unfortunately, the roe deer were difficult to locate. They left almost no scent and hid themselves deep in the forests. More common were the fallow deer, about the size of an American whitetail. At first, Courtaud tried to run them down as he had the roe, but they were much too fast for that. He tried stalking them, only to find there was always one sentinel deer on guard duty. He did not succeed until after a blizzard when they were caught among the drifts.

One afternoon, Courtaud came upon a lone fallow doe walking through a grove of birch trees. Warned by previous failures, Courtaud did not attack directly. Instead, he paralleled her course. Alarmed, the deer began to run. There was about a foot of snow and the deer's long legs could go through it and reach the ground while the wolf-dog floundered in the soft stuff. She easily outdistanced him and then unwisely crossed a frozen lake—the same lake where later Courtaud would meet the Lapp. On the ice, swept clear of snow by the wind, Courtaud could go faster than she and, putting on a spurt, began to overtake her. The frightened doe managed to reach the other side a few yards ahead of him, and once in the snow she started to gain. She stopped on a ridge to look back and, finding the wolf still following her, turned and ran along the ridge. Seeing her direction, Courtaud left her trail and cut across to intercept her. The doe spun around and ran, only to find herself in one of the "cups" scoured out of the side of the cliff by the harsh winds sweeping across the plateau. Before she could recover, Courtaud charged forward, knocking her over. While she struggled in the snow, he bit her through the base of the brain. She died in seconds. This time, he cached the surplus meat in the snow and lay over it for the next two days until there was nothing left but bones and a few shreds of hide.

Ever since he had come to the Schnee Fifel, Courtaud had encountered scent posts where one of the several packs of wolves that roamed the Ardennes had left their urine marks. The wolves used any conspicuous object as a scent post: a lone tree, a prominent rock, sometimes even a deer skull. The first time Courtaud had come on one of these posts and smelled the fierce, wild odor, he had cringed and looked about him fearfully. Then he had run to-the nearest ridge and scanned the country-side to make sure the pack was nowhere around. After testing the air, he was partially reassured and returned to the scent post, which was the stub of a dead spruce. He need not have been so alarmed. The scent was several days old. There were about ten wolves in the pack—the males had urinated on the stump and the females on the ground beside it—and Courtaud could easily tell the scent of each individual animal. They were well fed—the odor of the rich food drove the half-starved wolf-dog wild—and two at least were old animals, for their urine smelled weak and fetid. He noted with great satisfaction that none of the males was as big as he. In triumph, he boastfully urinated on the stump, showing that he could fling his fluid a handsbreadth higher than the others.

He paid another visit to the scent post a few days later. The pack had been there in the meanwhile and he knew at once by the odor that the males, at least, were furious. They had gone to great efforts to obliterate his contribution and then scratched up the ground around the post in their fury. They had also left musk from their tail glands. This gland is located on the top side of the tail, about three, inches from the base. It is surrounded by a circle of stiff black hairs that can be spread when the musk is. discharged. Courtaud sniffed the heavy musk thoughtfully. He had such a gland himself, but because of his dog's blood it was not functional. He was not quite sure what the significance of the musk was, but he strongly suspected it was a warning.

Even so, he was drawn to the pack. Not only was he

desperately lonely, he also wanted to be with animals that were so obviously well fed. Every week, as winter advanced, it was harder for him to find food. The marmots, his mainstay, had hibernated for the winter; catching birds was almost impossible and the deer were too fast. By now he had come to know the range of the pack fairly well; it was roughly marked by the scent posts, and also he knew what trails they followed. He began to follow them more closely.

Two days later he came upon the pack sunning themselves on an outcropping of black rock that projected above the snow. He approached them cautiously, cringing, his tail wagging, ears pulled down, and lips drawn back into an ingratiating grin. The wolves stood up instantly to study him. When he was a few yards away, he rolled over on his side, exposing his throat, and whimpered, moving his tail sideways. The wolves seemed more curious than hostile. Several even wagged their tails slightly in response. Greatly encouraged, Courtaud wriggled like a worm, moaning humbly. Then, without any warning, the wolf baron—the leader of the pack—charged him.

For a fraction of a second, Courtaud was uncertain of the baron's intention, but only for a fraction. The baron's tail was stiff and raised above the level of his back. The lips were wrinkled in a snarl and the ears erect and pricked forward. Courtaud bounded to his feet as the baron struck him and knocked him down. Now that the baron had shown his intentions, all the wolves in the pack attacked. Hopelessly outnumbered, Courtaud thought only of escaping. He was knocked down twice again and badly slashed on the shoulder before he could shake them off and run. Looking over his shoulder, he saw that after a few hundred yards, all the pack had given up the pursuit except the baron, who still followed him vindictively. Seeing that his enemy was alone, Courtaud stopped and again tried to show his good intentions by fawning before the baron. It did no good. For the second time the baron attacked. Again, Courtaud had no choice except flight. When he had made good his escape, he paused to look back. The baron, his tail stiffly out, trotted proudly back to his band, who surrounded him, licking his face, pushing him with their noses, and gently chewing his muzzle. Courtaud had seen men behave in this manner. When the Count Raoul returned triumphant from battle, his *seigneurs* would surround him in just this way, slapping him on the back, kissing him, and shaking his hand.

Courtaud gave up any idea of being able to join the pack. Alone, unskilled in hunting, he would have starved to death had he not found the sheepfolds in the scattered villages. By both night and day he raided them. In his ecstasy at finding so much good food, he killed recklessly, sometimes taking only a few bites from a carcass, sometimes killing merely for the thrill.

Never before had the villagers seen a wolf that would come openly into a village and showed no fear of man. They had never found it necessary to have shepherds; a few boys and girls were enough to keep the sheep from straying and the wolves had never dared to molest them. This animal—this *loup-garou*— charged the children if they tried to drive him off and gave every evidence of being as willing to attack them as the sheep. The village dogs were panic-stricken by this monster who was twice their size, with enormous, punishing jaws. Grown men armed with billhooks and homemade spears had to guard the flocks day and night, and they were needed for other duties. In their despair, the villagers sought help from the Flemish merchants, who sent them the Lapp.

After the *louvetier*'s death, Courtaud was afraid to continue his sheep raiding. He rightly connected the determined little man with his attacks on the flocks and did not want another such human on his trail. Yet sheep were his only source of food now. Alone, he could not catch game. There was nothing for it. He had to join a wolf pack or die.

TWO

The Pack

Courtaud was much more cautious how he approached the wolf pack this second time. He was growing weaker and he well knew the baron would kill him if the big wolf got the chance.

He began by following the pack, keeping about a hundred yards in the rear. The baron was the only wolf that showed any real animosity toward him, although when the baron chased him away, the rest of the pack would join in the attack. Courtaud always ran instantly. He made no more attempts to win over his enemy by exhibitions of submission, but trusted to his long legs. He soon satisfied himself that the wolves would not follow him any great distance. Chasing this "loner" was tiring and accomplished nothing.

Courtaud found an unexpected advantage in this constant following. After the pack had gorged themselves on their kills, they would retire and Courtaud, watching from cover, would steal in and eat their leavings. He drove off the other scavengers, like foxes and ravens, that also followed the pack. Unfortunately, there were seldom much leavings and often even the weaker members of the pack had to go without food. Rare indeed were the great days when the wolves were able to pull down an adult red deer or separate a half-grown calf from a hind so it could be easily killed. On such occasions, the pack made up for their long periods of fasting and gorged until they were drunk with meat and blood.

The baron especially resented Courtaud's constant trailing and tried to shake him off. He would suddenly turn off the plainly marked main trail and take the pack along windblown ridges bare of snow and down into the canyonlike ravines to where the rivers ran under their ceilings of ice. As Courtaud's nose was not especially good, these tricks would have succeeded if the wolf-dog had not learned to watch the ravens. The ravens followed the pack as he did and in winter were virtual parasites on the wolves, depending on them for food. It was impossible for the pack to lose the ravens. The birds' beady black eyes missed nothing, and whenever they were at fault they would soar high until they caught sight of the long line of wolves trotting single file through the snow. By watching the ravens, Courtaud was able to keep track of the wolves.

As game grew scarcer, the pack divided. Smaller packs could hunt more efficiently than a single large one. The main advantage of a large pack—that it could pull down bigger game than a small group of wolves could handle—meant little now, for the pack had already killed the few red deer too weak to defend themselves and so the wolves were dependent on fallow and roe deer, which had to rely on their speed rather than their strength. Courtaud followed the group that kept with the baron.

Then came an especially bad time. For a week it snowed almost constantly. Afterward, the weather became comparatively warm, followed by a cold spell. The melting snow froze, making a light crust through which the wolves broke. For a week they were unable to hunt and Courtaud, who had been half starved already, barely had enough strength to tail along behind when finally the snow became hard-packed enough to support the pack's weight.

Late one afternoon, while the pack was trotting along at their usual loping gait with Courtaud limping after them, the baron abruptly stopped, his nose up. The rest also stopped and sniffed the breeze. Courtaud, imitating them, could just make out the odor of some large animal perhaps a quarter of a mile away. He had never smelled anything quite like it, although he was able to identify it as a member of the deer family and therefore eatable. He trembled with hope, wondering if the baron would signal an attack. Very often, after studying a scent, the baron would decide against making an attack for some reason Courtaud could not understand. If he did so now, there was nothing left for Courtaud to do except lie down in the snow and die. He could not go much longer without food.

This time the baron decided to make the attempt. The pack gathered around him, wagging their tails excitedly and licking his muzzle as he conveyed to them by the motions of his body and his eagerness that they were going into battle. The baron swung off the trail and with the pack following him in single file, headed to where a stand of birch thrust their skeleton branches into the air. After them Courtaud shuffled along, glad it was they who had to break the trail through the snowfields.

The trees cut off the slight breeze and the wolves had trouble owning the scent. Courtaud could get only occasional wisps of it. Then, as they stood at a loss, the wind brought it to them strong and clear. The baron turned at right angles and bounded through the cover, the pack streaming behind him.

Before they had gone three hundred yards, they came upon a group of half a dozen gigantic creatures browsing among the birches. They were even bigger than red deer, the lone male having enormous antlers which, instead of resembling cande-labra, were broad and thick—shaped like a bird's wing. The creatures' muzzles were very long, some-what like the muzzles of enormous shrews, and from the throat hung a long bag of skin that swung as the animal moved. Although Courtaud did not know it, he was looking on some of the last elk, called moose in North America, left in Europe.

At sight of the wolves, the elk started running. Their longer legs gave them a great advantage in the deep snow and the wolves were speedily left behind. Seeing pursuit was useless, the baron stopped. As the rest of the disappointed pack turned back, still another elk jumped up from where she had been lying and started to run, only to find herself in the midst of the pack.

The wolves sensed instantly that this was a weak animal. She stumbled and did not move with the easy, swinging gait of the others. At once, they closed in from all sides. The baron seized her by the haunch. Another wolf locked his teeth in her belly. Others nipped at her feet. The elk fell, rose again, and for a moment was able to shake off her attackers. Then, as she tried to run, they were on her a second time, hanging to her rump and flanks. She managed to drag them a few yards through the trees before they pulled her down. Again she fought to her feet and this time struck the baron such a blow with one of her forefeet that he rolled over. She sprang forward to finish him off but the other wolves attacked her so fiercely from the rear that she was forced to turn on them. The baron regained his feet and limped away.

None of the rest of the pack dared to close with the big animal again, yet neither would they let her go. Leaning against a tree, gasping for breath, the cow watched them while the hungry wolves swallowed chunks of the bloody snow. When she finally reeled off, the pack followed at a respectful distance. All that night and the next day they followed her. When she lay down to rest, one wolf would leave the others and approach her, forcing her to stagger to her feet. If the full pack had been there, they would quickly have put an end to the business, but with only a few animals, they did not dare attack.

When night came, the cow tried to escape under cover of darkness. She nearly succeeded, for the wolves were tired and most of them sleeping. When at dawn they found her gone, they were furious. However, the blood trail was clear and they soon caught up with her.

The cow was weakening fast. Now when a wolf approached her, she was unable to rise. The pack saw the signs and closed in. Stiff though he was from the pounding he had taken, the baron charged in as befitted his rank and seized her by the throat. The rest swarmed over her weakly kicking body and soon it was all over.

Courtaud could hardly resist the sight and smell of the rich meat, yet he knew if he tried to approach he would soon be as dead as the cow. He had to content himself with eating bloody snow.

As he was some distance away from the carcass and his nostrils were not completely full of the blood scent, he was the first to detect the presence of the bear. Jumping back, he gave the warning bark. Instantly every wolf was on his feet, spinning around to face the danger. Through the trees was trundling the vast form of the bear. Although the wolf-dog did not know it, he was responsible for bringing the big brown beast out of his winter's hibernation. The avalanche that had killed the Lapp had also destroyed the bear's den and forced the great animal out into the inhospitable winter weather. Eventually he would find another den and return to his sleep, but this was an irritable old male who did not like his habits changed and stubbornly refused to behave sensibly. He had stumbled on the bloody trail of the wounded cow and had been following it hopefully. Now his patience was rewarded, for here was enough meat even for him.

The wolves gave back and the bear confidently waddled forward. Nothing, not even man, had ever dared to oppose him, and he minded the wolves no more than he did the ravens that had alighted around the hill, waiting their turn. When the bear saw the dead elk, he broke into a lunging gallop. The wolves opened to let him through and closed in from behind as he bent over to sniff the raw elk flesh.

Then the baron attacked. He darted in from behind, nipped the bear's ample haunch, and sprang back with a mouthful of fur. The bear roared more with astonishment than pain and swung around. Another wolf dove in from the side, but the bear turned on him so quickly he barely managed to escape. Again the baron got in a bite while a third wolf distracted the bear. Now the bear got his back against the dead elk, which afforded him some protection as he faced the wolves, his head swinging to and fro, spittle running from his huge jaws, his little eyes snapping with fury.

Each member of the pack responded to this challenge differently. A big black wolf hung in the background, refusing to go near the bear's great paws. A little white female almost silver in color ran fearlessly up to the animal, ducked her head down between her forepaws as though she were playing a game, and leaped aside at the last instant. A wolf that was almost orange ran back and forth, madly excited, in an aimless manner. A dark wolf sprinkled with yellow guard hairs watched every motion of the baron, rushing in to attack whenever the bear turned on the head wolf, always ready to distract the monster so the baron could make his play. He, in turn, was watched by a brownish wolf who did his best to duplicate the other's technique.

The bear would occasionally make short rushes, which the wolves easily avoided. Then he took up his stand against the elk and dared them to come on. This was far more dangerous for the wolves, but they refused to lose their hard-earned quarry. The baron took up a position on the bear's right while Yellow Hairs kept on his left. Brownie went to and fro between them, favoring Yellow Hairs. The bear rocked back and forth, his head moving in a snakelike fashion as he watched them. The baron and Yellow Hairs came toward him step by step, making sure to keep exactly the same distance from their enemy, tense to leap away if he charged.

Then the baron gave a sharp bark coupled with a short howl. It was a signal, for instantly Yellow Hairs leaped at the bear's shoulder. The bear made a snatch for him, using both forepaws as a man would use his hands, but Yellow Hairs ducked under the grab. At the same time, the baron bounded in and tore the bear's ear, throwing himself back just in time to avoid the long claws clutching for him.

Now Brownie moved in to distract the bear, although he did not dare to come as close as had the other two, and Silver helped him, dancing in and out so gracefully she seemed unconscious of the danger. The baron and Yellow Hairs had caught their breath and moved in again from opposite sides to repeat their previous maneuver.

Compared with the wolves, the bear appeared doltish, clumsy, and unsure of himself. Now, seemingly goaded beyond endurance, he suddenly charged Yellow Hairs, plunging laboriously through the snow. Yellow Hairs sprang back, keeping just out of his reach, luring the bear on while the baron darted in. With astonishing speed, quicker than even the wolves could move, the bear, who had apparently been intent on pursuing Yellow Hairs, spun around at the exact moment the leader sprang for him. Perhaps if the baron had not been stiff from the mauling the elk had given him he could still have avoided the clutching, claw-tipped paws, but the right paw hooked him. He snapped at it, trying to tear himself free, and the other paw clamped on his side. He was helpless, even though the entire pack hurled themselves on the bear in reckless disregard of their lives, tearing out mouthfuls of hair while Yellow Hairs even sank his teeth into the old male's testicles. The bear's jaws closed on the baron's neck. Courtaud, watching, wild with excitement, could hear the bones crack. Then the bear dropped the dead baron while he turned to deal with Yellow Hairs. The wolf was knocked down but managed to escape.

The bear sat licking his injured parts, growling to himself, while the wolves circled him. He was too sickened to eat and finally got to his feet and lurched away. The wolves followed him a short distance, but when he roared and turned on them, they fled. Once they were sure he was well away, they returned to the kill. Only Yellow Hairs took any interest in the dead baron. He sniffed the body for a long time before he joined the others at the elk.

When they had eaten and it was obvious that they intended to spend the night by the remains of the elk, Courtaud made his move. With the baron gone, he felt bolder. He came forward, tail held high. So exhausted were the pack by the long hunt, followed by the battle with the bear, that most of them did not even rise, only regarding him fixedly. Yellow Hairs did stand up and came toward him stiff-legged, his tail raised slightly higher than the level of his back. However, the wolf did not snarl or put his ears back. The two animals circled each other slowly. Then Yellow Hairs presented his anal region for Courtaud to smell, at the same time sniffing at Courtaud's.

This rite told each animal several things about the other. First, it established the other's sex, approximate age, general physical condition, and whether the animal was fearful or would fight if attacked. As there was no suggestion of adrenaline in the odor, both animals knew the other was confident and would put up a grim resistance to any aggression. This knowledge was reinforced by their actions. A nervous animal would drop his tail to cover his anal region so the other could not examine it. Yellow Hairs was clearly uncertain what to do. With the death of the baron, he was the most prominent wolf and would take charge of the group—at least until it reunited with the other packs, in which case there might well be another claimant for the throne. This strange animal—who did not move or smell quite the way a wolf should—had not made the sign of submission to him. If he had, Yellow Hairs would have accepted him at once. Unlike the dead baron, Yellow Hairs was not an aggressive animal; he was also too tired to want to fight, and the small pack was more ready to accept a newcomer than the full pack would have been because there was less competition for food and social position. Yet this new wolf refused to make obeisance to him as was proper. On the other hand, the stranger made no effort to establish his own authority.

The situation would probably have ended in a fight in which the other wolves, or at least Brownie, would have entered on Yellow Hairs's side. Luckily for Courtaud, at this moment Silver came over. Dainty and demure herself, she was clearly fascinated by the big stranger. She minced up to him, put her head down, waving her tail alluringly, and tried to play. As Courtaud stood on his dignity watching Yellow Hairs, she playfully pulled at the broad tufts of whitish fur that reached down and outward from his ears. Courtaud stood rigid at this familiarity, not quite knowing how to take it. Silver curtsied to him by putting her tail between her legs, lowering her haunches, and humping her back. Next she put one forepaw around his neck and licked him on the side of the mouth.

Seeing that Silver was so ready to accept the stranger, Yellow Hairs relaxed. He moved back to the others, keeping an eye on Courtaud as he went.

Silver continued her playful overtures, but Courtaud was not interested. He was too hungry. Turning away from the gay little female, he went to the elk and tore off a slab of flesh.

Immediately the whole pack was on their feet. It was one thing for this stranger to join them; sharing their kill was quite another matter. All except Silver, who plainly felt this big, handsome stranger could do no wrong, rushed at the wolf-dog with bared fangs and snarls.

Courtaud refused to run. He crouched, holding the precious meat in his jaws, rumbling deep within his broad chest. At the last moment, the pack halted, nonplussed. It was against all pack ethics to take meat away from another wolf. They might and usually did fight over a kill, but once a wolf had a piece of meat actually in his jaws, it was his. So they hesitated. Then Silver came over and lay down by his side, daintily nibbling at some fat, while Courtaud continued to bolt his portion, still growling. The pack continued to stand uncertain. If Yellow Hairs had given the signal, they would have fallen on this impudent stranger, but Yellow Hairs was still not sure of his authority and held back. Finally, some of the wolves came to feed on the elk merely as a sign of ownership, while the rest lay down again, allowing Courtaud to gorge himself.

Courtaud was now an accepted member of the pack, largely through Silver's good grace, but because of his youth and inexperience he was held in a subordinate position. He hardly had time to establish himself when they met one of the other splinter groups. By now, Yellow Hairs had been accepted as the new baron of his own group while a wolf with a black mantle over his back and neck had become the baron of the other pack. Courtaud took an immediate dislike to Black Mantle. His sole qualification for his new position was apparently a sullen nature and a quickness to bite, both most unusual characteristics in a wolf. He had a habit of marching up to a wolf and staring at him until the other animal was cowed into making the sign of absolute submission. Courtaud's submission was so obviously reluctant that Black Mantle attacked him. It required only a few slashes from the older wolf's long canine fangs to convince Courtaud that he was outmatched, and he lay writhing abjectly on the snow. For a moment it seemed as though Black Mantle would not accept his surrender, but something about the half-grown wolf-dog made the victor hesitate. There was a look in Courtaud's eyes and a set of his fangs that convinced the wolf baron that if he went too far, Courtaud would put up such a fight that even if the baron won, he would be left severely injured and perhaps permanently crippled. So he contemptuously turned away. Yellow Hairs did not seriously challenge Black Mantle's claim to leadership and returned to his subordinate position without question.

Gradually, Courtaud grew to know each member of both groups and how he or she was likely to react. There was Blackie, the big, lordly animal who turned out to be cowardly. There was Brownie, who lived in Yellow Hairs's shadow. There was White Mane, a gentle female who kept to herself. There were the Cubs, both about Courtaud's own age and obviously littermates, who were boisterous, good-natured, and inseparable. There was the Gray with a light face, who was so nervous that she always stayed away from the main pack for fear of attack. There was Orange, who, although full-grown, behaved like a mischievous puppy. There was the Old Man, an elderly wolf with teeth worn down to the gums, who was unable to hunt, had become a pensioner of the pack, and was allowed to accompany them even though he could hardly chew his food. There was also the varlet, a wretched animal, despised by all for no apparent reason Courtaud could see, who trailed after the others and had to be contented with scraps. It would be pleasant to report that Courtaud, remembering when he had been an outcast, took pity on the varlet and tried to make life easier for him, but unfortunately the truth was that Courtaud despised the underwolf quite as much as the others.

Later, a third group joined them, also part of the original pack. There were now about twenty-five wolves in the band, although the number was not constant, as some individual animals or couples would go off on affairs of their own for a few days or a week and rejoin later. Roughly three quarters of the wolves were youngsters two or three years old. The rest were mature animals. There were also two much older wolves, a male and female that kept largely to themselves. Not even the arrogant Black Mantle demanded that they do homage to him. From the respect paid them, Courtaud got the impression that nearly all the wolves were the offsprings of this original pair, except for a few, like himself, who for some reason or another had been permitted to join.

There were very few fights among the group. Black Mantle not infrequently felt it necessary to show his authority by mauling some animal, but the victim always submitted without protest, so injuries were never serious. There was occasional bickering between pack members, but if the quarrels ever turned into a real fight, all the other wolves interfered and attacked both the combatants impartially so the battle was broken up. Even so, there was a constant undercurrent of tensions, each wolf hoping to advance himself in the hierarchy. Mated couples were jealous of any wolf that showed too great an interest in either husband or wife, and there were constant disputes over food. So the pack was a group of individuals competing against each other, yet all forced to stay together for mutual assistance.

Right from the beginning, the gay, playful, and fearless little Silver had attached herself to Courtaud. She taught him games such as Catch the Bone. She would find a bone, bring it over to him, and drop it a few inches from his muzzle. When Courtaud tried to grab the bone, she would snatch it away and start running, with the big wolf-dog after her. He was faster but she was quicker at dodging. When at last he managed to get the bone, she would throw both her forelegs around his neck and lick the side of his mouth when he tried to chew it until both were rolling over and over on the snow, tussling and biting at each other. These bouts usually ended with them lying side by side, Silver giving him little love nibbles with her teeth so delicately that he could barely feel the touch, although Silver's jaws were quite capable of cracking open a deer's leg to get the marrow.

Courtaud enjoyed the play and Silver's company, but as he grew older he became annoyed by such puppy pranks. Because of his size and the sudden outbursts of ferocity that came from his alaunt blood, he had become the acknowledged leader among the young wolves, but it was hard to be dignified with the merry, vivacious Silver. Also, she could be something of a nuisance at times. He noticed the other females were submissive to males and never dared approach them without encouragement, so except when he was ready to make the overtures, he haughtily ignored her. If she came to him, he stood rigid, holding his head well up so she had trouble reaching it for her kissing, and sternly refusing to play.

The pack had had a good hunt and killed two fallow deer in the bottom of a ravine, an unusual piece of luck. Courtaud had fed well and like the rest of the pack slept late the next day. When he awoke it was late afternoon, almost time for the evening hunt. He stood up, yawned, stretched himself, and looked around for Silver. There was no sign of her.

Courtaud missed her. She was a nuisance, true, but a nuisance he had grown used to. He went looking for her. Some of the other wolves were awake and two or three of the females indicated that they were willing to romp with him, but he wanted Silver. She was nowhere to be found and Courtaud became seriously concerned. He looked everywhere for her and finally by chance caught a wisp of her scent on a puff of wind. He followed it and found her by herself behind a rock. She was lying stretched out with her long nose between her forelegs, watching him intently with her bright golden eyes, but she made no move as he came over. He nudged her with his nose, expecting her to roll over, crying with delight, but she remained still. When he nudged her harder, she whined angrily and nipped him—not a playful nip, but one that hurt.

Courtaud stood back, astonished and angry. Silver lay on her side, her mouth half open in a threatening snarl. This was no way for a female to behave to a male. Courtaud felt his alaunt blood rising in him. Silver, watching him intently, suddenly leaped to her feet and started running. Courtaud pounded after her. They tore up the side of a ridge and down the other, crossed a frozen river, and here Silver turned at bay with open mouth and ears laid back. Courtaud stood over her threateningly but she refused to cower. After a moment's pause, he turned and walked away, only to give a startled yelp. Silver had stolen up behind him and bitten his tail—hard. He whirled around and was after her again. This time she ran back to where the pack were lying under a stand of aspen and threw herself down between two of the biggest males who had previously showed her attention.

Puzzled, Courtaud went off and dug up a fine bone he had hidden in a snowbank. He brought the bone back and dropped it hopefully in front of Silver. She sniffed it disdainfully. Clearly she felt that he had a very poor taste in bones. Rising, she went off and dug up a bone of her own, which she chewed with every evidence of satisfaction. Courtaud went over to her and sniffed the bone. Silver watched him warily, ready to bite. Completely baffled, Courtaud turned away, only to find the bone dropped in front of him. Uncertainly, he picked it up, not knowing what to do. As he did so he felt a soft head rubbed against his shoulder and heard a low whine. Dropping the bone, he turned and saw Silver looking up at him happily. He grabbed her muzzle in his great jaws and moved it back and forth while she moaned with delight. They spent the rest of the evening lying side by side apart from the others, rubbing each other with their noses or kissing. From then on they were always together.

At last the winter was over. Streams formed by the melting snow poured down the gullies. The ravens began looking for nesting sites. The grebes returned to their favorite ponds. The first grass appeared and the wolves ate large quantities of it as a tonic after the months of cold. The young beech trees took on a translucent green and the woods were carpeted with anemones. Primroses appeared by the streams and purple vetch among the rocks. The adult female wolves were already in estrus.

Among the younger wolves, there was no breeding. The females were not able to breed until they were two years old; the males until they were three. However, attachments were formed that kept couples together as though they were "engaged," even though they could not breed for another year or so. Courtaud and Silver were as much a recognized pair as were the old pair who had originated the pack, although these were now too old for breeding. In sexual matters the wolves behaved much like humans. They usually mated for life, though this was not always true.

Black Mantle showed an interest in Silver but Silver would have none of him, keeping her tail tucked between her legs to cover herself and sitting down if the baron grew too attentive. At first, Courtaud was uncertain of Black Mantle's intentions, as he was too young himself to know what it was all about, but he did know the baron was molesting-Silver, so the next time the older wolf bothered her, Courtaud moved his bulk between them. Ordinarily, such a show of defiance would have meant a fight to the finish, but Black Mantle recognized the fact that Courtaud was defending his mate. A wolf of lower rank could defy the baron only on two matters: when he was refusing to be robbed of meat actually in his mouth, and when protecting his mate. So, with a snarl, Black Mantle moved away.

Finally there were three breeding pairs, each a member of one of the smaller units: Black Mantle and a determined female who had forced herself on him after Silver's rejection, Yellow Hairs and Gray, and one of the top-ranking males and White Mane. The rest were too young or too old or not compatible.

As soon as the frost was out of the ground, the happy couples began digging dens, generally in high areas that afforded a good view of the countryside and always near water, for the mother would have to drink several times a day to manufacture milk for her pups. The dens were quite elaborate, going twenty and sometimes even thirty feet into the ground. There was a large room at the end for the female and her pups and a smaller room near the entrance for the male. In their enthusiasm, the couple usually dug two or three other dens in likely places before the female made up her mind which she liked best.

One morning in April, Courtaud and Silver came on Yellow Hairs standing glumly outside, the entrance to his den, looking worried and hurt. They touched noses with him, then Silver went over to the mouth of the den to see if she could find out what was the matter. No sooner had she put her nose inside when a bansheelike scream made her jump back. The usual quiet Gray was squalling and hissing with fury. The three wolves outside stood astonished and then Yellow Hairs tried to enter. Such an explosion of rage followed that he hastily backed out again. Bewildered and a little frightened, the younger wolves moved off, leaving the mated couple to solve their problems in their own way.

It was two weeks before Gray would allow her mate to enter the maternity ward. When she did, he emerged half mad with excitement. After tearing around the area as though chasing his own tail, he hurried off. Hunting was simple at this time of year because the deer had young which were easily caught. Yellow Hairs returned carrying a dead fawn. He left it at the entrance and Gray devoured it. But it was another week before the mystery was solved for the rest of the pack. One morning, four furry, blunt-nosed, round-headed pups were found lying in the warm sun at the den's mouth while Gray and Yellow Hairs stood guard.

The whole pack were as delighted as though the pups were their own. Silver promptly adopted them to such a degree that Gray was rather resentful, even though she was glad of the opportunity to rest and go hunting. So many contributions of food were brought that even though most were buried, the spot was soon covered by blowflies and the cubs had to be moved to one of the extra dens. As the pups became weaned, not only the parents but all the wolves gorged themselves on food which they afterward regurgitated for the pups in a partially digested state. This served as pap for the youngsters.

The other two pairs had their pups a few days later, and each time there was the same general rejoicing. The pups ate so much and were so active, it required the combined efforts of the whole pack to take care of them. If all the wolves had mated and had offspring, the mortality rate among them would have been murderous. Even so, when the lush days of summer passed and winter came again, most of the *louvarts*—or six-month-old pups—would not make it to spring.

Courtaud continued to grow. He was now seven and a half feet from the tip of his nose to the end of his tail and weighed more than a full-grown man. His great poniardlike canine teeth were as long as a man's little finger and only Black Mantle could match the crushing power of his jaws. He had learned to work as a member of the pack, his most difficult lesson, for by nature he was independent, but he was still impatient and lacked the careful, controlled discretion of the pure wolves. To him, their caution seemed like weakness.

The third winter, the pack had been unable to make a kill for two weeks and the animals were starving. The elderly wolf who had followed them for so long was dead and now it was the turn of the old original pair. Unable to keep up with the pack, they had gone away together, united in death as they had been in life, and no one saw them again. Silver was growing noticeably weaker, although she continued brisk and gay. Often now Courtaud thought of the sheepfolds and how if the pack did not make a kill soon, he would be forced to return to stock killing.

Then one morning they came on the track of a red deer. The pack seldom bothered to follow a track unless it was smoking hot. Experience had shown them it was a waste of strength to track prey for miles, only at last to lose the line or find that the quarry was too strong for them. This track was not particularly fresh nor was it especially old. After sniffing a long time, Black Mantle made his decision and they started off on it.

Three hours later they came on their intended victim stripping bark from a birch tree. He was a ten-point stag. Ordinarily they would not have dared to close with him, but by now the pack was desperate. The fact that he was alone probably meant that he was old, so they circled him and Black Mantle and Yellow Hairs moved in to test him.

This old stag knew all about wolves. He turned and trotted away, to the great delight of the pack, who considered this a sure sign that he was afraid of them and could be pulled down from the rear while he ran in panic. They bounded after him, but the stag went only as far as a stand of pine. Turning, he wedged his vulnerable hindquarters among the trees so tightly that the branches snapped. Then he lowered his dagger antlers, his mane rose, his ears flattened, and he pawed the snow.

The wolves stopped at this awesome sight and reconsidered. Again the two leaders approached step by step, their legs bent under them for a spring backward. The stag let them get almost to him. Then he broke from the thicket and charged in a series of great bounds, his feet stamping the snow as he came. Both wolves fled, and only barely in time. At once the stag backed into his impregnable position and stood threatening them.

Yellow Hairs made one more attempt to find some weakness in the old warrior. He came on slowly, supported by the ever-faithful Brownie. The stag stood motionless until the wolf was almost on him. Yellow Hairs leaned forward, snapped, and jerked back. Still the stag stood with hanging head as though completely beaten. Yellow Hairs stole forward a second time, more confidently.

Suddenly the stag reared, coming down on the wolf with both forefeet. The hoofs cut like knives. Brownie rushed in, hoping to divert the attack, but the stag was intent on his victim. In seconds, Yellow Hairs was a mass of trampled bloody hide and raw flesh.

Black Mantle rose and turned away, giving the signal to retreat. The rest of the pack obeyed him; all but Courtaud.

The smell of blood, the excitement of the fight, all were too much for the wolf-dog. Ignoring pack etiquette, he hurled himself at the stag. Remembering his battle with the bull, he locked his jaws in the stag's nose and hung on, straining away as far as possible to avoid the hoofs. The stag tried to toss him, but he weighed less than half as much as the bull had and Courtaud was a far bigger animal than when he fled the castle. They struggled together while the pack watched in astonishment. Then Silver dashed in and fastened to the stag's hock. Brownie ran under the animal and attacked his belly. Now the rest of the pack surged forward and the stag was pulled down and torn to pieces while still alive.

From then on, the wolves regarded Courtaud with a new respect in spite of his youth. Even the older males lowered their tails humbly when he passed. Black Mantle hated him. Not only had Courtaud defied his authority and attacked the stag, he now began to usurp the baron's rightful place and led small groups of wolves on private hunting expeditions.

When spring came, Courtaud and Silver mated for the first time. When wolves copulate, the male's organ is locked in the female's body for a period of twenty minutes to half an hour. He cannot release himself and both animals are helpless. Black Mantle had never dared to attack Courtaud openly. He chose this moment to fall on his rival.

Hampered as he was, Courtaud tried to swing around to meet the attack, Silver helping him as best she could. The odds were too much against him. Black Mantle's right canine tooth ripped open his side and then the wolf baron had him by the throat. It was all over now.

Then Black Mantle let go. Brownie had seized him by the left hind leg. The baron turned on Brownie, but now both Orange and the Cubs, who had often accompanied Courtaud on his hunting expeditions, joined the combat. In their excitement they indiscriminately attacked all the others, but they served to break up the fight.

From that day forward, Courtaud knew that eventually he would have to fight Black Mantle for leadership in the pack.

THREE

Pack Baron

Silver was as bewildered by the miracle of birth as the other females had been, and Courtaud, for all his size and strength, was forced to wait outside the den for fear of being attacked by his hysterical mate. The den had been dug on top of a ridge that commanded a good view of the countryside, and Courtaud spent much of his time lying a little above the entrance where he could maintain watch. But Silver could not keep the glorious news to herself for long. Even before the pups' eyes were opened, she brought out one in her mouth for Courtaud to see. The tiny cub was nearly engulfed by the wolf's great jaws, for she was forced to carry it far back in her mouth to make sure that her daggerlike canines did not injure the morsel. She would not let Courtaud touch the mewling, writhing puppy, only sniff it respectfully from a safe distance; then she hurried back with it to the main chamber.

There was the usual group excitement among the pack which the sight and smell of infants always produced. When, at the end of a month, the pups were old enough to come out and play, the whole pack gathered around to watch their antics. All, that is, except Black Mantle. In spite of all the encouragement his mate could give him, the wolf baron had been unable to copulate with her that year. He was growing increasingly nervous and suspicious, constantly demanding abject submission from all the pack, ready to attack any animal that did not grovel before him. By mutual consent, he and Courtaud avoided each other, neither being eager for the duel both knew must come.

The pups were constantly wrestling and playing together, but as the days passed, these juvenile encounters became more serious. Courtaud rather enjoyed the pups' quarrels. Not so Silver, who was constantly separating them. All her wolf instincts went against serious fighting, for it disrupted the unity of the pack and nothing could be allowed to do that. To her wolf-dog mate, unity was less important.

The pups were intensely curious about everything and completely fearless. With the pack to protect them, they could afford to be. Either one or the other of their parents was with them constantly, quite ready to die defending the litter, and the other wolves were only slightly less devoted.

It must be admitted that after two months of doting motherhood, Silver did begin to grow restless. The pups were big enough now so when they pulled her tail, tried to nurse at her dry nipples, or roughhoused with her, they could be painful. Also, she longed to go hunting with the pack again. Luckily, at this moment the despised varlet ventured to approach. After writhing on the ground before the couple, he dared to eat some of the surplus food left around the den. The parents would have driven him off had not the pups been delighted by this new toy. They united in jumping on the varlet who, only too happy to have some notice taken of him, gladly submitted. He soon grew so adept at taking care of the pups that they would go to him rather than to Silver. If one of the pups wandered too far and refused to return when Courtaud gave his warning bark, the big father would grab the recalcitrant youngster with no gentle grip and drag him back to the den. Now the varlet actually interfered with the discipline, and would run to get the pup himself to make sure the youngster would not be punished. Courtaud permitted this liberty, much as a strict father will allow a nurse who he knows is devoted to his children to intercede for them.

When the other members of the pack found that the varlet had been accepted by the mighty Courtaud and his popular mate, they also accepted him and so the varlet was restored to full membership, Alas, it seemed necessary for the pack to have one individual to serve as a scapegoat, so another wolf was assigned to the position of varlet and forced to follow behind the rest.

After the pups were two months old, they could follow the pack for a few miles, although they were still too young to join in hunts. The pack would leave the small group of youngsters (there had been only one other litter that year) in some safe place to play while they set about the serious business of finding food. After a kill, they would return, collect the pups, and take them to the kill. This kept up until the pups were strong enough to keep up with the hunting pack, although it was still a long time before they could help in making the kill.

At this time, the young wolves began to join in the important ritual of howling. Howling among the wolves took the place of community singing among humans. Before departing for a hunt, the pack would gather together for a howling session. Each animal had a different voice and took care not to imitate the voice of another. By shaping their mouths and using their tongues, the wolves could produce a large variety of sounds. Aside from the pleasure they derived from these communal choruses, the howling also served to notify other packs of their presence, for the howling could be heard for miles. After a howling, the pack would keep quiet for half an hour or so, listening. If there were another pack within earshot, it would howl in reply. The wolves could tell the location and numbers of the strangers. This, together with the scent posts, helped the various packs keep to their own territories and avoid wars.

Besides the communal singing howls, there were individual howls that had special meanings. A deep, single howl followed by barks was the leader's means of assembling the pack. There was a high but soft call, usually given at night, that-meant the animal was lonely. An eager, deep howl was the mating call. An animal separated from the pack would go to the highest point he could find and howl. The others would answer him so he could find them. Different, packs had different calls, so the young wolves had to learn the cries of their own pack.

Most important of all the new experiences that the *louvarts* had to learn was the art and science of hunting. On this their lives would depend. There was a nice balance between the predators and their prey. If the predators found it too easy to capture their quarry, there would soon be no quarry left. If too difficult, the predators would cease to exist. Over the centuries, a balance had been created. Only the strongest and most intelligent of the predators survived. The others died, usually in the first winter.

Hunting usually took place at night when it was cooler and the scent was better. Late in the afternoon, Black Mantle as baron would go about waking the other wolves. First the pack would do homage to their leader by gathering around him with wagging tails, and lick his face to show their loyalty. This ceremony would be followed by a howl, much as soldiers sing a marching song before going into battle to keep up their spirits. Then the pack would start off, in single file, the baron leading. The baron knew the easiest paths, the ridges free of vegetation, and in winter the frozen rivers kept free of snow by the wind. The pack generally traveled at a steady lope, averaging about five miles an hour. They often covered fifty miles a night. One of the few old adages about wolves that is true is "a wolf lives by its feet."

The pack depended on four means for finding game. First was their knowledge of where game animals were likely to be. Second was coming on a fresh track. Third was airscenting the quarry— catching wind-borne scent. For this reason, they nearly always traveled upwind. Fourth, and most important, was sheer luck. Sometimes a single wolf would be dispatched to a high point to look around and report what he saw. Unlike hounds, which depend almost entirely on their noses, the wolves had excellent eyesight. When prey was located, the pack would perform an elaborate stalk, crouching down when the game animal lifted its head to look around, creeping closer when it resumed feeding. If the animal was big and powerful and stood its ground, the wolves were reluctant to attack. Instead, the baron and some of the biggest males would move in slowly, watching, carefully for signs of weakness. If they could detect none, the wolves would usually seek easier prey.

Courtaud could never understand this caution. His alaunt blood was all for a head-on attack. His great strength and size enabled him to engage quarry that the rest of the pack considered too formidable, for when the giant Courtaud charged in and took his fearsome nose grip, even the largest stag was held helpless. As a result, most of the pack admired the great wolf-dog. Black Mantle did not.

The rivalry between the baron and the wolf-dog became especially apparent in ibex hunting. These majestic goats with their sixty-inch horns made formidable quarry. They usually grazed in the open, so they were hard to stalk, and in addition the herd always had a sentinel watching. On the level the wolves could outrun them, but once the ibex reached the rocky sides of the mountains, they could easily outclimb the pack. They thought nothing of jumping forty feet from one ledge to another, and would even stop and watch the toiling wolves with what seemed to be amused contempt. Most wolf packs refused to bother with them, but Black Mantle had worked out a system for ibex-catching that was often successful.

Instead of trying to run down the ibex on the level, the baron led the pack along the highest part of the hills. If they came on a party of ibex feeding on the flat plateaus, they were above the goats. If the ibex stayed where they were, they were at the wolves' mercy, but to reach the safety of the heights they had to run the gauntlet of the pack. The wolves took only kids and females, not caring to tackle the heavy horns of the big rams—all, that is, except Courtaud. He attacked the rams by preference. As the rams were usually the last, allowing the more agile females and kids to go ahead of them, they were easier to catch. The pack depended on him to take care of the defending ram while they concentrated on the weaker animals, and the wolf baron hated the hybrid for his prowess.

There were also conflicts between them when hunting deer. Here the pack departed from their usual single-file method and spread out like hounds to beat the cover. Even if they could not scent the quarry, they could often hear the frightened animals crashing through the thickets. Usually they counted on the weaker animals dropping to the rear, but sometimes the wolves split into two packs and one group would drive the deer toward a spot where the rest waited in-ambush. Another trick was to take deer by relay running, one group chasing the herd until they tired, when the pursuit was taken up by a fresh lot. They also used decoys to distract the deer. A single wolf would dis-play himself where he could be easily seen. The deer did not automatically run at the sight of a wolf, for often the wolf might not be hunting and the deer did not want to expend energy unnecessarily, especially in winter. They would stand watching the wolf, who would trot past them in an unconcerned manner, stopping to scratch himself or mark scent posts. While the deer were watching the decoy, the rest of the pack would sneak up on the herd.

It was a dispute over deer that led to the final conflict between Black Mantle and Courtaud.

The pack had split again, and both the wolf baron and Courtaud were in the same unit. The unit, which numbered only six wolves, was trotting along when by chance they jumped a fallow deer. It so happened that Courtaud was in the lead, a most unusual circumstance as the baron generally went first, and he instantly took off after the deer. The deer went uphill and drew ahead of the wolf-dog, but then came a broad plateau swept clean of snow by the wind. Here Courtaud began to gain. The deer came to the end of the plateau, only to find the slope too precipitous, and after hesitating a few seconds, turned to the left. This pause was disastrous. Courtaud was able to cut across and intercept the fugitive. Just as Courtaud's jaws were about to close on the deer's haunch, Black Mantle with the rest of the pack burst from cover and pulled the quarry down. The wolf baron had seen how the deer was running and swung the pack to ambush him. Now the wolf baron sprang forward, snarling and with tail raised, to drive Courtaud from the kill.

This was too much. Courtaud hurled himself at his ancient enemy, confident that his superior weight and right to his prey would bring speedy victory.

Black Mantle had not become wolf baron without knowing how to fight. He avoided the full force of Courtaud's charge, swinging sideways and taking the shock of the wolf-dog's blow on his shoulder. As Courtaud tried to seize him by the throat, he was met by bared fangs that gritted on his. He struck again and again and always the fangs were ready for him. It was like two swordsmen, each parrying the other's thrust with his own blade. After the exchange, both animals had minor cuts on their lips and gums but were otherwise unhurt.

The rest of the pack stood back to watch, although several were whining unhappily. If it had been a fight between two ordinary wolves, they would have interfered, but the baron had begun this encounter and it was up to him to finish it. Had Black Mantle had any close friends in the pack, they would have joined him, but he was not a popular leader.

The baron stood with his head raised and slightly turned to expose the jugular vein, daring Courtaud to bite. This display of bravado should have caused the upstart to submit. Instead, Courtaud sprang for the tempting target. The baron was ready for him. Twisting, he caught Courtaud's bite on his shoulder, at the same time tripping the wolf-dog with one of his long legs. Courtaud went down, with the baron feeling for his throat.

In his eagerness to finish off his opponent, the baron neglected to guard himself, and Courtaud was able to fasten to his foreleg. The baron rolled with him like a wrestler. Courtaud lost his grip and both animals broke apart.

For an instant they eyed each other. Then the baron reared and mounted Courtaud from in front, grabbing him by the left stifle, the joint of the hind leg. Courtaud fought desperately, planting his hind feet well apart and straining to break the other's grip. There was no more growling or snarling; only a subdued grumble as the wolves struggled together. The punishment was more than Courtaud could take and he turned head and shoulders away from the baron. This was the signal of defeat and the whole pack knew it. Except by their tension they gave no sign; only Silver whimpered and ran forward, but even she did not dare interfere.

If the baron had relaxed his grip, Courtaud would have slunk away, permanently beaten. But in his fury Black Mantle strove to crush his enemy's leg. Wild with pain, Courtaud managed to writhe around and locked his jaws on the baron's muzzle. For a few seconds the baron continued to work his teeth in to reach the bone until he felt Courtaud's grip crushing his jaws. Then he let go, throwing himself down and trying to roll. He tore loose, but before he could regain his feet, Courtaud had him by the nose a second time. In his satisfaction, the wolf-dog actually grinned and wagged his tail. The baron tried to push him away with his forelegs, but Courtaud had locked his jaws. Blood was pouring from the baron's wounds into the snow and he was weakening fast. At last he went limp. Courtaud shook him a few times and then stood back. The other wolves came up to sniff and turn away. Black Mantle was dead.

Not even the adult males challenged-the big wolf-dog's right to leadership. Proudly he led the pack into territories where they had never ventured before, past white farmhouses glued to the sides of cliffs, along sheep trails that lay like tangled skeins of thread scarring the rocky ridges, under jagged peaks that soared upward taller than the spires of cathedrals, and over ranges so high they could look down on the woolly white clouds below them.

When the fog came in, cutting down on visibility, he took them into the great forests where the lines of trees stood like the pillars of a church and the soft snow held a lacework of tracks. Where the wind swirled, there were cups in the snow around the base of the trunks and the snow was blue in the shadows. And to the pack's astonishment and alarm, Courtaud would defiantly trot past the little villages, each built around a central fountain, and even use the stone crosses as scent posts—to the great alarm of the village dogs when they came investigating the next day.

Courtaud would not have been so successful a baron if it had not been for Silver, who trotted by his side, although slightly to the rear as became a female. Perhaps Courtaud did not know how greatly the slender little wolf influenced him. He took naturally to some of his duties as baron. He patrolled the pack's fief, checking the scent posts and making sure the neighboring packs kept their distance. He broke up fights and figured as the rallying symbol to the pack, as the Count Raoul had figured as a rallying symbol to his followers. As with humans, the wolves had to have an individual on whom they could fawn, follow with confidence, and feel was always right. They were prepared to follow the waving plume of Courtaud's tail to the death.

Silver sensed that the pack was uneasy because of Courtaud's unwolflike habits. It made them nervous to see him recklessly attacking formidable game; it was positively frightening for him to be contemptuous of man. The pack shrank back in terror when they saw Courtaud scatter flocks of sheep and challenge the child shepherds. Courtaud, not understanding their apprehension, ignored it.

Silver did not. The wolf baron liked to have her at his side and if she held back, he stopped to wait for her. When the pack showed reluctance to follow him, Silver hung back too. Gradually, Courtaud learned first to watch her for signs of alarm and then to watch the pack. In spite of his position as baron, he could not force the pack to obey him, for the pack was made up of independent animals. He was tireless, as was Silver, but when the *louvarts* began to limp, she slowed down, forcing him to do the same to spare the yearling cubs. Gradually the pack came to trust him, and if any wolf had challenged his leadership, Courtaud could have counted on the older males to support him. None had supported Black Mantle.

When spring came and fold after fold of the ridges emerged from their shrouds of snow, the roe bucks barked in the alder thickets, and Our-Lady's-mantles appeared in the sheltered nooks, several pairs of wolves had pups. The pack was well fed and felt secure, so several litters were born. No more *louvetiers* had been sent against them, for Courtaud had spread his raids over a vast distance and no one community suffered greatly. That autumn the pack reached the unheard-of number of forty-four animals. All the other packs fled before such a host, and the terrified peasants who came across the pack's fore swore there were a thousand animals following the giant *loup-garou* who had no fear of man.

When winter came, the growth of the pack brought increasingly serious problems. The great difficulty was finding enough food. The peasants now kept their flocks guarded in stone folds patrolled by men and dogs, and the wild game was hard to catch. Also, tensions increased within the pack; there were more quarrels, more competition for mates and rank. It would have been better for the pack to have split into smaller groups and for these to move to fresh hunting grounds, but none liked to leave the magic presence of the mighty Courtaud.

Early one evening while they were trotting through a beech forest, keeping a sharp lookout for wild pigs that might have come there after beechnuts, Courtaud came on man scent. He stopped at once, so abruptly that the following wolves nearly ran into him and Silver had to drop to avoid a collision. Courtaud sniffed cautiously, for although he was not afraid of man, he was suspicious of him. His educated nose picked up and separated a number of scents, much as a man interested only in certain objects can receive a number of visual impressions which he ignores while concentrating on the desired articles. In addition to many less interesting odors, Courtaud smelled the tracks of a man, a dog, and several red deer. Raising his head, he could airscent the deer. They were several hundred yards away in a thicket. The man smelled somewhat different from a peasant. In fact, his scent reminded Courtaud of the veneurs he had known at the castle so long ago. Courtaud could remember a scent better than most humans could remember a face. The dog was a hound. He suspected it was one of the heavy, bloodhound-like animals called limiers. The man, then, would be the *valiet de limier*—the veneur whose sole duty it was to work with a single limier, puzzling out trails.

A twig had been broken and put in the slot mark of one of the deer. Courtaud sniffed the slot. The twig meant nothing to him, except that it was heavy with man-scent, but the deer was clearly a large and powerful animal, probably a ten-point stag or better. Even with the full pack behind him, Courtaud would be hesitant about attacking such an animal. Nearby was a pile of fewmets, the stag's droppings. They had been disturbed by the man and seemingly some taken, for they were scattered around. The scent of the fewmets told the wolf-dog even more strongly than the odor of the slot that this was a dangerous animal.

Even so, there might be weaker animals in the herd. With Silver at his side, he assembled his followers and informed them by his motions that he intended to charge the herd. They responded by tail-wagging and licking. Then he led them deep into the grove, the pack following in single file.

They were in luck. Almost at once Courtaud picked up the trail of a hind with a half-grown calf and, judging from the calf's scent, it was sickly. When they put up the herd, it turned out that the calf could hardly run and the hind remained behind to protect it. Both were easily killed. Even the youngest *louvarts* fed well that evening.

The next morning, the blood-red sun was just breaking through the mists and the birds were beginning to whistle to each other, when Courtaud heard one of the attendant ravens screaming at something. He raised his head to listen, testing the wind. The breeze was against him, yet the bird was surely most upset. Slowly and reluctantly Courtaud got to his feet as the bird with an outburst of warning cries took to its wings.

Through the beeches a man was coming, holding a large limier on a fourteen-foot lead. Well behind him came two other men, each leading two raches coupled together.

The whole wolf pack were on their feet instantly and running, but not Courtaud. Far away came the sound of hunting horns, awakening old memories. The sight and smell of the men and the hounds stirred him deeply. Eagerly, he ran toward them. The distraught Silver tried to follow and then turned and fled.

The shocked men cried out at the sight of him. None of them was armed except with a dagger. The *valet de limier* snatched the bugle horn he wore on a baldric around his neck and hurriedly blew the *"menée"*—the signal that a wolf was about.

Courtaud stood wagging his tail and grinning happily. These men were not peasants. They were veneurs and veneurs were his friends.

Answering horn calls came from behind. The lewterers, who handled the hounds that hunted by sight, were bringing up the *lévriers*—the big, fighting greyhounds. Voices were calling *"À moi!* Tristan! Hector! Brun! Roland!" Courtaud was growing alarmed. This did not sound friendly. Still he remained, smiling and waving his tail.

The *lévriers* came tearing through the trees, not knowing what to expect but ready to fight anything, including the raches if they were uncoupled. When they saw him, the *lévriers* charged, clearly with the deadliest intent. At the same time, the men started yelling *"Le loup! Tayaut!"* and the cruel hiss of an arrow whispered past Courtaud's ear, followed by a "thuck!" as the head buried itself in a tree trunk, the shaft vibrating like a plucked harp string.

Courtaud needed no more. These men were enemies. He turned and ran, with the *lévriers* a spear's length from his brush.

Fortunately for him, there were a number of blowdowns and thickets in the woods which he knew and was able to avoid while the greyhounds plunged into them. In a few hundred yards he came on Silver, who had hung back to see what had happened to him. Side by side they raced on. In the open they would have soon been overtaken by the fleet *lévriers,* but the sight-hounds had no noses to speak of and were at a loss whenever the cover hid the wolves. The raches had been slipped now and were coming up strong, their baying rolling through the trees.

The wolves left the woods and Courtaud led the way up the side of a hill. Glancing back—as the ibex had often done when he was pursuing them—he saw that the *lévriers* were stretched out in a long line, one far in advance of the rest. He dropped down behind some rocks and lay quietly while Silver went on. In a few moments the leading *lévrier* tore past, intent on the white form before him. The greyhound probably never knew what hit him. He went flying up into the air and was dead when he hit the ground. Courtaud ran along the side of the hill toward a ridge he knew. While hidden from the hounds, he jumped over the ridge and waited.

He could hear them racing past; their cat feet barely touching the rocks. He waited until he could hear only one. Then he jumped over the ridge, killed the straggler with a single bite through the brain, jumped back, and was gone. The other two *lévriers* kept on, thinking he was still ahead of them. When the toiling raches arrived, they over-ran the scent where Courtaud had jumped back over the ridge and kept on after the greyhounds. When they finally realized that they were no longer on the line, it was too late for them to try back.

Courtaud heard Silver give the pack howl and went to where she was waiting for him on a spur. They trotted side by side to the top of a bluff overlooking a valley and howled together. Listening carefully, they could barely hear the answering call of the pack. They headed toward the noise.

They had to be careful, for the Ardennes were full of men and hounds of every description, especially the black St. Hubert's hounds bred in the nearby monastery of St. Hubert. These magnificent animals were generally considered the finest of all scenting hounds. Although not especially fast, they were staunch, had good noses, and were reckoned terrible fighters. Two of them were considered the equal of one wolf. The wolves could hear the vanchasers (the first pack to be released) tonguing on a hot line while the horns were sounded to tell the hounds they were on the right scent. This business of baying on a trail seemed strange to the wolves, as they always ran mute. A few moments later, the ten-point stag bounded past, his tongue protruding. The wolves hurriedly turned away as the pack swept past but they had no need to be alarmed. The hounds would not have quit the line for any other quarry, not even wolves.

Twice the wolves encountered nets strung across the game trails, partly to force the hunted stag to stay on a certain line and partly in the hope that he might entangle his antlers. The wolves avoided the nets easily—although Silver was frightened by the strange, man-smelling things—and finally rejoined the anxious pack, who smothered both of them with kisses and pats with their forefeet. Safely hidden, they listened while the midel, the second pack, were put on the line after the vanchasers had tired, and then the last pack, or partifters. These were slower but trusty, older hounds, for now the stag was tiring. He doubled back toward the wolves and all the pack rose in alarm, but the stag was headed for a pond into which he plunged in hopes of throwing off his pursuers. This was a trick he had often used with wolves and it was generally successful. The hounds followed him into the water, some even climbing on his back, but he would have succeeded in escaping if the hard-riding *piqueurs* had not come up. They forced their horses into the water and one of them stabbed the exhausted animal to the heart with his dagger.

The hunt continued for a week, for this was a *gran battue* intended to supply the local castle with meat enough for the entire winter. Virtually every animal encountered was killed; a wooded glade was turned into an abattoir, and wagons jolted over the rutted paths to carry away their loads of venison, pork, and goat meat. The wolves kept well away until the slaughter was over.

For the next few days, the pack lived high. There was enough waste to feed many packs of wolves. They grew so particular that they would touch only the best parts such as the fat clinging to the intestines. Gradually, the wasteful feast was over. The pack turned to the less-favored portions. Then to the hides and bones. Finally, when the last scraps were exhausted, they went hunting again.

But there was nothing to hunt. The Ardennes had been swept clean. Driven by hunger, they intruded on the fiefs of other packs, an unforgivable wolf sin, only to find these were also barren and the neighboring packs in as hopeless a condition as themselves. Then came the snow. For days it snowed, a white wall that blinded them and made traveling impossible. When the storm stopped, the hungry animals plunged and struggled through the drifts, uselessly expending their strength. Even when the snow packed down sufficiently to hold them, they were living in a dead world where nothing existed save themselves and a few birds.

Once again Courtaud led them to the villages, where the appetizing scent of sheep and cattle hung on the wind. The peasants had been busy reinforcing their byres with boulders, a tribute to the awe with which the mountain people regarded Courtaud and his pack. The *louvarts* were dying fast now and the females were weakening rapidly. Even Silver was no longer her gay self and Courtaud saw that she had not long to live.

One bleak morning, standing on top of a ridge looking over the white landscape, Courtaud saw far below him the lowlands, where there would be food and ease from the strangling snow. There would also be danger, great danger, but it was that or certain death. The packs had never ventured there because of their fear of man. Courtaud did not share this fear, dangerous as he knew man to be. To him, man was only another animal, to be dreaded no more and no less than a stag or an elk. On this historic morning which would never be forgotten in France, the great wolf-dog led his wild followers down from the Ardennes into the flatlands, toward Paris.

FOUR

The Man-Eater

The depleted pack was reluctant to leave the familiar Ardennes. When the wolves saw that Courtaud was leading them to the unknown lowlands, they hesitated and refused to go on. Even the loyal Silver whimpered and lay down. There was no way the wolf baron could force them to obey him; he was obliged to resort to pleading. He ran back and forth, whining, lying down to show his good intentions and then springing up to take a few more steps down the slope. At last Silver rose and followed him, and then that year's cubs. Several of the older wolves turned back, but when they saw and smelled the blizzard raging above them, they followed Courtaud as the lesser of two evils.

Perhaps they would have balked at leaving the well-known coniferous forests if by good luck Courtaud had not happened on a flock of blue grouse buried in the snow. The position of each bird was marked by a sunken spot where the heat of its body had melted the ice. Courtaud stumbled on the first one by chance; after that he found the rest by sight and scent. There were only a few of the birds so only a few of the pack got as much as a mouthful, but they were all encouraged by the presence of prey and went on more willingly.

After another few hours of trotting, the snow was so light that it was invisible except against the dark pines. Then they were below it, in oak and beech woods. Here they stopped for a rest, for even the adult wolves were tired. They slept for twelve hours before going on.

Compared to the windswept Schnee Fifel, here it was almost balmy. In sheltered nooks, hellebore was in blossom. They passed through a hazel coppice where the purple catkins were beginning to form, and in the morning they heard the larks singing as the birds rose in their circling flights. None of this interested the wolves. They were famished and except for the grouse there had been no sign or scent of food.

So far they had not encountered any traces of humans, for the serfs seldom went into the forests. To them, the forests were haunted places full of evil spirits and unknown dangers, but that night the pack came on a statue of Ardhuina, the ancient hunting goddess. It was well hidden in the forest, for if the priests had known of it, they would have had the old idol destroyed. Someone knew of it, though, and still worshipped there, for on the altar lay the carcass of a skinned fox and a dead owl, left as sacrifices. They had been partly eaten by ravens and magpies and the wolves quickly finished what was left. They spent the day here, sleeping under a giant linden tree that must have seeded itself in the waters left by the Flood.

In the morning, the ground was gray with hoarfrost and a scum of white ice lay in the hollows. Reluctant as he was to travel by day, Courtaud decided to push on. He had to find human habitation, for there would be food.

That afternoon they came on a village, but it was deserted. It had been sacked and burned. Here and there showed the sharp points of gables, known as "Knolles' miters" after the English leader who systematically burned every village he encountered. There was nothing but the blackened, charred bracken that had served as thatching, now fallen in. There was a little spilled grain that the birds had not found and the bones of men and cattle, all well-picked. Silver found the remains of a dead dog with a little meat on them. That was all.

For the next three days the pack traveled over country where not a rooster crowed nor a hen clucked. Every village they found was nothing but briars and bracken. The bridges had been destroyed and they were forced to swim the ale-colored streams. Courtaud stopped trying to get through the woods with their thick undergrowth and went openly along the deserted roads, barred by the shadows of the poplars that lined them. There was no danger here except from starvation. The pack met no passersby. It was said in those days that the roads of France were paved with corpses rather than stones, but unfortunately for the wolves, other scavengers had long ago disposed of the corpses.

France, which formerly had been the garden of Europe, was now a burned-out trash heap. This was the height of the Hundred Years War, which had been going on so long that no one could remember when there had been peace. The country was split between the English, the Burgundians, and the forces of the weak Charles VII. Meanwhile, bands of outlaws looted the helpless land.

Every day now wolves were dropping out of the pack, too weak from hunger to go on. There was game in the forests but they did not know where it was and they were daunted by the scent posts of the local packs they encountered. Not only was poaching on another pack's fief a deadly sin, but also Courtaud did not dare start a war with his followers in such a weakened condition. Most of them had not eaten for a week. Once they managed to surprise a bustard on the ice of a frozen pond and were able to outrun the big, fifty-pound bird. Once they trapped two large swans by a tangle of osiers. The woods were as full of squirrels as a lake is of minnows, but they were small and almost impossible to capture. They caught a few rabbits. Deer, their basic diet, seemed to have disappeared, for they found no sign of any.

After a night's hunting, they were resting in a half-overgrown clearing dating back to the golden days before the war, when serfs called *hospites*—men who were willing to clear new land—had been given their freedom and allowed to travel about, opening glades in the forest for cultivation. The morning mist lay low, but in the distance came the call of curlews. Courtaud was sleeping when the slight breeze brought to him the stench of men, horses, and leather. Instantly he was awake. He was about to rouse the rest of the pack when there came the jingle of bits, clump of hoofs, and low voices. The pack sprang up, and then copied their leader who had crouched down, his ears pricked to hear every sound.

A troop of men armed cap-à-pie—from head to foot—were riding down a path cut many years before by the hospites and now much overgrown but still passable. Each man rode a palfrey, leading his great destrier, or war-horse, on his right hand. The destriers, enormous animals coming from the Perche Hills, were known as Percherons. They could carry the weight of a man equipped with the heavy new armor, so massive it could withstand even the arrows shot from the terrible English longbows, which could drive an arrow through chain mail as though it were a cloak. These men were covered in plate mail from their great visored bascinets to the steel sabatons over their feet. They carried fourteen-foot lances whose butts fitted into metal sockets fastened to their stirrups. The war-horses too were armored *en-barbe*; that is, on their heads were peytrals, or helmets, on their sides flanchards, and on their flanks cruppers, both being strips of armor plating. The menie, or war party, moved in various units, each under its own flag: the square banners of the barons, the forked pennons of the knights, and the triangular streaming penoncels of the squires in the second rank.

The pack lay quietly, letting the host pass them, and even after the last had gone still did not dare to move. Finally Courtaud stood up, sniffing the air. The rest imitated him. He was about to leave the glade in a different direction than the men had taken when suddenly a stag, wild with fright, dashed past them. It had been put up by the army. For a moment Courtaud was prepared to give chase, but the stag was in prime condition and going far too fast. Regretfully he saw it vanish among the trees.

Far to the left came a series of halloos, given in different accents from the tones of the mounted men. Another group of men had seen the stag and were shouting, at it in sport. The sound of the horsemen was still audible but now it abruptly ceased. The menie had also heard the shouts and were listening. A few minutes later, Courtaud heard them leave the path and go through the woods toward the shouting.

The pack was impatient to be gone, running back and forth and whimpering. They hated anything to do with humans. Courtaud, however, had other ideas. He recalled from former days the oily scent of armor, the smell of horses, and the clank of arms. In those days, when he had always been well fed, it had mattered little to him, but he connected it with the smell of blood and blood meant food. To the unbelieving horror of the pack, he followed the menie, at a discreet distance.

The pack had followed him too long to stop now, although they shivered as they slipped among the trees, avoiding the worst of the underbrush. In the distance they could hear the horses crashing through the cover. Then the noise stopped. At the same time, the trees ahead of them thinned and they came to the edge of the woods.

They were on top of a long ridge and below them was open land covered with broom and heather. A few hundred yards away the land rose again to another ridge running parallel to the one where they lay, but bare of trees. A road ran along the top of this second ridge and another menie was moving over it, but a menie very different from the one that had passed the wolves. Most of the men were on foot and wore no armor but boiled-leather jackets with the Cross of St. George marked on them and wickerwork helmets with crosspieces of iron on the top. These men carried great bows longer than themselves, with quivers of arrows either slung over their shoulders or fastened to their belts. They also carried long stakes, bound with iron and sharpened at both ends. There were also a few mounted men in full plate armor, as well as baggage carts and sumpter mules heavily loaded. Courtaud watched the bowmen especially. He had a horror of bows and their ability to kill at a distance.

There was noise from the menie near the wolves. The men were mounting their destriers. A moment's pause. Then came the clear, high notes of a trumpet and the menie debouched from the woods. They paused for a moment to form ranks. Then the trumpet spoke again and the menie began to trot down the side of the ridge, their lance points flashing in the sun. They rode so closely together that a glove thrown among them would not have touched the ground. The necks of the horses behind lay on the cruppers of those in front.

There was a flicker on the hill as the opposing war host made ready to receive them. The archers took up positions on the flanks and with great mallets that had been slung over their backs drove their stakes into the ground slanting toward the oncoming horsemen. The mounted men took up their position in the center. The trumpet spoke again. At the signal, the lances of the attacking force swayed down until they were leveled low, the riders bending over until their heads touched the horses' manes. The big horses broke into a ponderous gallop, clods flying from beneath their hoofs like startled birds. The wolves could feel the roll of the hoofs through the ground, and they trembled.

On the hill, the bows of the archers swayed upward. For an instant they held motionless. Then a blizzard of arrows leaped away toward the charging horsemen. It was like a black snowstorm except that each snowdrop was tipped with steel. Horses went down on their knees, screaming, their riders pitching from the saddles. The rest pushed on, hurling over the smashed tangle of the dead and dying. Another volley of arrows sprang away. So deadly was the bowmen's aim that if a man raised his visor, he never closed it again. The archers had time for one more volley before the van of the charging menie reached them.

Repulsed by the stakes, the horsemen concentrated on the opposing mounted men. As they came together, there was a crash that made the wolves jump. After the first shock, the lances were useless and both sides drew their swords. Sparks flew as the swords struck on ailettes and pectorals that protected their shoulders and chests. Men went down with cloven helms, vomiting blood and spitting broken teeth. The pennons reeled and tottered. The wolves could smell the blood and hear the shrieks of the wounded as the horses trampled them. The archers dropped their bows, drew their daggers, and, running in, hamstrung the horses and dragged the men off their backs. In their heavy armor, the dismounted knights were virtually helpless.

Watching, the wolves saw a mounted man turn his horse's

head and ride wildly away toward the comparative safety of the woods. Two more followed him. Then half a dozen. Then all that was left of the attacking force shredded away in panic. The brief engagement was over.

The archers climbed over piles of the fallen, prying open helms and unriveting armor plate to see if the men inside were alive. If one was, and promised a large ransom, he was taken prisoner. Otherwise, the bowmen cut his throat. Some archers took four and five prisoners, enough to make them rich for life. The mounted knights disdained to hunt for loot so openly, but they rode about and if any man called to them, their squires took him prisoner.

After an hour or so the Free Company, one of the many bands of unemployed mercenaries who were virtually bandits, continued on its way with its prisoners. Such skirmishes occurred almost daily. It was the way the Free Companies made their living.

When the men were gone, Courtaud rose and, crossing the little valley, fell on one of the dead horses. He did not feed daintily. He tore off great gobs of flesh and bolted them. Slowly the others followed him, hungry but repelled by the man-scent. The *louvarts* were the first to eat, and then Silver. Gradually the rest of the pack set to. The human dead they did not touch; there was no need. There were plenty of horses. Soon ravens and magpies joined the feast, picking out the eyes of the dead as breaking through the hide was too difficult. The birds made no discrimination between horses and humans. Food was food to them.

For the next three weeks, the wolf pack followed the Free Company as the ravens had followed them in the Ardennes, and lived well. They grew used to the odor of humans and ceased to mind it. They also learned to eat human flesh. Occasionally the Free Company would find some village overlooked by former raiders and destroy it. After killing the inhabitants, they would slaughter the cattle and have a feast, but generally there were few cattle left, hardly enough for the men. It had always been difficult to carry cattle over the winter months because of the shortage of fodder. Now, with so much of the land laid waste, farming had become almost impossible, so except for a little breeding stock, all animals were slaughtered in the fall. The wolves would have gone hungry if they had been forced to rely on the leftovers of the feasts, but there was no need for that. There was always plenty of human meat and now that their dread of human scent was removed, they ate it readily. In this as in all matters, Courtaud led the way. He had never had any reluctance to have dealings with man as long as he was sure the man could not hurt him.

Occasionally a wolf would seize what he thought to be a corpse, only to have the corpse cry out and move. At first this frightened the wolves, but soon, they came to regard it as only an annoyance. They found that the badly injured people could put up no effective resistance. If there were plenty of genuine corpses lying about, they ignored the living; but if there was a shortage of food, they took the attitude that the wounded, in resisting, were trying to deprive them of their rightful meal. With Courtaud setting the example, they quickly discovered that humans were easy to kill—far easier than a red deer or an elk or an ibex. A wolf might go toward an injured man or woman and draw back when the person struggled. But when another wolf approached the person, the first wolf would defend his right to the quarry, seizing the victim and growling to establish that it was his rightful kill. The second wolf would then rush in and grab another part of the helpless wretch, and between them they would pull him apart. But they still would not attack an uninjured person able to defend himself.

The Free Company soon discovered that the pack was following them and regarded it as a great joke. They jested that it was now unnecessary for them to exterminate the French—the wolves would do it for them. "In other lands, wolves run from men. In France, men run from wolves," they boasted. They gave their leader the title of "Wolf Feeder." He was delighted.

As the Free Company penetrated deeper and deeper into the country and closer to Paris, they began to encounter increasingly powerful menies led by warriors who had become familiar with their tactics. These experienced warriors did not launch head-on attacks into the midst of the murderous arrow storm. They outflanked the company or pinned them down by surrounding them and strove to starve them out. In this the French chivalry had finally developed as much intelligence as a wolf pack, which would never dream of making a frontal attack on dangerous quarry if they could possibly take it from the rear, and always strove to wear down their prey before moving in for the kill. The Free Company may have been composed of brutes, but they were powerful brutes, skilled in war. Time after time they were able to break through the French encirclement and escape, but eventually they realized that this could not keep on. Reluctantly, their leader gave the order to leave the district.

The wolves now were left without the kind friends who had fed them, yet they no longer cared to suffer the efforts and privations involved in catching wild game. Indeed, they had almost forgotten the techniques. They had become virtual parasites on man. As the Free Company had gone, they would have to become raiders in their place.

They were now in a part of France that had missed the worst effects of the war. Here there were still castles that had been able to resist all attacks, and at the feet of the castles, villages where the inhabitants were still able to grow some crops and pasture cattle. These peasants depended mainly on their herds, for in time of trouble, the animals could be quickly driven into the enceinte of the castle, the drawbridge lifted, and the portcullis dropped. It would be a bold group of adventurers indeed who would undertake the siege of a castle. But the crops could not be so easily moved and in case of an attack would be lost. For that reason, only land within a, bowshot of the castle walls was cultivated. It could be protected by covering fire.

After a day's aimless searching, the pack came on a white-washed chapel in the woods that had miraculously escaped detection. There was nothing to eat, only the wooden image of a saint, but people had been there recently to put flowers in the shrine and the wolves backtracked them. Within an hour they came upon a cluster of mud-and-wattle huts huddled under the tower of a church, the only stone building in the place, to which all the winding lanes ran. Most of the hovels had enclosed yards where grew cabbages, onions, parsley, and sweet herbs. Behind the houses were larger vegetable gardens with cherry and apple trees. Beyond that ran the river, flowing past the gallows where the bones of two men hung. Near the river were the pens for the pigs and a few tethered cows. Small shelters housed ducks and geese. The mill was clacking away and at the forge the wolves could hear the smith's hammer strokes and see the sparks fly. The herdsmen were driving the cattle into the byres and the shepherds their flocks to the folds against the night.

To the east, built on a rocky outcrop by the river, stood the castle. The central keep was twenty times as tall as a man and had taken five years to build. So many villeins died from the corvées—the forced labor—that it had seemed at one time the count would rule over a desert when he had completed the work, yet because of it, not only the Free Companies but even the English armies had left the dread place alone. Yet even so, two men stood constantly back to back on the top of the keep, keeping watch over the lord's demesne, their horns slung over their shoulders to sound the alarm.

The pack lay and watched, invisible except for their red tongues and golden eyes. Luckily, the wind was in their favor—otherwise the serfs' dogs would have scented them—and they waited for sunset. Even after the church's bells had rung vespers, they remained still, although the glorious scent of live meat was constantly in their nostrils. The red light of fires gleamed through the cracks of the huts and still Courtaud refused to make his move. It was not until the compline rang from the church that he rose, stretched, and turned to the pack. The excited animals went through the formalities of the group kissing, patting with forefeet, and feverish tail-wagging they always indulged in before an attack. Then, with Courtaud in the fore, they advanced on the village.

For all his astuteness, Courtaud had not bothered to mark any particular byre or fold for his initial attack. He avoided the lanes and swung around behind the houses, the pack following him. The many scents confused him and he could not tell in just which buildings the cattle were.

Suddenly it seemed as though all the dogs in the village began barking at once. The sound excited the wolves rather than alarming them. A breath later came the frantic ringing of sheep bells as the sheep, mad with fear, dashed back and forth in their folds. Then came the roll of hoofs as the horses strove to escape even though they were hobbled. There was the sound of splintering wood as the cattle broke out of their byres.

The pack knew now that they had been scented and no more concealment was possible. Courtaud rushed at the nearest hut. He could smell cattle within, for most of the serfs' huts were both stable and home, the animals separated from the people by only a few palings. Wealthier peasants who owned a number of animals generally kept them in a separate building. There was a space of a few inches under the door and Courtaud thrust his long muzzle in, sniffing loudly. From within came loud screams and the sound of men's voices, shouting in alarm. Courtaud flung, his weight against the door. The wattle trembled but the leather hinges held. Courtaud tried again and again while the screams grew louder. Now an ox was bawling, a cow mooing, and pigs squealing. Again, Courtaud threw himself at the door. As he did so he heard the terror-stricken cry of a horse. The wolves had found one of the hobbled animals and were pulling it down.

Courtaud left the hut and ran to be in on the kill. Cattle, sheep, and horses were running, crazed with fear, and among them ran the wolves, sometimes hard to tell from the sheep in the darkness except that the wolves' yellow eyes shone green in the moonlight. In a nearby byre Courtaud heard the cattle slipping and falling on the soft dung they had voided in their terror. The wolves had gone mad at the sight of the running beasts and lost their usual discipline. Though there was quarry and enough around them for the taking, they struck at the doors of the huts to get at the beasts inside. An old deaf woman opened her door, thinking that it was one of her neighbors seeking entrance. When she saw her error, she tried to slam it shut again but a wolf seized the door in his teeth and worried it while the woman screamed. Courtaud passed another screaming woman. She had been caught in the garderobe, or privy, and the wolves had overturned it. She lay there trapped inside like a rabbit in a snare, screaming, although the wolves paid no attention to her.

In front of Courtaud, a cow went down on her knees and instantly he put his forelegs on the animal's shoulder, pushed her over, and ripped out her throat. Silver was right behind him.

Together they tore out the unborn calf and began to devour it. One of the *louvarts* joined them.

Courtaud felt something hiss past him and saw the *louvart* leap in the air, spin around, and then fall gasping. Hungry as he was, he dropped the calf and turned around. Men with bows were shooting at them from the open doorways and windows. Courtaud gave his warning bark, which Silver instantly obeyed, and both animals ran. Although no more oral warnings were given, the pack sensed and saw the fear of their leaders and followed at full speed. Within seconds they were clear of the village, frustrated and raging. They had been robbed of the great gorge they had promised themselves.

Down the road came a cart pulled by a pony and making a great noise, for the driver had hung it with tins, bells, and bird scares which were believed to keep away wolves. The man was Jean Dubois from Laon and with him were his wife and little son. In the cart was a tethered sheep which Jean was taking to Paris to sell. The road being bad from rains, he had been delayed, reaching the village where he had meant to spend the night long after dark.

Before Jean could cross himself, the wolves were around the cart. They paid no attention to the people, but Courtaud himself sprang for the pony's throat. Down he went with Courtaud's teeth in his neck. Others of the pack leaped into the cart and started pulling out the sheep.

Dubois was a man of great, stubborn courage and not many brains, for he tried to save the pony that was now under a pile of wolves. Jumping from the cart, he struck at the wolves with his peasant's billhook. They took no heed of him until he tried to force Courtaud away. To the wolf baron, he was on his lawful kill and he refused to retreat. Half a dozen wolves were tearing at the pony, who screamed the terrible scream of a horse in agony. Dubois tripped and fell over the body and the wolves, ripping the pony apart, made no distinction between man and beast. Dubois died with Courtaud's teeth in his throat. This was the first uninjured man any of the wolves had killed and had he not interfered, they would have spared him. Although they devoured the pony and the sheep, the pack ignored the woman and child who sat dead with fear in the cart.

The pack were still hungry when they went on, but Courtaud did not dare to return to the village. It did not take the wolves long to discover that the frightened cattle had scattered through the fields, where they could easily be tracked down and killed. So heavily did the pack feed that night that it was all they could do to drag themselves to the woods when daylight came.

When hunting wild quarry, the pack had never killed more than they needed. There was a good reason for this. Wild quarry was too difficult to catch. With the helpless domestic stock, they went wild. Many of the animals escaped mutilated but still alive. A cow had her belly badly torn, yet still reached the river where she drank till she could hold no more. Next morning, her owner had to kill her as she was beyond help. Several sheep were smothered when they piled up in a corner of the fold. Three horses had their tails bitten off where the pursuing wolves had grabbed them from behind and tried to pull them down. Others were badly slashed by the wolves' long canines. Of Jean Dubois, there was nothing left except the head and intestines.

Usually, the pack would have laid up for a day or two after such a gorge, but they had gone hungry so long that their bodies used up the nourishment rapidly. By evening, they were ready to take the trail again. The pack had spread out through the trees and Courtaud howled to bring them together—a howl that made the listening serfs cringe. Soon the shadows under the trees became alive. Hungry eyes in pairs glowed in the gathering darkness. They were prepared for another blood glut.

The wolf baron first made a sweep to see if any kine had escaped their notice the night before and were still wandering in the woods, but all survivors had been rounded up by the villeins. Only slightly disappointed, Courtaud led the way toward the village. As soon as it was completely dark, he would lead another attack on the folds and byres, scatter the kine, and then cut up the stragglers in the forest where his pack could not be shot at ambush from the huts.

A rising wind blew through the trees with a noise like horses galloping. A scud of rain was flung in their faces. Courtaud smelled thyme, and swung to avoid it, for the herbs always grew near water and he disliked getting his feet wet. Then they reached the edge of the woods and stopped dead.

All the village livestock were being driven toward the castle. There were several sounders of swine, a herd of cattle, three flocks of sheep, and horses, oxen, and geese. The drawbridge was lowered to receive them and the portcullis raised.

To Courtaud, this was a wondrous opportunity. One swift charge would scatter the livestock, which would then be at the pack's mercy. He rushed forward, making ten-foot bounds.

The wolves were among the domestic animals before the slow-thinking serfs realized what had happened. They then panicked, calling on the men-at-arms for help. The wolves flowed like water through the tame beasts, seizing their quarry by the hind legs and flanks. A cow, mad with pain and terror, ran dragging a wolf hanging to her tail. At last he pulled her to her knees. Another grabbed her by the nose. The cow used her fore hoofs as well as her horns but the wolf who had her by the nose stretched her out until his comrade could hamstring her. A horse went down with four wolves tearing at him. His hind legs kicked a few times and he was dead.

Courtaud had singled out a heifer. He seized her by the throat and by sheer strength jerked her head over heels so she came down on her back. The wolf baron turned over as well but recovered himself and stood back, allowing his vassals to finish the business.

Inside the castle, trumpets were sounding the alarm as though for an attack by a human menie. The archers on the parapet could not use their bows for dread of hitting the cattle and serfs, and none of the men-at-arms was eager to close with the wolves, for there would have been small need of a leech for any man they got their teeth into. As the kine poured into the bailey, the excited pack followed them, led by Courtaud.

The count alone kept his head, for he shouted, "By the Apostle whom the penitents seek, we have them! Porter, uphaul the bridge! Let the portcullis fall!"

Until now Courtaud had not realized that he was leading his pack into a trap. He had seen only the kine and sought to stampede them so they would scatter. Looking about him, he perceived they were surrounded by the castle walls and there was no escape save by the barbican by which they had entered. Drunk as the pack was by sight and scent of the rich feast around them, Courtaud turned and ran. Instantly the rest did the same.

It was in the nick of time, for the bridge was beginning to rise. Encouraged, the men-at-arms rushed forward with their pikes and Courtaud turned to face them with Silver at his side. The men shrank back from the snarling wolves, although they would have instantly closed with armed humans, who would have been far more dangerous adversaries. Then the porter released the portcullis suspended between the entrance towers.

Without turning his head, Courtaud could see it falling, for as wolves have eyes on either side of their heads they can see backward more easily than a man. The wolf baron was brave, yet not reckless. He turned and sped for the gateway with Silver beside him. It was a race between the wolves and the falling portcullis and all who watched held their breath. An instant before the portcullis struck, Silver slipped under it, but the larger Courtaud was not so lucky. He dodged under it, it is true, but one of the iron spikes caught him by the tail and held him.

A great shout went up and a dozen men sprang forward as the wolf baron struggled for his life, tearing at the flag-stones with his sharp claws and turning to bite at the tail that held him. "Throw a noose around his neck and strangle him," shouted the count. "I would have his fell whole and unmarked." While men ran to get a rope, Courtaud made one last great effort. He tore himself free, leaving the greater part of his tail on the spike. In three bounds he was on the upraising bridge where Silver had already passed, scrambled up it as though up a sloping wall, reached the top, and sprang clear. He fell into the moat, swam to the far side despite the arrows that splashed around him, and climbed the bank. For an instant he turned to look back, and then was gone.

The next morning the body of an old shepherd was found, together with his dead dog and all his sheep. The old man had not heard the reeve—who acted as the count's overseer—give the order to bring all livestock into the castle. Not one of the sheep had been eaten, although Courtaud had partly devoured the man, for his great fore was around the mutilated corpse.

This, then, is how Courtaud came to get his name, that is to say, Cut-Tail. From that day on, Courtaud never met a man he did not try to kill, and he taught his pack to do likewise.

FIVE

The Outlaw

Three weeks later the pack was lying up in a little glade they had come to regard as their home. A spring bubbled up here so strongly that the water seemed to be boiling over the white sand. In this sheltered spot white clover, tufted vetch, and star-eyed daisies were beginning to grow. Like a tent, a vast beech with silver bark overhung the glade, the tree's gnarled roots covered with climbing mosses. This tree was considered by the few humans who had ever visited the spot-as sacred to the fairies, and in happier times children had hung garlands from the branches as tributes to the Little People. A few of these faded garlands still remained.

The stump of the wolf baron's tail had almost healed by now. Silver had been an excellent nurse, keeping the raw flesh clean with her tongue and driving away the early flies and gnats. She herself had sustained an arrow wound in her shoulder that gave her some trouble, but she ignored it in worrying over her mate's mutilation. In addition to the pain, the loss of his great banner had humiliated Courtaud, as he had used his tail to signal his moods and desires to the pack.

The wolves had not confined their activities to the demesne of the castle where Courtaud had met his accident. They hunted over a wide area, seldom striking twice in the same place. They could travel seventy miles in a night, while a journey of twenty miles was considered difficult for humans over the miserable, robber-infested roads. So by the time one of their raids had been reported, they were many miles away in a different lord's demesne. As few lords dared to trespass on another lord's fief, this rendered the pack virtually immune from pursuit, as it did human raiders.

Both because of the loss of his tail and the problems of keeping the pack organized, Courtaud had paid little attention to Silver even after she came into estrus, so the female was forced to make the first advances. Often a wolf would select some object as a keepsake and prize it highly. Courtaud had selected the thighbone of the shepherd he had killed as a trophy and kept it buried near the spring. He would often dig it up to play with it and no other wolf was allowed to come near the keepsake. Like every wolf in the pack, Silver knew all about the bone and now that they had returned to the glade after a two-day raid, she dug it up and carried it past Courtaud with an air of great nonchalance.

For a few seconds, the wolf baron could not believe such sacrilege had actually been committed. Then he sprang up with a growl that ended in a roar of rage. Silver fled, still holding fast to the bone, with Courtaud after her. Once among the trees, she could outdodge him but as soon as she caught the angry scent of his anal glands, the little female knew that she had gone too far. She dropped the bone and darted away while the furious Courtaud retrieved his prized possession. He was contemplating running Silver down and punishing her after he had cached the bone, when he saw her stop as abruptly as though she had run into some obstacle and stand motionless except for her twitching nostrils.

Reluctantly, Courtaud shoved the bone under some dead leaves with his nose and then raised his head to test the air. He could detect only the usual morning smells: the dewlaid dust, the grass and herbs crushed by the pack's feet, woodsmoke and the scent of torches quenched at dawn from the distant village. There was also the odor of horses, ox-sweat, and the faint smell of dogs. He listened carefully. The first birds were cheeping, he could hear the dull blows of a woodsman's axe, and cows lowing to be milked. Nothing alarming.

Silver was alerted, although not alarmed. She seemed curious and somewhat interested in whatever it was she scented. Courtaud left his precious bone and swung at his easy stride to pick up the same current of air she had found. The moment he had done so, he also stopped dead.

A strange yet delightfully tantalizing odor was carried by the breeze. Like all wolves, Courtaud was intensely curious and would have investigated any unusual smell but this odor drew him with a fascination that was akin to a sexual drive. It awoke cravings in him that he could scarcely control. All he wanted was to find the source of that thrilling scent and roll in it.

The odor was that of long-dead fish. The heads, tails, and backbones of fish had been left to rot in a clay pot and then cupfuls of the rank, oily muck had been tossed along the trail at intervals. To any member of the canine family, the smell was irresistible.

The two wolves followed the odor as though in a trance. From a distance, the other members of the pack saw their preoccupation and followed. They, too, were seduced by the smell and followed it blindly. Then Courtaud encountered another odor.

It was musk from the anal glands of another male wolf. At the scent, Courtaud stopped, growled, and then pressed on fiercely. Yes, here was a spot where the impudent stranger had sprinkled a tree. Silver smelled the spot too and her tail rotated with uncertainty like a puzzled squirrel's. The urine smelled stale, as though very old, yet the sprinkling was recent. The yellow drops still glistened on the trunk of the tree. The ground around the tree smelled of cattle dung, yet there was no odor of cattle. Silver did not like any of this. She withdrew hurriedly, tail going between her legs, but not forgetting to use her nose. The manure smell persisted all along the game trail. Silver quietly got off the trail and retreated to the safety of the woods.

Courtaud was too furious to notice such niceties. All he knew or cared about was that a strange male had invaded his territory and deliberately left a challenge. The hackles on his neck rose, a deep war growl rumbled in his throat, and even the bewitching odor of the rotten fish, although now stronger than ever, was forgotten. The other males imitated his deep-mouthed threats and duplicated his actions as he contemptuously obliterated the foreign scent with copious splashes of his own urine.

The pack continued down the path, tension growing as they encountered another scent post. Silver followed nervously through the trees. She knew too much to interfere with a male defending his territory, yet something was terribly wrong, of that she was sure. Then the pack came to a sudden halt.

Before them was a circular enclosure of woven osier and from it came the strong odor of dog. Although the fence was too tall for the wolves to see over, in the center was a mound that stood higher than the fence and on top of it they could see a dog tied by a chain—the most terrified, abject dog in the world. He had long before scented the wolf pack and knew what his fate would be, for there was a feud to the death between wolf and dog. Unless they were hungry, wolves were indifferent to other animals except dogs. They never lost an opportunity to kill a dog.

Courtaud alone held back. He had been raised with dogs and was part dog himself and did not share the wolfish hatred for their first cousins. Still, seeing that the pack clearly expected him to lead them in the attack, he was starting forward when Silver burst from the thicket and flung herself before him in the attitude of extreme submission, lying on her back and wetting. She was whimpering as though in terror and Courtaud hesitated.

Blackie did not. Even though he was the most cowardly of the pack, he had learned that he could kill dogs easily. He had never been up against the hard-biting alaunts or the fierce *lévriers,* and the ordinary village dogs were helpless against the big wolf's powerful jaws and great weight. Now, for once seeing his usually redoubtable leader hold back, Blackie decided to assert himself. He rushed forward and with an easy bound cleared the fence. Wild with excitement, two other wolves followed him. The dog screamed with terror and despair.

The pack stood waiting to see the chained victim torn apart. Some of them ran back and forth, whining with eagerness to be in at the kill, but most held back, waiting for some signal from, their leader. Nothing happened. The dog continued to cower against the stake to which he was chained in the center of the mound but of the three wolves there was no sign. They had completely vanished.

Then there came a frightened yelp, seemingly from deep within the earth. Usually wolves take punishment in silence, whether in a trap or under the teeth of a pack of wolf-hounds, and only rarely do they venture a cry for help. Stiff-legged, testing every inch of earth he walked on, nostrils extended to catch the merest wisp of scent, Courtaud slowly approached the fence. After satisfying himself that it was harmless (the anxious

Silver, who had followed close behind him, was not nearly as confident), he reared and put his paws on the top of the barrier. So tall was the half-alaunt that he could just look over the edge.

Instantly the mystery was, explained. Just inside the osier fence a deep ditch had been dug with sides that slanted inward, making it impossible for the trapped wolves to climb out. The earth from the ditch had been used to build the mound so the dog would be visible from without. At the bottom of the ditch, the three wolves were running to and fro, vainly seeking a way to escape.

Furiously, Courtaud attacked the fence. He tore at the osiers, and finally Orange and then two more of the pack came to help him. Before long they had torn a hole in it and were able to look down directly into the pit, but then they could do no more. In his rage and hopelessness, there were several times when Courtaud was at the point of jumping into the pit himself. All his instincts were to help his entrapped comrades, but he was helpless.

From behind him came the alarm signal—the short bark followed by a quick howl. From the manner in which it was given Courtaud knew men were coming. Instantly the pack melted into the woods like smoke, only Silver momentarily hesitating. Courtaud alone stood his ground. If there was only one man and he was not armed, the wolf baron would defy him.

He caught the sound and smell of horses even before he could see them. From the way they moved, he knew they were being ridden. There were more than one and he knew that almost invariably mounted men were armed. Resistance was impossible, and yet he lingered a moment, hoping against hope there would be some way he could get his teeth into these hated creatures. Three horsemen came down the path, flecked with splotches of light. Their leader saw him and, with astonishing quickness, snatched a crossbow that hung from his saddle and, putting one foot through the iron stirrup at the bow's end, pulled the string back until it engaged in the release mechanism. There was something strange about the hand he used to cock the bow and the way he employed it. Courtaud was conscious of the strangeness but did not know what it was. The truth was that the man had no right hand; he had a crudely fashioned iron hook instead.

Belligerent though he was, Courtaud did not wait for more. He had never seen a crossbow before but he recognized it as some sort of weapon, quite possibly capable of sending a missile at him. When the man reached into a quiver at his belt and pulled out a short, deadly bolt, the thing looked enough like an arrow to confirm the wolf's worst fears. In two great bounds he was gone, long before the man could put the bolt in place.

The men dismounted by the fence and looked down into the pit. From their shouts and laughter, it was obvious that they were well pleased. In spite of Silver's almost inaudible whimperings, Courtaud crept back until he could see what was going on. If the men could have known how tempted he was to make a sudden rush and kill at least one of their number, they would have spun around and stood with their boar spears braced. Although they had all heard of the man-eating wolf pack, they did not believe the tales. Wolves never attacked men unless the animals were "wood"—that is to say, mad or rabid.

The man with the crossbow raised it and aimed into the pit. He squeezed the trigger and Courtaud heard the dull, flat crack of the release, so different from the twang of a longbow. There was no sound from the pit but the men shouted with satisfaction, and a few seconds later Courtaud could smell wolf blood and with it the odor of death as the stricken animal voided its bowels. Again the bow was cocked and another bolt sent on its fatal errand. This time there was a faint cry and Courtaud could hear the animal leap into the air and crash to earth.

Now the men changed their technique. The one with the hook put down the crossbow and, taking a hatchet from his belt, came toward the woods where Courtaud was hiding. The wolf sank down, his head between his forepaws, ready for flight or attack, but the man only took a few steps among the trees and cut down a forked branch. The stranger was as big for a man as Courtaud was for a wolf. His head especially was gigantic and Courtaud could have put one of his great paws between the man's eyes. The man was black as charcoal, with a broken nose that spread over his face and thick red lips that resembled newly sliced meat. He had no ears. He wore a jerkin of tanned leather and a cap of wildcat skin. His hose were of bull's hide fastened with strips of bark. Courtaud's twitching nostrils tried hard to pick up the man's scent, but he was too far away and there was no breeze there.

The man returned to the fence with his forked stick and slid into the pit with it. Courtaud could not see what was happening but after a short pause the man shouted to his friends, who dropped down into the pit beside him. A few minutes later Blackie was hoisted out, his long muzzle tied together with leather thongs and his neck strapped fast in the fork of the stick, which had made him a prisoner. Then they tied his feet together until he was helpless. Courtaud saw his old companion put on the back of a horse. One of the men gave the imprisoned dog some food and water to keep him alive and the broken fence was repaired. Then the men rode away.

When he was sure they had gone, Courtaud stole out and tried to pick up their scent. To his. astonishment, he could smell nothing but cattle dung. The men had buried the wooden sabots they wore and their leather gloves in a pile of dung overnight and this concealed their own scent. If Courtaud had not seen them, he would not have realized that man had found his retreat in the forest. Yet only for a time was the wolf baron at a loss. The men were not as cunning as they thought themselves. They had brushed against the leaves and undergrowth and by stretching up Courtaud was able to get their body scent in such places. He inhaled it deeply to be sure of recognizing it again, especially the scent of the big man with the hook. Courtaud had the feeling that it was this man who represented the real danger.

He was right. Gilles Garnier was a *braconnier,* that is to say, a poacher. He had been caught twice. The first time, the lord's foresters had found him in the woods with a limier on a leash. For that, he had lost his ears. The second time he was found with his crossbow cocked and a bolt in place. For that he had lost his right hand. If he were caught again—it meant death. So Gilles had become cautious. When he went to visit the willow nooses he used as snares for rabbits, he made sure that they had not been found by the foresters who might be lying up and watching them. He always went downwind of the snares with his limier, knowing the dog would signal him if men were about. He was careful where he spread his birdlime for the lord's fat pigeons that did so much damage to the serfs' crops. At night when he went fishing with a torch and a spear, he made sure all the foresters were either safe in bed or drunk. When he stretched nets across the game trails to entangle deer and an occasional wild pig, he first spent long days checking to be certain the foresters never visited those particular trails.

In spite of all his precautions, Gilles would long ago have been dangling at the end of his own, bowstring, had not he come to an unspoken agreement not only with the foresters but even with the lord himself. My lord's *valet de limier* did not track Gilles too carefully for fear that on the day of some great hunt, when the valet had harbored an exceptionally fine stag whose impressive fewmets, or droppings, had delighted the visiting nobles, Gilles would wait until the valet had departed and then alarm the animal so when the hunt arrived, there was no quarry and the valet would be in danger of losing his place. The foresters knew that if Gilles took his toll of the lord's game, he was even more zealous than they in protecting it from other *braconniers*. When Gilles found the nets or snares of another poacher, he would promptly inform the foresters and then they would get the credit for apprehending the scoundrel. If a wildcat were taking too many chickens, a wolf too many sheep, a goshawk too many pheasants, or an otter too many fish, a word to Gilles would stop the ravages—and the foresters could then report that due to their cleverness all was well. It was even rumored that if a traveler was seen with a well-filled purse at the local inn, the man never left my lord's demesne, although his body was never found by even the best-nosed limier, and the contents of his purse went into my lord's treasure chest, except for a few small coins. So as long as Gilles did not commit the major crime of killing a good stag, or take so many pigeons that the lord could not have his pigeon pie, the foresters turned a blind eye on his doings.

Now, however, it had been decreed that Courtaud and his pack were to be destroyed and Gilles was to be the executioner. If he failed, he would pay the penalty for his many crimes. So it was against this ruthless and experienced man that Courtaud found himself matched.

Naturally, the wolf baron, did not allow his pack to return to the fatal fence with its imprisoned dog, but as he soon found, Gilles had other devices at his command.

Returning early one morning from a raid on a distant village, Courtaud was aware of the smell of cattle dung. He stopped at once, as did the rest of the pack. Their glade was no place for cattle to be. Advancing cautiously, he came on some scattered bits of meat. This puzzled him. He cast around to see if he could pick up some man-scent. While he was about this task, he heard an angry growl from Silver. One of the *louvarts* had bolted a piece of meat. The youngster shrank back from the dominant female's anger and the rest left the meat severely alone. Stretching out one paw carefully, Silver scratched at one of the pieces. She could not tell why she distrusted the meat except that it had no business there. Under her sharp claws, the meat came apart. There was something inside.

Suddenly the *louvart* gave a yelp of pain and sprang into the air. He fell on his side, writhing with pain, gasping and trying to vomit. The rest of the pack gathered around anxiously and Courtaud left his sniffing and hurried over. The young wolf was obviously dying. When Courtaud licked his muzzle in an attempt to comfort him, the wolf baron could taste blood. The louvart was hemorrhaging internally. For an hour, the pack stood around their mortally injured comrade, whimpering with sympathy and desperate to help, but they could do nothing. Slowly the young wolf died in terrible agony, blood pouring from mouth and anus.

When there was no question that he was dead, Silver returned to the meat. With remarkably delicate touches she picked it apart. Inside was a short length of supple wood, sharpened at each end, bent into a circle held together with a horsehair. Silver scratched again. The motion snapped the hair—as stomach acids would also do—and the splinter of wood straightened out with a snap. It was strong enough to pierce the lining of a wolf's intestines. Even though none of the pack understood how the abominable contraption worked, they knew it was deadly and left the other pieces of meat alone, except to urinate on them to show contempt.

The pack, especially Silver, was learning to dread anything unusual in the woods, especially if it smelled of man. Courtaud, with his early training, still had no fear of man as man. His fearlessness nearly proved his undoing.

They now no longer went to the glade, apprehensive of what they might find there, but spent the days on a low tor that rose out of a marsh, covered with the silken tassels of bog grass. The wolves liked this place because they could see for several hundred yards in any direction and nothing could approach them unobserved. They did not realize that if they could see, they could also be seen.

They were lying about one afternoon, waiting for the sun to drop low enough to go hunting, when the wind brought an odor that sent every wolf to his feet. It was the scent of Blackie.

Courtaud waited only long enough to make sure and then plunged into the swamp with the rest after him. Even the usually ultracautious Silver pressed on eagerly. A hundred yards into the forest they came on a curious arrangement of sticks that looked like a figure 4. The odor of Blackie's anal glands was overpowering. It was coming from the contraption.

Silver began to whimper and crouched. This was surely man's work. Courtaud pressed on. The scent was coming from the horizontal crossbar. Directly above this bar was suspended a boar spear, weighted by two great stones, its razor sharp head pointed downward.

Incredible as it seems to a human, this sinister arrangement did not alarm the wolves—except for Silver, and she would have been equally alarmed at the sight of a silver spoon hung from a string. None of the pack was able to realize that this was a deadfall, or to grasp its ominous implications. The reason for this is simply that nothing in their lives had trained them to cope with such a device. It was entirely foreign.

Only a little doubtfully, Courtaud went over to sniff the crossbar. Yes, here was the strong scent of Blackie's anal glands. He was about to touch it with his nose when he was pushed aside.

Blackie had mated-the year before and his mate, a young female, had been passionately attached to her big lover. She had mourned him continually since he had been carried off, growing so thin she could scarcely keep up with the others. Now, mad with excitement and hope, she flung herself forward, defying even the omnipotent leader. She struck the fatal crossbar. The falling spear pinned her to the ground and she died almost instantly.

These triumphs over the pack were valuable to Gilles beyond being able to produce dead wolves. Courtaud and his pack had begun to be regarded with superstitious fear throughout the district. Never before had the serfs seen wolves that deliberately preyed on people. The cunning of the pack seemed to them supernatural. When raiding a village, one wolf would seize a pig or chicken—anything that could be counted upon to set up a loud noise—and run with it. The tumult drew off the men and dogs, and while they were gone the rest of the pack would attack. Whether or not the wolves deliberately decoyed the men away, the serfs thought they did. Knowing that the pack would attack women rather than men, some of the boldest foresters dressed as women and went out alone as living bait for the pack. The wolves were never deceived. The peasants thought that they could detect the imposture only by some fiendish guile. It did not occur to them that men walked differently than did women and the wolves were able to detect the slightest shades of altered behavior, just as they could tell with uncanny skill whether a red deer was strong enough to put up a determined fight or not.

Gilles had had trouble, even with the foresters, getting anyone to help him against these werewolves, but when he was able to show that the wolves could be killed by such obvious devices as pitfalls, deadfalls, and *aiguilles* (as the sharpened sticks in the meat were called), people began to lose their awe of the pack.

There was one group of humans who did not bother the wolves, and the wolves did not bother them. This was a party of charcoal-makers who lived in the forest. These men were always well armed, so the wolves left them alone. For their part, the men had no wish to provoke such dangerous adversaries, so there was a truce between them. In bad weather, instead of lying on the tor, the wolves would congregate in the woods under a great oak near a path often used by the charcoal-makers for their great, unwieldy carts with creaking wheels pulled by a team of oxen. So used did the wolves grow to these men that they let the carts pass within a few yards of their lying-up grounds without doing more than glance at them.

After a spell of wet weather, the wolves were lying in their usual spot when the carts appeared toiling along the road. In them were the charcoal-makers, covered with smut as usual, lolling against the sides, glancing only casually in the direction of the oak. They had hardly appeared when Courtaud leaped up and bolted for the woods, instantly followed by the entire pack.

The carts came to a stop and the foresters disguised as charcoal-burners leaped out, cursing in astonishment and disappointment. Bows were produced and unstrung, for there would clearly be no need for them now. Most bewildered of all was Gilles Garnier, who had kept hidden in the bottom of the first cart. For the first time, the *braconnier* began to wonder if the tales of the cut-tailed wolf were true and he had super-natural powers. How had he been able to tell that this was not one of the charcoal-makers' carts and the men in it were his enemies? The wind had been blowing from the pack to the carts so he could have scented nothing The carts were identical with those used by the charcoal-makers.

The carts were identical except for one item. The charcoal-makers' carts had squeaking wheels. The wheels of the carts used by the foresters had been greased. Courtaud missed the familiar sound and instantly knew something was wrong.

Soon Gilles had another problem to puzzle him. He had a trap of wood, shaped something like a sabot, except that within it were two flexible sticks with a flat piece of wood between them. When the flat trigger was forced down between the horizontal side sticks, they snapped together, holding the leg of any animal that had been careless enough to step on the trigger.

Gilles had a number of these traps made by a wheelwright in return for a haunch of venison. Now, by chance, after the wheelwright had put out the traps to weather, the pack raided the village. Several of the wolves ran across the traps, which, not being set, caused them no damage. Gilles was delighted when he was told of this, for it clearly showed that the supposedly clever animals had no fear of traps.

Even so, Gilles was taking no chances. He buried the traps in the dung pile for two days and when he removed them he wore leather gloves soaked in blood. He had bags on his feet which had also been buried in the manure pile and, when he carried the traps into the woods, he was careful not to rub against any branches. He located several of Courtaud's scent posts and buried the traps around them. To help him set the traps, which had to be done by two people using short poles as levers to press back the flexible side sticks, he took along his blowsy woman, who was almost as strong as he was and was the only human being in the world who cared for him. Like Gilles, she wore blood-soaked gloves and had dung-soaked bags on her feet. After the traps were set and buried, Gilles covered them with dead leaves and then sifted earth over the leaves. Lastly, he smoothed the earth with Blackie's tail. When he had finished, it seemed incredible that any creature could tell that something was concealed there.

Yet Silver could. When the pack paid its weekly visit to the post, Courtaud smelled the dung odor and pulled back. Remembering how that smell had in the past been connected with danger, he went about sniffing at twigs, although this time they told him nothing. While the rest of the pack hesitated, Silver looked around: It had rained since Gilles and his woman had set the traps and this the poacher had regarded as great luck, for it washed away any trace of man-smell that might linger behind. But the rain also dampened the dead leaves and caused them to sink into the traps. Silver noticed the minute depressions. With the greatest of care, she extended one foreleg as far as it would go and scratched until she touched the trap. In the damp air, she could scent the fresh-cut wood and knew it had no business to be there. Taking infinite pains, she slowly uncovered the trap. Then, after several false starts, she seized the strange object in her teeth and shook it as she would a rabbit she was killing. The flat trigger pan was dislodged and the side sticks snapped together. The effect was that the trap exploded in her face.

Silver dropped the weird object and she and the rest sprang back. For a long time they did not dare return, but as the trap lay there and did not move again, they inched toward it. This time it was Courtaud who picked it up and shook it, but it would not explode for him. Now Gray, a sharp little female, located another trap and succeeded in digging it up and springing it. Soon it became a game. When all the traps had been found the wolves collected them in a pile and took turns urinating on them.

When Gilles returned to the place with some foresters and their limiers (they had expected the wolves to run off with the traps on their legs and that they would need the hounds to track them) and found what had happened, they were more convinced than ever that the wolves were in league with the devil. How else could it be explained that the wolves had had no fear of the unset traps in the village and yet, once they were set, had taken such elaborate precautions to spring them? The animals had certainly never seen traps before; Gilles was one of the very few men who knew their use.

The explanation was simple, although it never occurred to the men because they were men and could reason and so supposed that the wolves could do the same. The village was full of man-made objects and the wolves expected to find them there. The forest was not. Therefore, a man-made object in the forest was highly suspicious. The wolves had no idea of the nature of a trap or how it operated. If the traps were set in a village street, whether concealed or not, the wolves would have walked straight into them. This the men did not realize, and so never used the traps again.

The whole pack had come to recognize Gilles Garnier as their implacable enemy, yet even though he often came to the woods alone, they did not dare to attack him. He was always armed and they knew him to be dangerous. They were many and he was one and a single determined charge would have settled the affair, yet they did not dare to make that charge, not even Courtaud. But let the *braconnier* be at a disadvantage—like a stag that had allowed himself to get mired in a bog or gone lame—ah, that would be another matter.

The pack now maintained a sort of patrol through the forest. The sentries kept in sight of each other. If one saw something alarming, he crouched or took cover. If another wolf saw him, he would do the same, and in a surprisingly short space of time the alarm would be passed throughout the pack. Then several of the older wolves would secretly trail the intruder, always keeping carefully upwind of him so he could not scent them—for the wolves, as did the men, attributed to the other species their own abilities.

Courtaud awoke late one fine spring morning and lay luxuriating in the little hollow he had dug as a bed the night before. A cuckoo and a throstle were singing and he could smell the strong scent of the pines around him as well as the coolness of the woods. The pack now seldom slept twice in the same place. This time they had selected a coppice of birch, beech, and oak that formed a finger of the forest that stretched down into the pasturelands of a lord's demesne. Below them a river wiggled past, frosted with white foam. Mist was rising from the hollows like the breath of cattle on a frosty morning. Far away they could see a peasant harrowing with a harrow of thorns tied to the tail of his horse. Behind him walked his wife, breaking the clods with a mallet.

A roebuck barked in a thicket. Courtaud wriggled contentedly. He had managed to pull out most of his old winter's coat on brambles and felt much better. The long, matted fur had itched. Most of the pack were asleep but a few were up, eating grass as they always did in the spring or turning over stones with their long noses to look for mole crickets.

Silver trotted over to him. She humped her back, put her ears down, and playfully waved her forepaws. Courtaud lazily sniffed her lips and licked them to see if she had found anything to eat. Nothing but crickets. He was feeling mildly peckish himself.

Somewhere a jay began to scream. At the sound, the whole pack froze. The freeze was against them and, cock their ears as they might, they could hear nothing but the jay.

One of the sentinel wolves came running up. She was a female and she squatted nervously to urinate. Courtaud went over to her while she lay down, tilted her head to one side, and raised a paw. Another of the sentinels appeared: a male. He stopped to look over his shoulder, barked, and then growled. He also scratched fiercely with his hind legs. There were intruders in the forest.

Courtaud decided to investigate personally. He set off, back-tracking the two wolves by their scent. Silver came too and several of the older animals. The rest waited.

When the sentinels showed by their nervous motions that they were coming near the place, Courtaud gave a "spy hop"; that is, he gave a great jump straight up. He could just make out something moving, so he swung around downwind. Instantly he recognized two scents: one was Gilles Garnier and the other was a dog. He did not know the dog. He also recognized the odors of two harts: a comparatively young animal and one much older.

Gilles and the dog were moving upwind so the dog could scent anything ahead. That was perfectly natural to Courtaud. He always by preference traveled upwind for, the same reason. Now he followed the two like their own shadows.

He came to a little bed of flowers where the man had been digging. Courtaud sniffed the spot suspiciously, suspecting another trap. The flowers were yellow and seemed to be encased in little hoods of leaves. The man had dug up several and taken the roots. Courtaud skirted the place and pressed on after his quarry.

Soon he was in sight of them. With the dog, he had to be far more wary than if Gilles had been alone or with another man, but Courtaud did not realize this, for it never occurred to him that men had no sense of smell. Still, as long as the breeze remained steady he was safe.

The limier was straining on his lead, although far too well trained to give tongue. A moment later, the two harts appeared moving among the trees.

The larger hart had antlers with six tines. The smaller animal was a spike buck that went ahead of his companion to test the wind and expose himself to any danger. Such close friendships between two male animals, one much older than the other, often occurred. Gilles dropped the limier's lead, paused a moment to study the direction of the wind from the movements of the leaves, and moved behind a crab apple tree. He raised his crossbow but the younger hart saw the motion and froze. Gilles remained motionless in spite of the torture of the gnats that buzzed around his face. After a long wait, the hart relaxed and the deer began to feed.

Gilles steadied the bow against the tree trunk and squeezed the trigger. The bow gave its flat report and the younger buck sprang into the air, then darted away with his older companion after him.

Gilles recocked his bow and called over the limier, which had sunk down and awaited quietly the outcome of his master's hunting. The poacher sat down with his back against the apple tree and, taking out a rosary, said it three times. It was not an act of piety. Gilles knew that a wounded deer, if not pursued, will lie down. In forty-five minutes the animal will stiffen so that it cannot rise again. At the end of the required time, Gilles picked up the lead and put the hound on the harts' trail. As they moved off, Courtaud followed them, with the pack trailing him.

At once, the wolf could smell the odor of blood and knew the deer had been hard hit. He could not see the scarlet stains on the dark leaves although they stood out distinctly. Being color-blind, the wolf saw the red as black. Gilles could not smell the blood but could follow the red splotches easily even without the hound's nose.

They had gone only a few hundred yards when they came on the dead hart with his friend standing beside him. The older deer bounded away as soon as he saw them.

Gilles took something from his pocket and, putting down the crossbow, bent over the dead animal. With a small knife he made holes in the body and put something in them. Courtaud grew tense with excitement. His mane stood up and his tail stiffened. The other wolves, knowing the signs, also pulled themselves together for an attack. The wolf baron knew that at last the man was in his power. Gilles was weaponless, bent over, and completely unconscious that Courtaud was near. The wolf baron began his stalk. When the man straightened to rest his back, the wolf dropped down. When he bent over again, the wolf resumed his stalk.

The limier was growing increasingly restive. He could not clearly scent the wolf, yet he was sure something was wrong. He began to whine. At the sound, Courtaud charged.

He was on the stooping man in five great bounds. Ever since that day long ago when he had seized the bull by the nose and found this grip gave him an advantage, he had gone for his opponent's head by choice. Courtaud's great jaws closed on the poacher's skull. It would have been quicker and better to have broken the man's neck, which the big wolf could have easily done. Instead, Courtaud tried to crush the man's skull. One of his great canines sank into the *braconnier*'s temple. Gilles screamed with pain and terror and tried to stand, but Courtaud's weight dragged him down. The wolf locked his jaws, crushing the cranium and tearing the scalp loose. Gilles never screamed again. He died in the act of striking backward with his little knife.

While Courtaud devoured his kill, the pack moved in and attacked the dead deer. For three of them, it was a fatal mistake. Within an hour, they went into convulsions, retching in a vain attempt to vomit up their lethal meal, and fell with blood pouring from their mouths.

Courtaud sniffed at their muzzles. He recognized the odor of the yellow-flowering plants with the tiny hoods. The same odor was also in certain places on the dead hart. Courtaud had no idea that the innocent-seeming plant was known to humans as monkshood or wolfsbane, and contained the deadly poison aconite.

From then on, the pack never ate anything they had not killed themselves. Courtaud went a step beyond that. He seldom ate anything but humans, whom he was convinced were safe food.

That evening, Gilles's woman found what was left of her husband's corpse. She threw herself on it and refused to leave, even after she saw the eyes of the wolf pack gleaming green in the moonlight as they closed in on her.

SIX

The Battue

It was a cold, wet morning. Every hill had a cap of mist; every leaf was fringed with pearls of moisture. Rain squalls, driven by an east wind, whipped across the open fields and infiltrated the woods. In a tangle of hazel scrub the pack was lying up near their kill of the evening before—a woodcutter and his yoke of oxen. The pack had killed the oxen and Courtaud the man. The wolf baron had cracked the woodcutter's skull, a method of killing that was to become his trademark. The wolves were lying on a sodden mass of last year's bracken, most of them sleeping, although occasionally a wolf would slip through the scrub to drive the ravens away from the kill, the pack always being fiercely possessive of anything they regarded as their property.

Courtaud and Silver were lying together, one of his long fore-paws across her neck and her muzzle nestled under his chin. The wind was blowing from the kill to them, so if humans discovered it, they would know immediately even in their deep sleep. Both were somewhat more nervous than usual. The day before they had found a dead horse in the forest where a horse had no right to be. More suspicious yet, the animal had been dragged nearly half a mile. They had followed the drag from curiosity and found a local pack at the carcass. As they had no use for the animal, refusing to eat anything they had not killed themselves, and respecting as much as they could the territorial rights of the other packs, they had withdrawn discreetly. Still, it was vaguely disturbing.

The wind shifted slightly and brought with it the smell of smoke. Instantly the pack awoke. They all looked at Courtaud. The wolf baron opened one eye, yawned, sniffed, and went back to sleep. The pack at once relaxed.

Now came the sound of a horn, being blown a great distance away. A man could not have heard the sound, but Courtaud stiffened and cocked his ears. He recognized it as an oliphant, a hunting horn. Not only did the wolves have a much greater hearing range than did men—they could hear notes both higher and lower than could humans—they could also identify a greater variety of sounds. By a slightly different intonation in their barks, growls, howls, and whines, they could convey to each other very fine shades of meaning. The horn meant that there were hunters in the forest. They were probably after game, but it was unsettling.

The wailing note of the horn bothered the wolves' delicate ears. One of the younger males put back his head and howled. Courtaud rose and gave the youngster a hard look that sent him cringing. This was a time to listen, not to make noises themselves.

Seeing that the wolf baron was alert, the rest of the pack promptly rose and stood listening and sniffing. The wind shifted slightly again—it was cold and damp, perfect for carrying scent—and the smell of smoke became very strong. With it came the odor of men, horses, and dogs—many of them.

Courtaud trotted off, dodging through the thorn thickets and scrub. The pack followed him, wading up to their bellies in the ground-clinging mist and pouring like water through the trees. For once, Courtaud did not go upwind, for that was where the danger lay. So he could not smell what might be ahead of him, and that bothered him as much as if he were forced to run with his eyes shut.

The wolf baron was right in fearing danger. In a forest glade, a great assembly had gathered at the rendezvous. For once, several lords had agreed to suspend their constant feuds and join forces to take the man-killer "by force," that is, to hunt him down with hounds. Five hundred serfs had been impressed as beaters. The night before, the lords' provosts had gone from hut to hut telling the villeins that their lord demanded a "love boon"—a day's labor in addition to their usual tasks. They would receive no pay, as killing the wolves was for their benefit, but it would be a "wet boon," that is, each man would be given a free flagon of beer and a dish of pease porridge. Even though the peasants feared and hated the wolves, they were reluctant to turn out. A day lost in the spring of the year was a serious blow to their ragged economy, and fighting their way through underbrush all day was more than most of the half-starved creatures could endure. Many of them would have run away if possible, and they had to be closely watched by the provost's men.

The nobles looked forward to the sport. They were seated around a great fire where servants were cooking food, Unloaded from the leather-topped panniers strapped to the backs of mules. A cask of the light wine which came from that *pays,* and was therefore called champagne, had been breached, and cup after cup was being filled. Whereas the serfs wore their simple tabards and smocks, the nobles were magnificent in jerkins of velvet with strappings of gold, hose of broadcloth fastened by points tipped with silver, and velvet shoes. Many had felt caps with hawk feathers held by a jeweled brooch. Their baldrics were gold chains. Their saddles were also gorgeous, often being of gold covered with engravings of various wild animals. The seats were covered with buckram and over this was another cover of silk, the flaps hanging far down. Every man was armed with either a lance or a sword. In hunting the lordly stag, etiquette permitted only the use of a dagger, but wolves were vermin which could be killed in any way by any means.

To hunt down the man-killers, there was a pack of four hundred raches, which resembled foxhounds: thirty *lévriers*, the fighting greyhounds; and ten great alaunts with spiked collars. Only these giant dogs had any chance against a wolf single-handed. The raches were coupled together—an old hound being coupled with a young one—and the berners who handled them kept them well away from the short-tempered *lévriers* and alaunts. One of the great problems in using these fighting dogs was to keep them from attacking the raches once they were slipped.

In addition, there were the foresters, many carrying spears with notched shafts, each notch standing for a wild boar it had killed; the mounted piqueurs, who acted as whippers-in; archers with rain-slacked bowstrings; and the horse-holders. There were many horses, for each rider would need at least one remount before the day was over. The horses varied from the delicate-looking snow-white Libyans to the powerful Spanish barbs and the graceful Andalusians. Men were still coming in, with mustaches and eyebrows dripping moisture from the woods, rubbing the cramp out of their bridle hands while hailing old friends.

A little apart stood the head *piqueur*, or huntsman, wearing much-stained hunting leathers and with a blanket tied behind his saddle, for long experience had taught him that on a wolf hunt one never knew where he might spend the night. He was an old man, his hands knotted like a furze root and his face mottled with red dots like a trout's belly. Over his shoulder hung an oliphant made from the horn of the almost extinct auroch, the great wild ox that still inhabited remote parts of Europe. It was on a horn like this that Roland had called Charlemagne back from a distance of eighty-four miles, according to the legend. The head piqueur was listening to the report of the *valet de limier* whose wise bloodhound had winded the wolf pack and shown his handler their location. To the piqueur's disappointment, Courtaud's pack had not been decoyed by the dead horse. The horse had been dragged to a place in the forest where it could easily be surrounded, thus trapping any wolves feeding on the carcass. Now the piqueur foresaw a long hunt ahead of him.

He went over to the gentlemen drinking around the fire, bowed, and explained his plans, drawing a map of the area in the ashes with a stick as he talked. There was considerable discussion, as every lord felt himself to be an authority on hunting. The piqueur listened politely while trying to conceal his impatience. Every minute they delayed gave the wolves that much more opportunity to slip away. He was relieved when the nobles finally decided to launch *l'attaque* and the count said, "Take your trysts, gentlemen."

The piqueur spoke to the head berner as he mounted his Orkney hunter. The berner ordered five of the oldest, steadiest hounds to be uncoupled and called them over to him by name. He also mounted and, with the *valet de limier,* started off, the hounds following. These chosen hounds were the *rapprocheurs,* which would start the quarry. A forester followed, with a group of men carrying stakes sharpened at one end and a running noose attached to the other. These men hoped to be able to surround the pack and plant their stakes around the wolves in a circle. When the Wolves tried to escape, some of them at least would run their heads into the open nooses and be caught.

A blood-red sun began to show through the mist. Birds started whistling to each other from the trees and a woodpecker scolded. The *valet de limier* touched the piqueur's boot and pointed downward to a broken stick he had left when he had been here earlier with his hound, the break pointing in the direction of the hazel thicket where the limier had indicated the pack to be. He and the hound had had to be careful to keep downwind of the thicket, to prevent the wolves from smelling them.

The men with the stakes and nooses were sent to surround the thicket, but even as they left, both the piqueur and the berner knew from the actions of the *rapprocheurs* that the pack was already gone. Still they waited. A hail came from a forester who had stumbled on the dead oxen and the woodcutter. The men hurried to the sound. The piqueur cursed and shook his head at the sight of the half-eaten corpse, and the berner turned away hurriedly before he became sick. Here were plenty of wolf tracks as well as the print of Courtaud's great fore. Following the piqueur's orders, the berner put the *rapprocheurs* on it.

The scent was stone-cold, for Courtaud had not returned to his kill during the night so the hounds could not own it. The men had to guide them, following the tracks in the soft earth, which meant nothing to the hounds, until they reached the woods. Here the scent had been caught and held by the bushes and while the men were helpless, the hounds were able to track. Slowly they moved off, heads down, tails wagging. The scent was so light they did not feel justified in giving tongue. The men waited outside the hazel tangle for the hounds to throw their voices.

They waited the length of time it would take to say six Hail Marys. Then came the deep, bell-like voice of Brochart, the oldest of the *rapprocheurs. "Oyez à Bro-chart!"* cried the berner. *"Ça va!"* ("Hark to Brochart! To him!")

Suddenly all four of the other hounds burst into full cry. *"Le loup!"* ("They are on the wolf!") *"Tayaut!"* ("The game is raised!") shouted the *valet de limier,* mad with excitement. The head piqueur put his oliphant to his lips, but the berner shook his head and the huntsman waited. Above the babble of the *rapprocheurs* could still be heard the methodical, well-spaced bay of Brochart, one cry every fifteen pulse beats. Brochart was going in an entirely different direction than the other hounds. He was paying no attention whatever to the eager baying of his comrades, who were obviously on a hot scent.

The piqueur looked at the berner irritably. "Either all the others are wrong or old Brochart is at fault. I am calling up the vanchasers."

The vanchasers were the first of the three running packs to be loosed, each pack having approximately fifty couples of hounds. "Wait!" said the berner, still listening intently. The piqueur sat fuming with impatience. His horse, sensing his nervousness, began to cavort. The piqueur pulled him up savagely.

A crashing in the scrub made all three men start and the *valet de limier* half-drew his hunting knife. A *daguet*—a young, spiked buck—burst from the cover with a couple of the hounds virtually on his flank. The *daguet* paused for a moment, kicked at the hounds, swerved for a moment to toss at them with his foot-long spikes, and then with one easy bound cleared a hedge of restharrow as tall as a man.

The second couple of *rapprocheurs* appeared, hot on the *daguet's* line. *"Le change!"* shouted the piqueur. "Assemble! War! War!" He spurred his horse to turn the hounds while the berner shouted at them. The piqueur's whip cracked and the startled hounds shrank back.

In the distance still came Brochart's steady bay, now going in a rhythmical sequence about as fast as a man could breathe. "*Oyez à Brochart!*" cried the berner. "*Menée!*"

The piqueur sounded the "*menée*" the signal that the true line had been found. For the first time, the two couples of *rapprocheurs* paused to listen to their comrade. Then they turned and dove into the scrub.

Leaving the *valet de limier*, who was on foot, the two mounted men turned their horses and galloped around the hazel thicket. As they came out in a stand of beech, they heard all two and a half couples of hounds give tongue together. Then in the distance came the "*laisser courre*"—a series of short blasts—and the "*vue.*" The wolf pack had been sighted.

The head piqueur at once gave the call to uncouple the vanchasers. These horn calls were a difficult and clumsy way of signaling: the horns were capable of producing only one note, so to make the various calls the note had to be cut short, prolonged, or a series of blasts had to be made—three long calls followed by two short, for example. To add to the problem, all the nobles had their own horns, which they enjoyed blowing either, to signal each, other or simply for amusement. This time the head piqueur was fortunate enough to have his message received promptly. Listening intently, he heard the piqueur who had the vanchasers answer the summons with his own horn, and a few minutes later had the satisfaction of seeing the man come trotting up, followed by the first pack. After them came the hunt, straggling among the trees. A wildly excited serf came running up to report that he had seen the *rapprocheurs* (the ignorant fellow simply referred to them as "five dogs," knowing nothing of hunting terms) and that they were hot on the trail of the wolves. One of his friends had seen the wolves themselves and had promptly climbed a tree. The wolves were in full flight, but might at any time stop and turn on the *rapprocheurs.*

The berner was very much afraid of just this disaster, and he loved his hounds. Taking the peasant up behind him, he galloped off, the peasant showing him which way to go while the piqueurs brought up the running pack. Within five minutes they sighted a forester, waving his hand and shouting. He had seen both the wolves and the *rapprocheurs* and run up to within twenty steps of where they had passed. Closer he did not dare go, for fear his scent would foul the line.

The second piqueur brought up the vanchasers, now bunched so closely together a large rug would have covered the whole pack. He put them straight on the line. It required an agonizing few minutes for the hounds to make sure of the line—there were so many of them that they got in each other's way—and even after they had hit it and given tongue, they ran about in circles trying to decide which way the wolves had been running. The head piqueur set them right—every second counted now—and at last they all streamed away, the forest full of their baying.

It was *l'attaque.* Every horn sounded a fanfare. Everyone was galloping, lapwings flushing under the horses' feet as they crossed a field. The head piqueur, his head touching his horse's mane to avoid branches, was calling *"Volez, mes chiens! Après! Mes valets! Mes amis!"* ("Off you go! After them, my helpers, my friends!") Incautious riders were swept from their horses' backs by the trees and suffered serious falls. Some horses also went down with broken legs. These were put out of their pain by a dagger stab in the joint between the first and second bone in the neck, the stroke being delivered from above. The death of either animal or human was not allowed to delay the hunt for a moment. The cry of the pack, the silver mountings on the horns flashing in the sun, the brilliant costumes of the nobles, all vanished among the trees.

The wolves, as usual, ran in a straight line. In various places in the forest, nets had been hung on sticks set at an angle, in the hope that the wolves would knock them down and become enveloped, but Courtaud led his followers safely through the obstacles. He also avoided archers placed to intercept him and swept around a series of stake-and-binder fences intended to guide the wolves into a pitfall covered with a lid of woven vines. Ahead were more nets, these designed like pusses so if a wolf ran into one, the net pulled together at the mouth and held him. Seeing the pack was turning away from these devices, the head piqueur sounded *"le bébuché,"* to let the rest know that the quarry had left the district. The call was answered by the third piqueur, coming up with the midel, the second pack. The head piqueur waved to this helper to bring the midel around to turn the wolves if possible. The man did not understand the motion and came straight on. He crossed the wolves' trail and the hounds, following him, caught the scent and burst into full cry. Swerving together like a flock of birds, they took the line. The head piqueur swore. Now the second pack was largely wasted. There was still one more pack—the partifters. If possible, these should be brought around to head the wolves so they would be caught between the two packs.

So far, the wolves had been running together. Now they began to scatter. The hounds also scattered, following different trails. The "recheat," or recall, was blown but only a few of the raches answered it. Brochart, the wise old *rapprocheur,* was brought up riding on the horn of a piqueur's saddle, and put down. He was allowed to work out the line of Courtaud while the berner whispered to him, *"Swef, mon ami, swef!"* ("Go softly, friend, softly!") Among the scores of scents, the uncanny nose of the old hound finally picked out Courtaud's and gave tongue. The remains of the pack were put on while Brochart was allowed to rest. His running days were over and the head piqueur said sadly, "Ah, if we could only put old noses on young legs!"

Courtaud and Silver were running together. They went straight across country, stopping for nothing. They tore through a village, scattering humans and animals in their rush, plunged into a river, swam it, climbed the far bank, and kept on. The hounds lost them in the village and when the head piqueur tried to cast them in a circle, outside the miserable huts where there would be no confusing scents, the hounds could find nothing, for the river had cut off the wolves' trail. Brochart was far to the rear and the head piqueur was at a complete loss. The few serfs who had stayed up with them were of no use. They were taking a malicious satisfaction in destroying the crops of these strangers.

The second piqueur galloped to his side and pointed. "See those cattle!" he exclaimed.

In a field a hundred paces on the far side of the river a head of cattle was running panic-stricken, the herd boys unable to control them.

The head piqueur needed to see no more. He glanced up and down the stream, hoping to find a bridge. There was none. He sounded the recheat and, once he had the hounds around him, shouted, "Avaunt, sire, avaunt!" ("Forward, sir, forward!") and, sounding his horn, forced his horse into the swift current. A few hounds followed him. The rest held back until the whips and cries of the piqueurs sent them into the water.

The dripping hounds climbed the far bank and loped after the rider, guided by the sound of his horn as much as by sight. They were scattered over the field like the stars in heaven. The head piqueur spurred forward, watching the ground. He came to where the cattle had started to run, swung to the right, and blew the "apel." The nearest hounds ran to him, casting around hopefully but unsuccessfully.

A young hound suddenly gave an eager, doubtful yelp. The rest of the pack stopped questing and stood with raised heads, watching him uncertainly. The youngster spoke again, his adolescent bay unlike the deep note of the older animals. At last, an old hound trotted over and tested the spot while the puppy stood back, watching anxiously. A few sniffs, and the old hound burst into full cry. That was enough. In a moment every hound in the pack was racing to the spot. *"Oyez à Beaumont, oyez, assemble à Beaumont!"* cried the head piquer. "Beaumont has found the coward with the short tail!" The pack streamed away, screaming with excitement on the hot scent. *"Bien aller!"* ("All goes well!") joyfully proclaimed the piqueur's horn, and the triumphant cry was taken up by the horns of everyone still able to keep up.

Ahead of them came the notes *"Hoo, hoo, hoo, ra, ra, taho!"* The piqueur's heart leaped. By some miracle, the berner in charge of the partifters had managed to bring his pack around to intercept the wolves. The fresh pack would be slipped in the wolf's face—*"le relais."*

The head piqueur blew "Hoo sto, hoo sto, mon ami!" ("Keep going!") and heard the response. Oh for the fast *lévriers*, but they had been left far behind. He did not know how many wolves there were and only hoped that the raches could hold them. He had never seen any scent hounds that would stand up to a wolf, but they might be able to hold the man-eaters until the alaunts could be brought up. Actually, the killing was virtually always done by men.

A groom galloped up leading a fresh mount, which the piqueur accepted gladly. They must have gone nearly ten leagues.

Wolves, he knew, could run for double that distance; more than the stoutest hounds could do. That was why the partifters were so vital.

Ahead came an explosion of noises—hounds screaming with rage and excitement, and over and over the horn notes of the *"vue."* The newly uncoupled partifters must have run right into the wolves and were now hunting by sight. The piqueur put spurs to his fresh horse and sped after his own pack.

The noise ahead increased, but now it was mixed with yelps of pain. The wolves were among the hounds. The piqueur groaned to think how many good hounds would be lost and then hardened his heart. It was worth it to get the man-eater.

The noise died down. The wolves must have fought their way clear. Ahead was a newly plowed field and here the midel lost the scent. The piqueur drew rein beside a thatched cottage with mud walls. The sun had come out, turning the thatch to gold. The distant hills were still veiled by a white mist and flocks of gulls rose from the field, their shrill cry not unlike the cry of the hounds at a distance. On the slope of the hill, sheep were standing watching, each with a lamb at her side.

The piqueur rode through the field looking for tracks. He could find nothing. Sounding his horn, he took the pack across it and cast them on the green slopes on the far side. They swept over the slope like low-flying swallows. Then they hit the line, came together, and rushed forward. The men could hear them break into full cry.

The second piqueur was a light man on a fast horse. He moved into the lead. His horse, going all out, stepped into a badger hole and went down, his rider flying over his head. No one stopped to aid the man. The hunt was too important.

They came on some astonished serfs who were repairing drainage ditches. Yes, they had seen the hunt pass near to them.

There were two wolves: a great one and one much smaller. They pointed the direction and the men spurred on.

They topped a rise and there, less than a mile away, saw two speeding specks going up a distant slope, followed at a respectful distance by what was left of the three packs, mostly the partifters. At this moment, a cart appeared with a berner and ten of the *lévriers,* the greyhounds. The berner had guessed how the wolves would run, commandeered a peasant's cart, and, coming by back roads, had arrived in time. The head piqueur was happier to see him than he would have been to see a vision of the Blessed Mother. One of the *lévriers* was handed up to him and he held the gazehound high so he could see the distant quarry, knowing well that scent meant little to the *lévriers.* The greyhound studied the distant forms, struggled to be put down, and set off, his lithe body nearly forming a ball as he sped over the ground. His comrades hurled themselves out of the cart and followed him, although they had no idea what the quarry might be.

Now, indeed, the horses were taught what spurs were for. The *lévriers* might attack the raches in their excitement. In fact, children were none too safe from them, especially if the children panicked and ran. The horses were tired now and stumbled, but their riders forced them on. A wood intervened, but they found a path through and dashed on in single file. On the far side, they saw the two wolves with the *lévriers* closing in on them. The greyhounds had fanned out, exactly as wolves did when running down a deer, so no matter if the quarry turned right or left, there would be a hound to stop him. The leading *lévrier,* the most aggressive of the lot, was pressing forward now while the others moved to support him. This powerful beast was snow-white and had learned to trip quarry by grabbing the hind leg and tossing. As soon as the game was down, the other hounds would rush in and finish it. The *lévrier* was trying to pull down Silver, but Courtaud kept between him and the little female.

The wolf baron swerved suddenly to the right. The *lévrier* on that side put on a burst of speed to cut him off, but as the hound came up, Courtaud gave a flirt of his head. The *lévrier* shot into the air, turned over, and hit the ground. It said much for his pluck that he regained his feet and tried to go on, although now on three legs.

A quickset thorn hedge grew here by stones yellow with lichens and a line of beech trees alive with screaming crows. Here Courtaud and Silver halted, their hindquarters protected by the hedge. Far away, the head piqueur saw the hounds eddy about the spot, knew what it meant, and sounded the *"l'hallali"*; the quarry had turned at bay. He had only his hunting knife and would prefer one of the gentlemen equipped with sword or spear to close with the wolves.

The raches swarmed about, calling down curses on the wolves, but none dared to close. The white *lévrier* charged in. He and the wolf met jaw to jaw, their teeth clicking, as they fought for a hold. Suddenly the *lévrier* folded his forelegs under him and made a plunge for the wolf, sliding in on his belly. He fastened to Courtaud's foreleg and began to shake. Courtaud rolled with him. Two of the other *lévriers* came to their leader's help, but Silver fought them off. The white hound lost his grip and they broke apart.

Courtaud stuck out one of his forelegs. The *lévrier* made a lunge for it and Courtaud seized him by the muzzle. In his efforts to fight back, the hound drove one of his own teeth through his upper lip and could not get it free. He was helpless. The fearful jaws clamped down on him and the *lévrier*, kicking wildly, died.

The head piqueur came up. He looked around and found he

was alone. There was one dead hound and there soon would be more, even if the wolves did not break out of the encircling pack and escape. There was no help for it. He dismounted and, drawing his dagger, forced his way through the raches, now mad with excitement and ready to close on the wolves since the man was here. The remaining *lévriers* rushed in as the piqueur raised his dagger, sighting along it. Courtaud saw the motion and charged. The raches shrank back while the *lévriers* tried to hold the wolf and Silver strove to protect Courtaud's exposed flanks. In the tumult, the piqueur was knocked off balance and fell. As he went down, Courtaud's teeth locked on his face. Smothered under the struggling hounds, the man was unable to use his dagger. When Courtaud could no longer take the punishment of the teeth tearing at him from all sides and let go, the man no longer moved.

The raches and the *lévriers* were now fighting among themselves. The two wolves broke out of the melee and sped away together just as the foremost riders appeared and sounded the "*vue.*" But not a single hound could be found to follow them as they vanished over the next rise.

SEVEN

Paris

It was not until long after nightfall that Courtaud dared to give the long assembly cry of the pack. After the first few notes, Silver raised her muzzle and joined him, tired as she was. They howled together for a few minutes and then stopped to listen. For a long time there was no response, and then so faintly that even their ultra-acute hearing could barely catch it came a dozen short, barking answers. Courtaud waited nearly half an hour before he howled again, and this time the replies were nearer and more distinct. He could recognize the individual animals now—White Mane, Gray, Brownie, and the Cubs. By dawn nearly all of the remnants of the pack had gathered around their leader and his mate. Most were limping, several had been savaged by dogs, and three showed spear or arrow wounds. They were so weary that they collapsed and lay like dead animals for five hours.

Although the wolves had no way of knowing it, the humans had paid a disastrously heavy price for their victory. A score of horses were dead or foundered; half that number of men were crippled by falls. The head piqueur was dead. The count of the *pays* lay in his castle helpless with a broken collarbone, never to ride again. Not even the head berner knew how many hounds were lost, dead, or crippled. The serfs were too exhausted to do more than token work in the fields for the next month. The game was so scattered that hunting would be almost impossible for weeks to come—and game formed a vital part of the nobles' diet. The cost and damage of the battue was a hundredfold greater than the ravages of the wolves justified, and with the dispersing of the wild game, all the local wolf packs were virtually forced to live on the humans livestock. Also, the quality of the surviving game would be permanently injured. By their careful "testing" of prospective quarry, the wolves tended to take only the oldest or weakest animals, thus culling out the herds and eliminating the unfit. Human hunters showed no such discrimination; in fact, they deliberately hunted only the best beasts, as these provided the finest trophies and gave the best meat. On castle walls, for generations after the *gran battue,* the great hunt, the poor quality of trophy antlers bore silent witness to the degeneration of the herds.

Still, despite its fantastic cost, the battue accomplished its purpose. Courtaud resolved to leave the district. It was proving too dangerous. The other wolf packs also were forced to migrate. Courtaud's pack had long ago given up depending on game. Human stupidity and persecution had forced them to turn to stock killing and, when the opportunity offered, to be man-eaters. Now, the other packs were being compelled to follow the same course. As if by common consent, the packs began to leave the *pays* and drifted south, following roads now largely deserted because of the ceaseless war. But after a few days traveling, they began to pick up the scent of herds of cattle, flocks of sheep, and droves of pigs all being driven toward some common point. They followed the enticing odors hopefully, Courtaud's pack always in the lead, until one morning the great wolf-dog led his followers to the top of a little hill covered with boulders among which they slipped like ghosts. From their height, they looked down on a city bisected by a slowly flowing river.

The city was protected by a double fosse or system of moats—the outer fosse being dry and the inner flooded—and by a tall wall studded with towers. At the center of the city in the midst of the river was an island shaped like a boat. Here stood a fantastic cathedral with twin towers that speared the sky. Walled bridges ran from the island to the mainland where stood the greater part of the city, crossed by two great streets at right angles to each other, which ran straight as lances through the tangle of buildings. The pack looked down over a jumble of roofs covered with green mold, chimneys sending up blue plumes of smoke, a cat's cradle of twisting streets overhung by balconies that projected so far out that people could carry on conversations from one to another, tiny squares, spires of carved stone as fine as lace, black-pitched market sheds, mansions with gardens, and an occasional round tower topped with a leaden cone. There were two great fortresses—one known as the Bastille and the other called the Louvre, meaning "wolf den," so named because it had once been the site of a pile of rocks where wolves made their homes before the expanding city engulfed it.

Between the city and the hill where the wolves lay was a low section of land, now swampy from the spring rains. A paved road ran across it, starting at one of the city gates and vanishing among the pollard willows, poplars, and alders that marked the beginning of the forest. A gallows stood by the city gate with two bodies hanging from it. There were a few farms that reached to the foot of the hill. Near the forest were piles of seasoning cordwood, waiting to be hauled to the city. The hill itself was so rocky and inhospitable it was largely left barren, except for a few vineyards and a number of windmills scattered about where grain brought from the outlying manors was ground.

Human observers would have been impressed by the sight, for fifteenth-century Paris was one of the great cities of Europe, but the wolves were concerned only with the odors coming from the place. From the slaughter pens of the Marché Palus rose the delightful scent of fresh meat, and the whole place reeked with the tantalizing smell of food. The hungry wolves licked their thin muzzles and yearned after the rich harvest, but the city seemed impregnable. The elaborate fortifications of Charles V could have withstood the assault of an army.

Although the wolves could both see and scent herds of kine being driven along the highway to the city, they hesitated to attack the helpless creatures and their handful of drivers. The terrors of the battue were still too vivid in their minds and they were in unknown territory, always an uncomfortable sensation. Fortunately, they found that the hill was full of rats, part of the overflow from the city that teemed with them as a carcass teems with maggots. Rats were hardly a satisfactory quarry for wolves, yet they made do. Somewhat more substantial were the martens that inhabited the hill and lived on the rats. These giant weasels were usually arboreal, but they had left their trees to prey on the rats, which were far easier to catch than squirrels, their ordinary prey. The martens were trapped, in turn, by woodsmen, who sold their beautiful soft pelts as miniver. So many martens lived on the hill that it had been named after them and was known as Montmartre.

The martens had an unpleasant odor and soon the wolves sought more satisfactory food. At night they drifted like shadows through the farms, moving so softly that they seldom disturbed the sleeping dogs, and always going upwind so they could tell what lay ahead. They were able to catch a few frogs along the banks of the river. On special occasions they were lucky enough to find sleeping wildfowl. They always moved in single file, each stepping in the footprints of the leader. Perhaps they had developed this habit in the mountains when it was easier to go through snow if the trail was already broken.

They soon came across the signs of many other wolves; for Paris was a magnet for all the packs within miles. Trash, offal from the stockyards, and not infrequently a stray corpse were disposed of by being thrown over the walls. The wolf packs acted as a garbage disposal system. Indeed, the city would have been in a bad way without them. They kept the surrounding area reasonably clean.

The resident wolves knew the hours when the garbage would be thrown out and timed their visits accordingly. Courtaud and his pack did not, and so for a time they did not meet. Then early one morning near the Porte Sainte-Antoine, Courtaud came on a scent post that made him bristle, growl, and scratch backward angrily with his hind feet. It was clearly the scent post of a dominant wolf baron who had marked out this particular territory for himself and his pack. An ordinary wolf leader would have respected the property rights of the incumbent pack, but Courtaud, with his alaunt blood, was not intimidated. What did give him pause, however, was his rival's size. He had to exert himself to fling his urine as high on the stone gatepost as had the other.

The old varlet—the outcast wolf bullied by even the weakest of the pack—had long since disappeared and his place had been taken by a small, two-year-old male who had joined the pack a few months before, exactly when or how none could remember. This new varlet was quite clever and acted as court jester. When there was a kill, the varlet would rush forward, growling savagely as though he meant to take on the whole pack. One of the young males, eager to show his authority, would promptly charge him, whereupon the varlet would pretend-to go lame, limping about on three legs and moaning pitifully, yet all the time drawing closer to the meat. When his attacker hesitated, the varlet would limp close enough to snatch a mouthful and then, his leg miraculously healed, go racing off. The varlet was not content merely to trail the pack; he skirted around them and not infrequently made important discoveries.

Courtaud was so busy effacing the boundary marks of the strange leader—and the pack were so occupied in watching him—that they grew careless. Suddenly the varlet plunged into the midst of them, tail between his legs, yelping in terror. Only a matter of the gravest importance would induce the varlet to force his way among his superiors, and every wolf knew it. Instantly the wolves lost all interest in the gatepost and stood rigid, every sense alert. The varlet's mane was bristling and he snarled. Something was coming.

A hundred paces away, the frogs had stopped croaking. Then frogs ninety paces away became silent, and then eighty. Whatever it was, it was coming toward them. There was no wind and Silver, the cautious, was prepared to flee, but Courtaud stood his ground. The nearby frogs hushed and now the pack could see figures in the low-lying morning mist. They instantly recognized them as wolves. A moment later, they could scent them and Courtaud promptly identified the scent of the leader who had marked the gatepost.

The resident pack came on, either unconscious or indifferent to the strangers. They did not move in single file, but were scattered about in a disorderly fashion behind their big leader. They behaved, looked, and to a certain extent smelled more like dogs than wolves, because for months now they had been scavengers, living off the city's refuse, and as a result had lost much of their wild nature. There were many more of them than Courtaud's pack, but ordinarily the forest wolves would have made short work of these mangy carrion-eaters. Unfortunately for Courtaud and his followers, they were weak from their long trek from Champagne and half-starved.

The leader of the pack, who had a black streak across his muzzle, was almost on top of them before he paused. There were so many wolves about Paris that he did not at first recognize these as a new pack. When he did, his mane rose and he moved forward stiff-legged, with his tail raised higher than the level of his back to show his superiority. Much to his surprise, Courtaud approached him in the same way, instead of lowering his tail and cringing.

The two males came together slowly, both sniffing audibly to gauge the other's potentials. They circled each other head to tail, neither allowing his anus to be sniffed, while trying to get a whiff of the other's scent glands which would carry so mush information. Courtaud stood higher than Black Streak although he was not as heavy. Black Streak was clearly an experienced fighter. He had lost one ear and was heavily scarred from numerous battles. He recognized in Courtaud a younger, more active animal, but also knew he was half-starved—the poor quality of his scent showed that—and tired, for he moved stiffly.

Black Streak seemed to give up, for he turned his head away— always a sign of cowardice. For an instant, Courtaud relaxed, and it appeared as though the two packs could come to an understanding without fighting. Abruptly and with astonishing quickness, Black Streak spun sideways and struck Courtaud on the shoulder with all his weight. Courtaud reeled and nearly went down. As he staggered, the resident pack moved forward as one wolf; they had seen other wolves who challenged their leader go down in just this manner. Courtaud managed to keep his balance and snapped at Black Streak's throat. Black Streak was forced to twist around to parry the bite, and as he did so, Courtaud in his turn swung sideways and hit Black Streak with the full force of his body, instantly reaching for his opponent's neck. The big leader threw his head backward to avoid the bite and for a moment went off balance. Courtaud closed and threw him on his back. Now it was the turn of Courtaud's pack to sway forward, but Black Streak regained his feet. He feinted first at Courtaud's foreleg and then at his throat, forcing the wolf-dog to jerk his head back and forth to meet the thrusts. Courtaud gave back and they stood facing each other and snarling, neither willing to resume the struggle.

Suddenly there came the vicious whir of arrows and sullen "plunks" as they embedded themselves in the ground. The wolves were off and running even before the twanging of the bowstrings reached them. Archers were amusing themselves by releasing at the wolves from on top of the wall. Back on the hill, Courtaud's pack counted noses, or rather checked scents. An old female was missing. The pack howled in unison until the sun came up. It had an especially doleful note, unlike the cheerful music of a howl before hunting or a conversation with other packs. They seemed to be mourning their dead. Perhaps they were.

From then on, Courtaud and his pack avoided the city and its tempting garbage. Instead, they explored the surrounding country far more carefully than human scouts could have done. Not only did they observe marks and signs that even the most acute woodsman would have missed, they memorized dozens of scents. By the end of a week, they knew every stone wall and every hedgerow-enclosed field, and had learned to check certain bushes where sometimes they found a thrush caught in a snare baited with berries. They also knew the pens where the cattle were kept and where the chickens and ducks spent the night. They never touched so much as a pullet, for this was their home range and they did not wish to draw attention to themselves. With any luck, next spring they would dig their dens among the rocks of Montmartre and raise their pups here. No wolf, no matter how stupid, ever dreamed of killing within several miles of his home den area.

The wolves soon learned to watch all that went on along the road that led north from Paris through the forests. Paris was the great market of France, and along this road was driven daily enough food to feed all the wolves in Europe. Only for a few miles was the road paved. Then it turned into a dirt path that was a mire in wet weather. Still, the pack continued its patrol, for they sometimes found sick or dead animals that had been left behind. The varlet proved surprisingly useful here. He turned out to have an excellent nose and was often the first to discover some abandoned horse or cow. If the animal was dead, he took care to get a full gorge before bringing over the others. If it was alive, he relied on the pack to kill it for him and then, by crawling on the ground and whimpering like a hungry puppy, managed to get his share.

Once the pack got to know the country and became more confident, they stopped relying on abandoned animals for food and openly attacked the cattle, sheep, and pigs. The herdsmen were peasants, usually dressed in undyed sheepskins with galligaskins wrapped like leggings around their legs. They were armed with staffs, spiked clubs, or at least *le pardou,* the peasant's short knife. Even Courtaud preferred to leave these men alone, but the driven animals were another matter. They could be easily stampeded, often simply by the wolves' scent, and once scattered were easy prey. So regularly did Courtaud's band patrol the highway and so ruthlessly did they extract their levy, that the herdsmen learned to hamstring one old cow and leave her for the wolves. Thus distracted, the pack would allow the rest to pass in safety. The herdsmen told each other, "It is better to sacrifice one animal that the rest may go clear."

These were good days for the pack. Courtaud overcame his man-killing propensities, to Silver's relief. She had learned to eat human flesh when the pack followed the Free Company, but deliberately attacking humans always bothered her. It was not normal wolf behavior and therefore disturbing, After feasting on whatever animal had been given them for tribute, the pack would return to Montmartre, terrifying the women cutting rushes for baskets by the river and making the curlews fly up before, them as they crossed the little valley between the hill and the city wall. Once on the hill, they would sleep among the boulders until it was time to go forth again.

This golden period was suddenly brought to a close. In the nearby town of Meaux was an English garrison, composed largely of bowmen with a few men-at-arms. They collected taxes from the townspeople and the local peasants, but not in unreasonable amounts, and so were not especially disliked except for being foreigners. They were not strong enough to be a threat to Paris, nor did the Parisians care much what happened to Meaux, so an armed neutrality existed between them.

A group of butchers, who objected to the toll Courtaud's pack took from the cattle driven to Marché Palus, hired a small group of the English bowmen to guard the herds while they were passing through the wolf king's domain. The next time Courtaud confidently intercepted a herd of steers headed for the Porte Saint-Antoine, he was astonished to find arrows flying past him, singing their deadly wasplike buzz. The wolves fled and took refuge in a thicket of dense gorsebush. Later they made several other tentative attempts to cut out steers from the herds, only to be met with more arrows. Finally they were forced to give up and return to rat and marten hunting on the hill. The city dwellers were still kind enough to throw their garbage over the walls, but Courtaud was not a garbage eater except through necessity. He prepared to take his band on a search for a new home.

Then, one morning in July, Courtaud and his followers were awakened by the sounds of kettledrum and trumpet, and, raising their heads, they saw the sparkle of armor as a procession rode out of the Porte Saint-Antoine. At the head flapped the banner of the Count de Richemont, governor of Paris. Actually, the count was the leader of a band of *écorcheurs*—the grisly "flayers" who spared no one, French or English. The count lived for loot and, as long as he was able to enrich himself, it was a matter of indifference to him whether Charles VII, Henry VI, the Duke of Burgundy, or the devil ruled in France. Although his *écorcheurs* were officially the Parisian garrison, and maintained at public expense to fight the English, the count used them solely to protect the wealthy corn factors who had a monopoly on grain brought into the city, which they sold to the people at enormous profit. However, the price of bread had reached such exorbitant heights that the people were rebelling, and the count had decided that it would be wise to distract them. Meaux with its little English garrison lay only twenty-five miles away. The count decided to make a token attack on Meaux, then return to Paris and announce a brilliant victory.

It must be admitted that the *écorcheurs* had their side of the question. Most were either former peasants driven off their land by the never-ending war, wandering mercenaries who knew no other life, or the fragments of feudal levies who could now exist only by looting. Whenever it was pointed out to them that they were little better than bandits, the *écorcheurs* invariably replied,

"We must live." It was an unanswerable argument. The wolves were in much the same situation.

It was a long time since the pack had seen a war party, but they recognized it instantly, remembering the time when they had followed the Free Company. Ordinary wolves would have been terrified by the sight, sound, and smell of so many men and horses; these welcomed it. The armor flashing in the sunlight, the forest of tall lances, the military trumpets, were well known to them and connected with food. Driven from their home range, prevented from hunting their natural prey, they had learned to depend on humans. They had no other choice.

The wolves were not the only animals to recognize the significance of the menie. Ravens, croaking with anticipation, materialized from barren hillsides where two crows would have been a crowd. An eagle appeared, floating on rigid wings with the long flight feathers spread like the fingers of a hand to feel for the slightest updraft. He, too, was a scavenger, for all his noble appearance. Foxes slipped noiseless as cats through the furze. They would follow the menie for a while at least, but the ravens would follow it for days, trailing it as in the Ardennes they had trailed the wolf packs. The wolves also followed, and made little attempt to conceal themselves. They knew the men had other matters to concern them besides wolves.

Courtaud's pack was the only true pack-in-being around Paris at this time. There was a good reason for this. The resident wolves had split up into small groups or breeding pairs as they did every summer. Because they had been driven out of their range, Courtaud's pack had not bred that year and had remained together, not knowing the country well enough to separate. However, they were followed by a few loners and strays. Some mated pairs whose pups were old enough to make short trips also tagged along at a discreet distance. When the pups grew tired, they would be left in a group at some easily identifiable spot under the care of an old "auntie," who watched over them until the parents returned, hopefully with food.

The little expedition with its hidden attendants made a brave show as they rode down the valley of the Ourcq. The wolves trailed them slowly, stopping to eat berries and some of the sharp grass that acted as a tonic. A few of the *louvarts* amused themselves hunting voles, but the older wolves kept close to Courtaud. The pack poured themselves through the willows and padded across the patches of flowering heath, conscious only that the irritating odor of the flowers tended to stifle important scents. Then ahead of them came the smell of pines, arrowheads, iris, and above all the coolness of water. They had reached the Marne, which flowed past Meaux. Animals and humans stopped to drink.

By mid-afternoon, the spires of the cathedral of Meaux appeared above the poplars. Here the menie halted and the wolves did likewise. The count's strategy was simple. His *écorcheurs* would make a surprise attack on the serfs' huts that surrounded the walled and moated town. They would seize everything worth taking (which meant mainly livestock, for the serfs had little else of value), kill as many of the peasants as possible, burn their huts, hayricks, and standing grain, and then go through the motions of laying siege to the town. They had no real chance of taking Meaux, so after a week or so they would return to Paris. This was the standard pattern of medieval warfare. By destroying the serfs, you cut your enemy off from his source of food without endangering yourself. From the point of view of men-at-arms, this was the perfect way to fight wars. It was also perfect for the wolves.

One of the *écorcheurs* had been born in Meaux and he acted as a guide. After the horses had been rested, the menie left the shelter of the forest and charged forward at full gallop. They were not wearing the enormously heavy armor recently adopted as a countermeasure to the murderous bodkin shafts of the English longbows, and their horses were the light, fast barbs and *roussins.* The surprise was complete. In their excitement, some of the raiders rode into the peasants' huts, the better to cut down their victims, but most devoted their efforts to rounding up the livestock. Meanwhile the bells in the cathedral tower were ringing the alarm and the town gates were shut, but the raiders paid little attention to that. A crowd of miserable captives was herded to the village square, where the count sat on his powerful hackney surrounded by his personal bodyguard. Another contingent of the *écorcheurs* was busy firing the huts. Soon the watching wolves saw the pale flame of burning thatch and smelled the smoke. The odor of blood was even stronger and far more exciting. Several of the *louvarts* grew restless and began to move forward. Courtaud ignored them, but Silver and some of the older males sent them back with growls and nips. These young wolves were always a problem. Too old to be considered pups, they took pride in their independence, yet lacked the discipline and experience of the full-grown animals.

The *écorcheurs* then attacked the convent of Saint Agaire, which stood outside the town walls. The convent had witnessed many sieges and never yet been harmed, better protected by fear of the saint than by the stoutest walls and moat, but now its time had come. The nuns were dragged out to be raped and murdered, the altar torn apart in the hope it might contain treasure (it held only the bones of the saint), and the treasury looted of its gleaming candlesticks, which turned out to be merely gilded, much to the count's disappointment. One of the *écorcheurs,* a savage from the Baltic, climbed the tower to tear loose the glistening weathercock, which he thought was a golden idol. Others slaughtered the livestock, and soon half-raw shoulders and joints were being devoured. The convent's wine cellar was emptied and the drunken men fought with each other and played games with the saint's bones.

The ravens were already at work and Courtaud rose and moved toward the feast. The varlet, the only wolf not subjected to pack discipline, as he was an outcast, had been darting about for some time, grabbing whatever he could find that was eatable. Suddenly they saw him racing back, his tail as usual between his legs, and leaving splashes of yellow urine as he ran. The pack stopped and it was well they did.

Unnoticed, the gates of the town had quietly been opened and the drawbridge dropped. Out poured a little menie of men-at-arms, supported by arrow hail from the walls. Although the force was less than a quarter of his own following, the count was taken aback. Most of his men were scattered, many dismounted, not a few drunk. Fortunately, he had kept his own bodyguard mounted and beside him. Shouting "Saint Denis for France!" he drove his spurs into his hackney and the bodyguard leveled their lances and charged. The oncoming wolves found them-selves between the two forces and barely managed to escape. A minute more, and they would have been trampled.

The menies came together, each shouting its own war cries. The shock was terrible. Men and horses went down and in that press, those who fell never rose again. The lances splintered or had to be dropped as the work became too close. Swords were drawn, the sharp steel shivering on bone or sliding through soft fat. The dust rose and covered the scene, while under the pall a series of individual fights continued. Young pages hovered outside the melee with daggers in their hands, ready to dart in and dispatch any fallen man with a stab through the visor slit. The wolves waited beyond the pages for their turn.

Horses ran from under the dust cloud with broken girths and trailing reins. The temptation was too much for Courtaud. He sprang after a horse and seized it by the tail. The horse struggled to free itself, kicking. As the iron-shod hoofs struck close to him, Courtaud let go the tail. The abruptly released horse fell forward on his head. Instantly half a dozen wolves, led by Silver, were on him. He was torn to pieces while still struggling.

The dust cloud was lifting now. Tired men leaned panting on their swords, their armor smotheringly hot in the sun. They tried to come together again, but the ground was so slippery with blood they kept falling. Some of the most determined tore off their shoes of jointed mail and fought barefooted.

The dismounted and scattered *écorcheurs* were beginning to rally, and formed ranks for a charge. From the town walls, a trumpet called once—twice—urgently. Of the English force, all those who could ride heard the warning and turned back. The *écorcheurs* had reformed and now launched their charge, but before they could overtake the diminished group of Englishmen, they came within bowshot of the town walls. At once a black blizzard burst from the ramparts and the air was filled with the drone of the arrows. The raiders gave back as saddles emptied and horses, running mad with feathered shafts sticking in them, stampeded through the press. At the gate, a group of knights dismounted and held the way while their squires led their horses into the town and the rest of the menie crossed the bridge. Then it was raised with a clang and the French heard the English give their traditional three cheers.

Not for many months had the wolves eaten as they did that evening. Flies covered the corpses like freckles but the scavengers did not care. The riderless horses were so exhausted they stood with their heads down and could be easily hamstrung by even the most inexperienced *louvart*. The parent wolves often crippled the helpless animals first and then watched while the young wolves duplicated their actions. None of the men watching from the walls doubted that the wolves were taking advantage of the situation to teach their young how to kill, although it is quite possible that the older wolves were not consciously giving the pups lessons. They were drunk with blood as the *écorcheurs* had been drunk with wine. Never with wild game would the pack have considered for a moment such pointless, wholesale killing, nor would the opportunity have ever occurred. They gorged that night until many of them literally could not move and lay as helpless as the drunk *écorcheurs*. They had found a paradise for wolves.

The count's force had been so badly mauled by the unexpected sally from the town, that the next morning he prepared to depart. The tired wolves were awakened at dawn by the clank of armor being donned and the neighing of horses. They listened without interest. There was enough food here for a week at least. Then came a sound that made Courtaud and Silver, at least, lift their weary heads. It was the rumble of horses' hoofs on the hard ground. These newcomers consisted of a Free Company under the leadership of a man known as Téte-Noir. They were mainly German and under ordinary conditions would have proved as great a threat to the French *écorcheurs* as did the English. Téte-Noir and his men had been pillaging the already pillaged countryside when they had seen the smoke of the burning village and decided to investigate. There was no use in their attacking the *écorcheurs,* for the raiders had no loot except a few pigs and chickens. So a truce was struck. In Meaux there was plenty of loot and Téte-Noir had two men who knew how to construct catapults that could throw a two-hundred-pound stone 350 paces. Using the captured peasants as labor, they could also construct scaling ladders and *pavois,* the wooden shields supported by props that could conceal two men and be carried close enough to the walls so the crossbowmen could reply to the English archers.

But first a leader had to be decided upon. Because of their proximity to Paris and the chance that the city might send the Count de Richemont help, Téte-Noir swore an oath of allegiance to the count. Kneeling, he placed his joined hands between the count's hands and swore to obey him. Now the count was the acknowledged head of the combined forces.

Meanwhile, more and more wolves were leaking in through the forest and along the deserted roads. They could smell the carnage five miles away when the wind was right, and also many had been watching the menie ever since it left Paris. These new arrivals presented a problem. The various packs were suspicious of each other and quarrels were frequent. Last to come was Black Streak with his followers. So well fed and so confident had Courtaud become that he contemptuously allowed the impressed Black Streak to sniff his anus. Black Streak knew that this lordly animal—who had also been first on the ground—was his master. He lowered his head and Courtaud majestically took the upper jaw between his teeth and shook it firmly. It was the sign of dominance. Black Streak would now recognize Courtaud as leader and obey him; at least until they returned to Paris. The other wolf leaders came forward, lowered their tails, and held out their unresistant muzzles to be gripped in turn. When the ceremony was over, Courtaud was the king wolf of all the packs.

For the next two weeks, the besiegers busied themselves with preparations for the attack. The captured serfs were set to binding together great bundles of faggots to serve as fascines to fill in the moat; those who had some skill with an axe were employed cutting down trees to fashion the ladders, *pavois,* and catapults. The women were also useful. Their hair was cut off and twisted into ropes for the newly constructed catapults. Human hair had proven to be the best substance for this purpose.

The wolves had greatly increased in number. The men swore that there were over two hundred of them. Perhaps this was an exaggeration, but in any event they were growing constantly bolder. After they had devoured the corpses of men and animals killed on the first day, they haunted the camp. Armed guards had to be put over the horse lines and cattle pens. It seemed as though the wolves, once accustomed to the idea that men were there to provide food for them, became resentful if the men did not oblige. In any event, they became more aggressive. As they staged their attacks principally at night, the French arbalisters with their powerful but clumsy crossbows could do little against them. Even when the arbalister was able to see a wolf, it took him nearly a minute to wind and cock his crossbow and the wolf seldom waited.

At last the day came for the assault on the town. The serfs had filled in part of the fosse with their fascines and many had died in the process in spite of the covering fire the arbalisters gave them from behind their *pavois.* Now the newly constructed catapults destroyed much of the hoardings that covered the ramparts and provided the archers with shelter. The moment for the supreme effort had come.

The Germans led the advance on foot, for no horse could have been controlled under the English arrows. With their spurs removed to keep them from tripping and their lances shortened to five-foot length, the Germans plodded forward, their heads lowered against the arrow storm. Their armor was so heavy that if a man tripped, he was unable to rise again without help, but nothing but a steel quarrel from a crossbow could pierce it. Still, it had its vulnerable points. If a man, stifled by the heat, removed the steel gorget protecting his throat, he drank his own blood as a broadhead tore through the chain mail which had once been considered adequate protection. Meanwhile the more lightly clad *écorcheurs* followed under cover of the *pavois* while the catapults and arbalisters cleared the walls.

A battering ram on wheels was brought up, protected by a shed covered with raw hides so the besieged could not set fire to it. The ponderous contraption was rolled into place and the ram began to crash against the town gates. As it did so, from the machicolations—covered stone gutters that ran down the walls—boiling oil was poured on the attackers. Men were broiled alive in their armor. On the parapets, the English archers discarded their, bows and flung down paving stones that the town's inhabitants pried from the streets. Women tossed burning hoops dipped in tar around the heads of the attackers.

The *écorcheurs* ran forward with their scaling ladders and swayed them up against the walls. One group was able to get grappling hooks caught in the drawbridge and pulled it down by main strength, breaking its rusty chains. The gates collapsed and the heavily armed Germans waddled in, moving like sleep-walkers but unstoppable.

Courtaud dared to rush forward, with Silver half a length behind him and the rest of the pack following. They found dead and dying men behind the abandoned *pavois* and Courtaud, wild with excitement and the smell of blood, attacked them with an almost hysterical fury. Courtaud's pack joined him, and Black Streak, after a little hesitation, led the city wolves forward. The wolves rushed in, tore off great hunks of flesh, and then ran back to swallow them before returning for more, but Courtaud refused to retreat. He gorged himself where he stood.

In the marketplace, the English were making a last stand. At their head stood a young knight, waving his sword. He raised his hand too high, exposing the *"défaut de la cuirasse"*—the weak spot under the arm. A crossbow quarrel struck him and he fell. At the sight, the English surrendered—with the condition that their lives and personal property be spared. The victorious besiegers agreed, as there was no advantage to be gained in overcoming the little knot of desperate men. Instead, they looted the town.

It was a great victory for both the *écorcheurs* and the wolves. Neither realized until much later that with the English bowmen gone, the herds of domestic animals driven to the Paris market would no longer have bowmen guardians.

EIGHT

The Capture of Courtaud

The hut was hidden deep in the forest and so rickety that one would go outside to sneeze, yet it had an air of comfort. It was made of crossed laths chinked with hardened mud and possessed a chimney rather than allowing the smoke to seep out through the thatch, as with most peasants' homes. There were two rooms, one for the family and one for the beasts: the yoke of oxen, the cow, ten sheep, and the pigs. There was horn in the windows that let in light while keeping out the cold in winter, and there were even shutters. The mother had blown up the fire in the ingle and set her copper kettle on to boil. Meanwhile, she nursed her baby while spinning with her distaff. Because the house was so isolated, it had escaped the Free Companies' raids, and on this August evening everything was especially calm.

Under the apple tree in the tiny yard, two little girls were spreading dried dung on the vegetable beds and working it into the soil. There would be time for another crop of lettuce and peas before the first frost. They had been chattering together. Now they became silent. An uncanny hush had fallen over the woods. No bird sang or insect chirped. Even the stones and trees seemed to hold their breath. The children looked about nervously and wished that their two older brothers had not taken Roland, the dog, with them when they went to drive home the cow.

There was a stone wall surrounding the yard. A stone fell from it. The children were about ten paces apart and the one nearest the house looked up. She was just in time to see a giant wolf with a short tail spring down from the wall and seize her sister.

At the children's screams, their mother put down the baby and, still clutching her distaff, rushed out. She screamed too when she saw her oldest daughter's head almost engulfed in the wolf's mouth. Half insane with terror, she attacked the murderer with her distaff. So furious was her assault that Courtaud dropped the girl and retreated. The mother snatched up the unconscious child and held it protectingly to her breast. Courtaud circled her and sprang on the other child. This child was smaller, and in spite of her screams the wolf dragged her off toward the wall. Still holding the limp body of the older child, the mother tried to pursue him, but Courtaud sprang over the wall with his prey in his mouth.

He would have made his escape had not the two boys come up with the cow and Roland. For a few moments the boys saw only their hysterical mother, clinging to the senseless body of their sister, and did not realize what had happened, but Roland scented the wolf. He bounded over the wall and in a few seconds caught up with the kidnapper. Roland was only a sheep dog and weighed less than half as much as Courtaud, but he attacked instantly. Courtaud refused to drop the child and was at a disadvantage. He tried to run, but the gallant Roland forced him to turn. Brave as the dog was, he dared not come to grips with the wolf. Instead, he barked as loudly as he could.

Now the boys came up. There had been rumors of man-eating wolves that had reached even this lonely cabin and one boy had a homemade bayonet, made by tying his peasant's knife, the *pardou,* to the end of a stick. He charged Courtaud with his crude weapon. The wolf ducked and ran, still carrying his little victim, with Roland in pursuit. This time Roland grabbed the wolf by the leg. It was a fatal mistake. By the time the boys caught up, Roland lay dead and Courtaud, with his victim, had disappeared.

The boys hesitated. They could not bring themselves to go into the tangled underbrush, especially as they had no means of trailing the man-eater and did not know how many other wolves might be about. Weeping, one boy carried the corpse of poor Roland back to their home while the other walked backward with his bayonet at the ready. There they had to help their mother with their other sister, who had recovered consciousness and would not allow anyone to touch her. She thought that she was still in the wolf's grip. At last by main strength they dragged the shrieking girl inside and laid her on the communal bed. Meanwhile, Claudette, the cow, had run off and without Roland to help, they were a long time finding her and bringing the frightened animal home. It was almost dark by the time they returned and found their father there with the yoke of oxen and a cart piled high with wood.

In spite of the hour, once the oxen and Claudette were safely bedded down inside the house and the wattle door made as fast as its leather hinges would permit, they set out to follow the wolf. The father took his axe, the oldest boy his bayonet, and the youngest a pitchfork. The father held a torch made of strips of fir bound together with flax and soaked in grease. They found the spot where Roland had been killed and then proceeded more slowly, the youngest boy carrying the torch so the man could have both hands for the axe. They found some traces of blood and then some shreds of clothing caught on a gorsebush. A few paces further on, they came on the head of the child. There was no sign of the body.

All three stood sobbing around the pathetic remains of the child, for in those times people made no attempt to hide their emotions. Yet they were practical also. It was now almost pitch-dark and there were rustlings in the bushes that made them think the wolf had not gone far. Peasants might mourn their dead, but they had to think also of the living. The little head was reverently gathered up and they returned to the comparative safety of the hut.

As soon as it was light the next day, the boys set out to get help, each taking some weapon. The father stayed with his wife, as she needed his help with the mauled girl, who kept dozing off, only to awake screaming that the wolf had her. By noon, over a dozen men had assembled—woodcutters, charcoal burners, simple serfs, every man with at least one dog and some home-made weapon. The dogs were put on the line, but the scent was cold now. They did make one discovery: a pile of freshly turned earth. With their knives the men dug up what was left of the child's body and returned with this poor trophy.

When Courtaud came back that evening with Silver and found his cache robbed, he was furious. He growled, tore up the ground with his hind feet, and went into such a rage that Silver, trying to lick his mouth to quiet him, was afraid to go near the maddened animal and kissed the air a foot away. Courtaud trailed the posse back to the hut, even jumped the wall and stood on his hind legs looking in at a crack in the horn of a window, trying to find what the thieves had done with his kill. Frustrated, he went away at last with Silver following. On the path, they came on an old woman spinning with her distaff as she walked, followed a few paces away by her husband with a mattock over his shoulder. Without hesitation, Courtaud in his rage charged the woman and tore her throat out before her startled husband could come to her help. Then he and Silver dove into the broom and vanished while the frenzied man tried to staunch the flow of blood from his dying wife's jugular.

Not only Courtaud's pack learned to prey on the livestock being driven to Paris; the other wolf packs joined them. Ever since the siege of Meaux the packs, once terrified of man, had learned that, if a wolf took a few precautions, men were comparatively harmless. With the English longbowmen, it had been a different matter. An archer could discharge twelve shafts a minute and hit a wolf at 250 paces with each one. An arbalister could discharge his crossbow only once in the same period and the weapon was, by its very nature, not as accurate as a longbow because the fletchering of the bolt scraping along the flat of the bow affected its flight. The French had short bows but they were weak things, the archer drawing to his chest rather than to the angle of his jaw, which made aiming difficult and limited his range. The French had never learned the art of making the powerful longbow.

It was Courtaud who taught the city wolves how to outwit the arbalisters and handle the stubborn cattle. The cattle must never be allowed to form a defensive ring. Wolves, with their ingrained habit of testing all prey before attacking, tended to approach the driven cattle slowly, watching for weaklings, slinking to and fro and hoping to cut out some likely prospect. Courtaud attacked instantly. He had discovered places along the road especially suitable for ambush—a particularly dense patch of elder, a pile of rocks, a stand of pine and spruce that had grown up where the woodsmen had cut down the hard timber—and in such places he lay up with his followers. When a herd was driven past, he would suddenly attack, scattering the cattle in all directions. Before the arbalisters could cock their weapons or the mounted men level their lances, wolves and cattle were inextricably mixed and spread through the forest. The wolves would then cut off a small group and drive them to a safe place for the slaughter. The wolves showed amazing ability to herd hoofed prey, an ability they had often used in the past to drive deer into a cul-de-sac so they could be the more easily killed. So selective did the packs become that they would kill only the best and tenderest heifers, and then eat only the choicest bits, leaving the rest behind. Once having selected a victim, they would knock other cattle out of the way to reach the chosen animal. Courtaud himself had little interest in the cattle. His target was the humans, but he enjoyed panicking the herds.

Courtaud became increasingly wedded to human flesh. He seemed to become addicted to it, as a man might to drink or drugs. He had to be careful how he approached the well-armed men who guarded the cattle, but shepherds driving their flocks to Paris were generally unarmed and helpless. The wolf king was known to run over the backs of the closely crowded sheep to get at the shepherd. Big and powerful as the wolf-dog was, he was actually no match for a man armed with a stout cudgel or even a knife, but his size, ferocity, and the legends that began to attach themselves to him usually paralyzed his victims with terror. It was said that he was not a wolf at all but a bear, a lion imported from Africa by some noble, or a demon. As the arrows discharged by nervous bowmen invariably missed the swift-moving animal, it was believed that they bounced off his hide and he was invulnerable. It was said that he had power to strike men dumb so when they encountered him they were unable to call for help. Men were, indeed, struck dumb at the sight of Courtaud—dumb with fear.

The drovers listened anxiously for the howling sessions the wolf packs indulged in before starting out on a raid. They learned to recognize Courtaud's deep voice from among the others. If the wolf king howled, they abandoned their flocks and ran panic-stricken for the safety of the city walls. Yet in spite of the terror that the king wolf inspired, there were still men and women brave enough to visit the fatal hill of Montmartre to collect the wolves' droppings. These droppings brought a large sum in Paris, for it was well known that wolf dung, mixed with honey, was a sovereign cure for sore eyes. The wolves even grew used to these human scavengers as they did to the ravens and foxes, and ignored them. The scavengers, in turn, were grateful to the wolves and hoped they would never leave the hill. Also indebted to the wolves was the Count de Richemont, for the butchers who paid the count a considerable sum to protect their interests were able to increase enormously the price of meat under the plea that the wolves were preventing all but a few scattered herds of livestock from reaching the city.

Other wolves besides Courtaud learned to become man-eaters, but because of his great size and short tail, he was easily identified and all kills were credited to him. A mother sent her little daughter to bring in the cows. When the child did not return, the mother went to look for her. She fell over the child's sabots, the crude wooden shoes hand-carved by the peasants. Farther on, she found the remnants of her daughter's clothes, but of the child herself, no trace was ever found. In this case, Black Streak was the murderer. He had eaten what he wanted of the child and then buried the rest deep in the forest, yet Courtaud was blamed. On another occasion, an old woman saw cows feeding in her wheat field. She dispatched her young son to drive them away. The boy used his sling to send the cows running and then returned home—to find the partly eaten corpse of his mother lying across the doorstep. Here again, other wolves were responsible, but to the peasants it was all the work of the werewolf of Paris—Courtaud.

At this time Charles VII, King of France by the grace of God and the courage of Joan of Arc, whom he had left to die at the hands of the vengeful English, came to Paris, although he disliked the city which had been so often hostile to him. The king was a little man with small eyes and a large nose, thick lips and a sallow skin. He was suspicious of everyone, and with good reason. Charles had been a weak, futile young man and was in many respects a most unkingly king, yet he still felt a certain responsibility toward his people. Among other matters, he heard the story of Courtaud, or rather what by now might be called the legend of Courtaud, and listened astonished.

"Is there no *louvetier* that can rid us of this monster?" he demanded.

An old courtier who in his youth had been a famous hunter spoke up. "There is Boisselier, captain of the city guard, my lord. He is part English and therefore part wolf, so he can think like a wolf."

This seemed reasonable to all present. It was well known that the English were related to wolves: their names showed that. The father of Alfred the Great was Aethelwulf; their great national hero was Beowulf; the archbishop of Canterbury had been a Wulfheln and the archbishop of York, Wulfstan. So Boisselier was summoned.

He was a tall blond man, with hair the color of a cornfield, who kept to himself, and if he had been in paradise would have left it to hunt wolves. Although he was a bastard, he was allowed to fly a tiercel gentle, a male peregrine falcon, as his father had been a gentleman with a coat of arms, but, strange man that he was, he preferred to fly the peasants' goshawk rather than the noble's peregrine. This was because flying falcons required open country and a large retinue of mounted followers, while a single man could wander through the fields and woods with a goshawk on his gloved fist and fly it at any prey that appeared, whether rabbit or swan, and Boisselier liked to be alone. Though he hunted sweet game—that is, the hart, the hind, and the fallow deer—he was especially famous for his skill in the pursuit of foul game—which is to say the boar, the sow, the fox, the otter, and above all the wolf. Unmarried, he was rumored to have sexual relations with female wolves who told him all their secrets. Indeed, so closely entwined with wolves was he that he even used his nose like a wolf, sniffing at scent posts and getting down on his hands and knees to smell the earth where a wolf had lain. Some said he was a werewolf who could change into a wolf at will and run with the packs.

That Boisselier loved and admired wolves was well known, yet no one thought it strange that he devoted his life to their destruction. It was natural for a man to kill what he loved. There was a close bond between the English and French nobles who intermarried, praised each other's skill with arms, visited at each other's castles, and equally despised the common people. This mutual attachment did not prevent their constant wars, and, indeed, neither would have known what to do without the other to fight, for fighting was the only career for a gentleman. As was suitable for the eldest, Boisselier's older brother was a man-at-arms and had fought on both sides. It was equally proper that the second son should be a hunter. If there had been a third son, he would have been a priest. Such matters were arranged by custom, which was to say by God.

So Boisselier was summoned to come before the king and knelt before his sovereign. He had thought about Courtaud often and knew what had to be done. He was convinced that unless Courtaud was indeed a werewolf—and Boisselier considered this quite probable—he could be taken, if not at the first attempt, then on the second or third.

"He must be trapped in his den of Montmartre, my lord," said the master huntsman respectfully but with the authority of an expert. "It is a notched, knuckled crag where the devil might say his matins at midnight, yet there is no other way. When he kills it is generally late in the evening, and so great is the fear he inspires that no man will venture out at night to bring me the news. By the next day, the scent is cold. The attack must be made on his castle shortly after dawn while the dew still holds the scent and he and his menie are still asleep."

The campaign was discussed in detail, exactly as though Courtaud were the captain of a band of *écorcheurs*. Silver was always referred to as his "chatelaine," Black Streak as the "seneschal." The dominant males, most of whom were well known not only to the *louvetier* but also to many of the nobles present, were called "seigneurs," "men-at-arms," or "squires," according to their supposed rank. There was even some question whether anyone not of gentle blood should be allowed to attack Courtaud, as this would be discourteous to the wolf king, just as no base-born man was permitted to kill a royal hart of ten points or more. Under the circumstances, Boisselier thought it permissible for anyone to kill the wolf, though several nobles considered this as outrageous as the English custom of allowing yeoman archers to take nobles prisoners. Some even sneeringly suggested that it was Boisselier's English blood and illegitimate birth that made him favor such an idea. The king was forced to intervene. He pointed out that as wolves are creatures of evil and therefore pagans, they are to be classed with Saracens. The great Pope Urban II had said that any device used against the heathen was allowable. This settled the question.

"I will need five hundred beaters," continued the *louvetier.* "And two thousand deniers to pay them. Otherwise, it is useless to make the attempt."

The Count de Richemont looked hopeful. He had no wish to see Courtaud killed and his pack broken up. The wolves were such a convenient excuse for keeping the price of meat high and increasing his profits. Charles was known to be tightfisted.

However, the king had a simple solution to the problem.

"Count de Richemont," he said, addressing the smug *écorcheur,* "as governor of my city of Paris, you will supply the money and the beaters. The audience is at an end."

Boisselier set about his plans with his usual care. With his goshawk on his fist, he spent many hours on Montmartre flying at rabbits and martens until he knew the ground well and where the wolves were likely to lie up. The next consideration was the hounds. In general, French hounds had good noses and strong voices (the last an important consideration in dense cover) but little stamina. They had to be used in relays. As it was difficult to tell how the wolves would run in the rocky slopes of Montmartre, relays would be difficult if not impossible. Still, Boisselier did not despair. First it would be necessary to find the line of the king wolf himself. Boisselier resolved to use for limiers several couples of Talbots, English black-and-tan bloodhounds. Once the line was clear, he would slip the *chiens fauves de Bretagne.* There were long-coated, tawny hounds with inferior noses and poor tongues which were apt to riot, that is, chase any game they encountered instead of being "staunch" and staying on the scent of the chosen quarry. On the other hand, they had one great attribute: they were brave and determined. Once the wolf king had turned at bay, the *chiens gris de Saint-Louis* would be released. These great brutes were rough-coated and their thick hair served as armor in a jaw-to-jaw fight. According to legend, they had been imported from the Near East by Saint Louis because he so admired their courage.

Two weeks passed before Boisselier was ready to make his attempt. Some wolves were killed by crossbow quarrels from the city wall, and Boisselier cut them open, putting dead sheep and pigs inside the carcasses before throwing them to his hounds, to encourage them to attack the otherwise unappetizing quarry. Beaters were collected, some through bribery and some by threats, and equipped with rattles and other noisemakers. Peasants were ordered to burn all dry fields around Montmartre and cut down brush along waterways where wolves might lie up, so the pack would be sure to be on the hill.

Then came the morning for which the *louvetier* had prayed. The hill was shrouded in a morning mist as thick as milk. No one could see three paces ahead and, what was more important, the fog held the scent. There was such a profound calm that the mist hung like a motionless white veil.

The beaters were assembled and sat around fires waiting until the more tardy nobles could mount their horses and join them. The men's feet were wrapped in rags, as their sabots would make too much noise on the stony slopes and the wolves were not to be alarmed until the right moment. Priests moved among them, blessing the men and the hounds. The fast *lévriers* were taken around to the open group on the far side of the hill where it was expected the wolves would break. When all was ready, the beaters spread out and began their advance.

As the sun rose, the mist began to curl and roll. The *valets de limiers* went ahead to the *brisées*, the rough, uncultivated country, with their Talbot bloodhounds, watching the ground intently as they moved up the hillside. They were looking for Courtaud's great fore. The first man to find it was promised a gold ecu.

So far they had moved in silence. Now there was a little disturbance. A peasant was sent back to find Boisselier. He returned in a few minutes with the *louvetier.* The remains of a woman had been found, partly buried. The loose soil was scraped away and the gnawed body, wrapped in a cloak, was sent back. Then the advance continued.

The mist was rapidly dissolving now as the heat of the sun sucked it up. There was another delay. They had encountered some underbrush and the beaters refused to enter it for fear of the wolves. Yet it was vital that each patch of cover be beaten as they went forward and all the men keep to their appointed places, else there would be holes in the net being drawn-around the hill. Boisselier went from beater to beater, ordering, cajoling, begging. It was no use. The fear of Courtaud and the sight of the torn corpse was too strong. At last, a priest was brought up. He promised them an indulgence if they pressed on. Reluctantly, they consented.

Boisselier sounded his horn to signal the advance, as with the hill surrounded, silence was no longer necessary. From all around the base of Montmartre, other horns answered him. The beaters shouted and swung their rattles. The *valets de limiers* could be seen only occasionally now among the boulders and twisted trees.

Back in the city, bells tolled a dirge. It was for the dead woman. The beaters crossed themselves and muttered prayers as they pressed on.

One of the Talbots spoke, for the English hounds were not trained to run mute like the French limiers. The beaters glanced back at Boisselier, who was coming behind them with the berners, each man leading two of the *chiens fauves* coupled together. The beaters hoped to see the hounds slipped, which would relieve them of the hard, dangerous work ahead, but

Boisselier refused to uncouple the pack. The Talbot had probably picked up the scent of a wolf, but it could be any wolf. The *louvetier* was interested in only one.

Another Talbot spoke. Then silence. Then still another hound gave his deep, bell-like cry. Then baying broke out all along the line, punctuated by the blowing of the valets' horns. They had found Courtaud's fore.

The *chiens fauves* were straining at their leashes, but Boisselier gave the signal to release a number of mongrels that were yapping and wriggling with excitement. There was a good chance that the wolves would make a stand of it among the rocks—at least until they saw the men. It was better to have mongrels killed than valuable hounds.

Boisselier sounded his horn and shouted *"Haleile, là! Tayau velleci allier!"* ("Get going, there! Into the cover, come on, keep together!") Thus encouraged, the curs dashed forward, Boisselier following close behind them. One of the *valets de limiers* was waiting to show him the fore, marked by a broken twig stuck beside it. Boisselier needed only one glance to know it was truly Courtaud's. A man could put his whole hand in the giant paw mark. He gave the valet his gold ecu.

The mongrels had disappeared among the rocks, but their frantic yelling could be heard. Boisselier gave the order to slip the *chiens fauves*. They were put on the line of the great fore while Boisselier chanted *"Harlow, chiens! Harlow, velleci, allier!"* "Hark, dogs! Hark! Come on, keep together!") For a few moments the hounds cast about, their tails wagging madly as they caught tantalizing wisps of scent without being able to own the line. An eager yap. Another. Still another. Then the pack streamed away in full cry after the curs.

"Hay fuit, là, chiens! Hay fuit, là, là, là!" ("Seek 'em, dogs! Seek 'em there! There! There!") cried the beaters. Ahead of them

was an explosion of sounds. Every man knew what that meant. The foremost dogs had engaged the wolf.

Courtaud had been awakened shortly after dawn by Silver's whimperings. She had been hurt in the left leg a few days before by a stone from the sling of a shepherd, and still limped. He had been bringing food to her, but he could not bring water, and she had been forced to limp to the moat to drink after nightfall. She had borne her suffering with a wolf's usual stoicism, so it was unusual for her to make any complaint. He lifted his head to listen, although the mist smothered all noises.

Then he felt vibrations through the earth. A great number of creatures were coming. The other wolves were on their feet now, nervous and puzzled. They looked to him to lead them away, not realizing that he would not leave Silver.

Black Streak came over and fawned. Courtaud ignored him. Finally, Black Streak turned away, disappearing in the mist. Other wolves followed him.

Silver stood and managed to hobble on three legs a little distance. The mist was dribbling away down the hill. Courtaud saw the distant line of dots that was the beaters. He lay down again. Perhaps they would miss him. He saw the hounds too. Still, they might take after the other wolves. It was better to do nothing.

There were men on horseback and these he watched carefully. He cared little for the hounds. He was supremely confident that with Silver at his back, together they could beat off any number of dogs. The men on foot were too slow to overtake him. Even Silver in her crippled condition could easily outrun them. But in open country, horsemen could ride him down while he was hampered by the hounds. He did not know, that the horsemen were finding it impossible to ride among the rocks of Montmartre. Even Boisselier, seeing the situation, had called up his head piqueur and turned over the handling of the hunt to him. The accompanying nobles were amused. They thought Boisselier was afraid of coming to grips with the werewolf. They did not know that the *louvetier* had other plans.

Quiet as the mist itself, Courtaud and Silver glided away among the rocks. They did not try to leave the hill. Instead, they made for a certain rocky defile they knew. Here they took their stand, Courtaud at one end, Silver at the other. Nothing except armed men could dislodge them from this position.

They heard the Talbot give tongue, and Silver shivered while Courtaud prepared to go down fighting. Neither had any doubt that the limier was on Courtaud's trail. Next came the horns and finally the screaming of the mongrels on the hot scent. Courtaud's mane stiffened and rose at the sound. It would not be long now. Then the foremost dog appeared.

The mongrels swirled around him like crows around a hawk. Courtaud killed one so quickly that the dog following did not see what had happened until his own head was crunched by the wolf's jaws. The rest gave back, screaming with rage and excitement, not daring to close. A big animal that looked as though he might have some alaunt in him became hysterical at the sight and smell of the wolf that stood there with his lips pulled back to show his fangs, yet making no sound. The mongrel hurled himself forward, and at the sight half a dozen dogs followed him. Courtaud slashed with his left fang and the big dog reeled back, one eye gone and his cheek laid open. Courtaud chopped left and right among the dog's followers and at each chop there was a yelp or a death scream.

Now the *chiens fauves* came up. They swung around the defile, hoping to take the wolf from behind, only to find Silver guarding the pass. She was smaller than Courtaud, yet not a hound dared to close with her. Many were bigger than she was, yet none had her terrible, punishing jaws. Behind him, Courtaud heard the battle raging. He wanted to come to his mate's assistance but did not dare to turn away. Anyhow, by the sounds, Silver was doing quite well for herself.

The fierce *chiens gris* were slipped. In their eagerness, they knocked to one side the other dogs, who were only too happy to let them through. Courtaud retreated so only one hound at a time could reach him in the narrow pass. He broke the jaw of the first of the *chiens gris* to engage him. The second locked jaws with him and they went down together, while two more of the *chiens gris* managed to crawl over their comrade and attack the wolf. Biting hard, Courtaud still could not rise against their combined weight. He crushed in one hound's chest, disemboweled another with a slash of his canines, and then managed to struggle to his feet. He heard the shouts of the men, *"Hon velleci aller, velleci aller!"* and blasts on a horn. They were hurrying to the hounds' help.

The *chiens gris* had not as yet discovered Silver, and the other dogs had left her alone to join in the attack on Courtaud. Standing alone, spittle running from his mouth as he snarled, with a half-circle of dead or dying dogs in front of him, Courtaud saw her slip away. He saw the form of the head piqueur struggling over the rocks, holding a boar spear, and heard the man shout, "Forward, for the love of Saint Hubert, or we lose every hound!" With Silver gone, the wolf king was no longer hampered. He charged through the pack, scattering them, although two or three tore hair from his sides, and, avoiding the man, bounded over the rocks and was gone.

Behind him, the piqueur's horn warned the fewterers waiting with their leviers that the wolf was coming. Courtaud dodged among the boulders, crossed the hill, and burst out of the broom so unexpectedly that the fewterers were caught off guard in spite of the horn call. The grey-hounds were dressed in armor to protect them, and this armor slowed them down. However, as the wolf would have to run through them while the greyhounds were slipped in his face, with the *chiens gris* coming up behind, it was thought that they could delay him long enough for the mounted men to use their lances.

Courtaud was out of the cover and halfway down the hill before the startled fewterers could slip their hounds or the horsemen could mount. Here a miracle occurred, later attributed to Courtaud's supernatural powers or possibly those of his father, the devil. There was one last patch of mist in a little hollow. Into this Courtaud vanished and the greyhounds, unable to see their quarry, plunged in after him only to lose the grey shape in the mist.

The *chiens gris* were pouring down the slope, running the breast-high scent with their heads well up, throwing their tongues like trumpets. They would have no trouble in the mist but before they could reach it, the wolf would be through and away.

Boisselier was there riding a palfrey, a curious mount for a hunter. But wait! Sitting on a pillion behind his saddle was a great, spotted cat twice the size of the *lévriers*. The strange creature resembled a leopard but with much longer legs and a small head. It had an elongated, slender body and, although clearly a cat, was built more like the greyhounds than a feline. Strangest of all, the animal was hooded like a falcon.

Boisselier shook the reins and the palfrey cantered forward. She was single-footed and moved so smoothly that the blind-hooded cat had no trouble keeping his balance on the broad platform. Boisselier rode toward the far side of the mist pocket from whence Courtaud must emerge. Several horsemen raced past him on their fleet barbs, some with lances, others waving swords, yet Boisselier seemed undisturbed. They were still a long way from the mist pocket.

Two of the *lévriers* came out of the mist, looked about, and went back in. Until the scenting hounds came up, they were helpless.

Cries went up from half a dozen voices and there was much blowing of horns. Courtaud had exploded out of the mist and was headed for the distant forest. Between him and the first of the trees lay a broad, freshly plowed field. The steeds, of the mounted men who tried to follow him bogged down in the soft mud, and in any case the wolf had too long a lead. From all sides men were shouting *"Le guépard de course! Le guépard!"* ("The hunting leopard! the leopard!")

Boisselier reached back and slipped the hood from the cat's head. As the animal stood up, balancing carefully on his pillion, it could be seen that he had a black streak running from the corner of each eye to his mouth, exactly the same lines that falcons, the fastest of all birds, have. For a few seconds the great cat looked around, until he spied the fleeing wolf. Then he lowered his head, crouched, and somewhat gingerly sprang to the ground. With his feet on a firm surface, he lost all hesitation and started after Courtaud at a long lope that did not appear fast, yet covered the ground at an amazing speed.

The men whooped and the horns cheered the spotted one on. Quickly the cat built up speed. His great bounds now took him clear of the ground and his yellow eyes never left the form of the speeding wolf. Rapidly he gained on his quarry, yet refused to close with him. The men roared with disappointment.

"Wait!" said Boisselier confidently. Courtaud was still going downhill. The cat did not dare risk springing on him when both might roll down the slope and one of the hunting leopard's long legs get broken. He contented himself with running by Courtaud's side almost as Silver would have done.

Courtaud could clearly see and smell his pursuer. He had no idea what the creature was but it did not seem especially formidable. He was much bigger and the animal appeared to regard him curiously rather than aggressively. It did not snarl, spit, growl, or show other symptoms of rage. Courtaud put on an additional burst of speed to leave it behind, yet it kept easily at his side. Then they reached the level ground.

One quick look showed Courtaud that he had far outdistanced the mounted men. Of hounds and *lévriers,* there was no sign. He had only to dispose of this strange creature that refused to leave him. He spun around and slashed.

The cat reared like a horse and, so rapidly that the eye could barely follow the motions, struck left and right at the wolf's head with his forelegs. The claws on the cat's feet were blunt but on the inside of each foreleg he had a dewclaw that was usually folded flat against his fur. Now the dewclaws were extended almost at right angles. Each claw was nearly as long as one of Courtaud's long canines, hooked and terribly powerful. Courtaud went down, yet kept his head in spite of the strangeness of the attack. He bared his teeth, expecting the cat to follow his assault by biting. Instead, the cat stood back with one paw upraised, watching. Courtaud rolled, trying to seize the cat by the other leg. The cat leaped clean into the air and then struck again, a raking blow with both claws. Fur flew and Courtaud tried to rise, but the cat was mad with rage now, striking repeatedly with incredible speed, and Courtaud could not regain his feet for the fury of the blows. He managed to twist around and grab the cat by the shoulder. At the same moment, the cat grabbed him by the back of the neck, not shaking him as a dog would have done, but crouching down and sinking his teeth deeper and deeper.

So powerful was the strange animal that Courtaud could not break the grip, although he felt the pounding of horses' hoofs and heard the riders' yells as they came up.

It was not Boisselier, but one of the lighter men on a faster horse who arrived first. Hardly touching the reins, but throwing his weight back in the saddle, the man slid his mount to a halt, kicking his feet out of the stirrups at the same instant and leaping to the ground. He forced the metal handle of his riding whip between Courtaud's teeth and used the thing to bind his jaws together. Other men came up and tied the wolf's legs together with their leather points, the laces used to tie their hose to their doublets. Courtaud, the wolf king, was at last a prisoner of his enemies. None of his pack, not even the devoted Silver, could help him now.

NINE

The Trial of Courtaud

The torture chambers were in the donjon of the Bastille. This one was entered by a trapdoor in the ceiling which led to a narrow stone staircase built against the wall. It was lighted by three deep loopholes. In the center of the domed room was a stone pillar with chains riveted into it, the stone worn away in places by the rubbing of the prisoners' backs as they writhed in pain. Hung from the ceiling were two iron cages large enough to hold a man. The floor was covered with sand to soak up blood and along the wall were arranged the terrible instruments of torture, painted red or black. There was a fireplace with a grill for heating irons.

Behind a long table sat three figures wrapped in black cloaks with the hoods pulled so far down over their faces that they seemed to be masked. At one end of the table sat a pale-faced, thin man with a pile of books and manuscripts before him. He was the clerk; the three men were judges. The torturers, naked to the waist and wearing masks, stood among the fearful tools of their trade with folded arms. Seated on benches were a number of men and women who had borne witness against the accused.

One of these was Boisselier, captain of the city guard and newly appointed head *louvetier* to the king.

The strangest sight of all was a wooden trestle, equipped with winches, to which apparatus Courtaud was tied. He was dressed in a tight suit of flesh-colored cerecloth with a chestnut-brown wig and a long white beard. His muzzle was tied together with leather thongs. His forelegs were tied to ropes passing over a revolving drum at the top of the rack while his hind legs were similarly secured to another drum at the bottom. Both drums could be rotated by the winches.

Courtaud had long since ceased to struggle. He lay still, staring at the copper-colored light thrown by the smoky cressets set in iron sconces fastened to the wall. The central judge, who was seated on a wooden throne somewhat higher than the others, began to speak.

"Wolf who liest here at our mercy, can you speak?"

Courtaud made no response.

"It may be that you are a warlock or magician and if so you can understand my words. Does not Holy Scripture tell us, 'For without are dogs and sorcerers and whoremongers'?"

"Revelations, twenty-first chapter, eighth verse," intoned the clerk.

"Do not attempt to deceive us, for we know well that it is possible for men to assume the bodies of wolves and other animals. Did not Baron Plato say that a man who eats a human entrail becomes a wolf? Did not Petronius in the *Satyricon* tell of seeing a man take off his clothes and make water around them so that he might become a wolf? Was not Sir Actaeon turned into a stag? And lastly, did not the great Pope Innocent II change Hugues de Champ-d'Avesne into a wolf for his wickedness, and has not William of Auvergne, bishop of Paris, left records of diverse godless men who became wolves? So we are not to be tricked in this matter, wolf."

"*Bestia laedens ex interna malitia*" ("The beast suffers from an inherent wickedness"), added the clerk.

"Know too that thou art a beast born evil. Zephaniah says of a sinful city, 'Her judges are evening wolves.' The blessed Apostle Saint Paul has told us, 'After my departing shall grievous wolves enter in among you, not sparing the flock.' Our Lord Himself has warned us, 'Behold, I send you forth as lambs among wolves,' and again, 'Beware of false prophets which come to you in sheeps' clothing but inwardly are ravening wolves.'"

"Zephaniah, third chapter, third verse. Acts of the Apostles, twentieth chapter, twenty-ninth verse. Saint Luke, tenth chapter, third verse. Saint Matthew, chapter seven, verse fifteen," added the clerk.

"Know, too, that it is useless for you to plead that this curse was laid on you by some witch or other worker of magic, for the learned Benedict XIV has said that in such cases the witch or magic-worker has but laid a fresh sin on his or her conscience."

"*Nec enim rationem patitur nec ulla aequitate mitigatur, nec prece ulla flectitur esuriens populus*" ("For the hungry people neither submits to reason, nor is it appeased by any equity, nor is it persuaded by any entreaty"), explained the clerk.

There was a pause, but Courtaud still said nothing. At length the judge continued, "Wolf, your food has been human flesh and you slaked your thirst on blood. Wherever you walked, the earth rotted away. Your breath poisoned the air for a hundred leagues. As animals are subject to man, they are therefore subject to the same canon law as man which now condemns you."

"*Quantum remedium est ut verberetur cum hie sit multum inobediens*" ("The penalty is that he be beaten as often as he has been frequently disobedient"), chanted the clerk.

"The Mosaic code orders that an ox which has killed a man

be stoned to death, so what shall be your fate who have ridden so in this country that it be all wasted?"

"*Excommunicatio afficit animam, non corpus, nisi per quondam consequentiam, cuius medicina est*" ("Excommunication affects the soul, not the body, unless by a certain consequence it is the body's cure"), the clerk pointed out.

"So after hearing the testimony of these witnesses [here the judge indicated the little group on the wooden benches], I therefore condemn you to have your privy members torn off and burned in front of your face, your snout cut off and a human mask substituted for it, and you are to be hanged on the gallows by the Porte Saint-Honoré at noon tomorrow as a warning to all evildoers."

The judges rose to show the trial was at an end, but before they could leave the room, Boisselier had sprung up.

"Now in the name of Christ who made His image to float to Locques on the waves, I would rather be stark naked in Russia than endure such a sight. You show the poor brute no gentleness. Let him die, for he is more wicked than Judas, but let him die like one of gentle blood by the axe or the sword."

The judges glared at him, while the clerk looked shocked.

"You love the church but little to doubt her wisdom," snapped one of the underjudges. "This is close to heresy Your Words demand the fire."

"I know not if they deserve fire or water. I speak the truth. Be pitiful and show mercy."

The head judge said angrily, "And what of the people he has slaughtered?"

"He is a king. A king is worth nothing without he be feared."

The Count de Richemont was present as a witness and now spoke up. "I believe this animal to indeed be a seigneur among wolves. I have it on good authority that he inherited his position not from his father, *la béte de Saint-Riquière,* but rather from his mother, *la demoiselle La Vendée,* whose mother in turn was a *loup-garou* of note and seizin of these forests by her liege lord, the devil himself."

The judge hesitated and considered the point.

"Yet an example must be made to warn the other wolves not to molest us," suggested the third judge. "They must depart from hence and go to their own fief. It seems that every month more come to the walls of Paris."

"The wolves will stay as long as they are fed by wars and by men," retorted Boisselier. "Not a night goes by but half a score of bodies are thrown off the walls—beggars who have died of hunger, men killed in tavern brawls, whores whose pimps need them no longer. We are baiting the packs in and then training them to like the taste of human flesh."

"These are sore words," reproved the head judge. "I for one refuse to receive this brute to mercy."

"Sir, saving your displeasure, I am a mean man without enough land to rub down a pack horse, yet I know wolves. It is the wars that encourage them. If my lord the Count de Richemont and his *écorcheurs* had not destroyed the English at Meaux, there would be bowmen to guard the livestock on the highways and the wolves would have been starved out."

"See how this bastard adventures himself!" retorted the count. "My lords, you should be grateful to my *écorcheurs,* for without them your serfs would leave your fiefs. It is only fear of my men that keeps them on the land."

"That answer pleases me nothing," angrily replied the head judge. "Let the sentence be carried out at noon tomorrow."

Everyone bowed as the judges left the room. Boisselier followed them soberly. He separated himself from the other witnesses and was broodingly walking along one of the corridors of the old fortress when he felt de Richemont touch his sleeve.

"Do not let my words set you in a pride," said the *écorcheur* softly. "For I swear to you by Him who turned water into wine, I wish no ill to old cut-tail. How could I, for is he not of my trade? No, I would not seek his death for all the gold of Ponthieu!"

"You lie falsely. I tell you so to your teeth!"

"Think you so? Then now is the time to take bit in teeth. Hear my plan."

Boisselier decided to listen.

So it happened that that night, under cover of darkness, Courtaud heard men enter the donjon. He was cut loose from the rack, wrapped in a cloak, and two men carried him up the stone stairs. Here a warden stood with a cresset but there was the jingle of money and he let them pass. Courtaud did not struggle. Once he had been tied, all spirit of resistance left him. He seemed resigned to his fate.

Courtaud smelled fresh air—or air that was fresh compared to the donjon. It was full of smells he did not bother to identify, most unusual for him. He was carried down the silent streets to a postern which again was opened after money clinked. Boisselier bent over him and with his dagger cut the bonds that held Courtaud's feet. At last, the wolf began to struggle.

"Quiet, wolf, your succors have not failed you," whispered Boisselier. "Yet hear me, wolf or king or demon or whatever you may be. Take your pack and go elsewhere, for by the Apostle whom the pilgrims seek in Nero's meadow, if you remain here killing more helpless folk, I will play a tune on your ribs that you will not care to dance by."

"Nay, not so," came de Richemont's voice. "Stay, Sir Wolf, and take your toll of the kine along the highway. Both you and I must make a living. Yet spare the humans as Boisselier says. Surely there are enough fat beefs and tender sheep to stay your hunger."

Courtaud felt the strap confining his muzzle cut, yet he remained lying motionless on the ground. He was too weakened and dazed by his experience to run and too cowed by his captivity to show spirit. To the men, he appeared to be listening and they explained at length what they expected of him. Even the experienced Boisselier believed animals could understand human speech, at least to some extent. He never willingly killed a large animal like a stag or a bear without first explaining to the quarry why he had to die. He did this for the same reason his brother, the man-at-arms, allowed a prisoner to say an act of contrition before killing him, when it was convenient. It was part of the code of chivalry and then, too, there were such things as ghosts, both human and animal. Many men took for granted they would meet a favorite horse, or hound or hawk, in heaven. Some animal ghosts returned to earth if they had been unjustly treated, so why take chances?

Even after the men had left him, Courtaud remained motionless. Gradually his nose began to distinguish different scents and his eyes to pick up impressions. Finally he rose stiffly and walked away. He tried to run but he was too stiff. Slowly, he hobbled down to the moat and drank deeply. After several attempts, for his hindquarters were weak, he jumped into the moat and swam clumsily across. On the far side he had trouble climbing out and fell back several times. At length he grabbed a tuft of grass with his teeth and pulled himself up the bank. After resting awhile, he went on toward Montmartre.

Among the boulders, he came on the cache of one of the pack, marked with a squirt of urine. Courtaud hesitated. To disturb another wolf's cache was against all wolf custom, like taking meat away from a fellow pack member, but he was starving. He dug up the cache, which turned out to be part of a sheep, and bolted it. He had not eaten for three days. Then he went on.

He came on one of his own scent posts and sniffed it suspiciously. His own scent was strong. Still, Black Streak had also wet the spot more recently. Courtaud growled and scratched with his hind legs. He noted, however, that Black Streak had taken care not to obliterate his mark. Instead, the number-two male had wet on the ground beside it, like a female. This showed that although Black Streak had ideas about taking over command of the pack, he was still hesitant and not sure if Courtaud would return. The wolf king scratched more fiercely and growled louder. He wished he felt stronger after his captivity.

The moonlight lacquered the leaves of the dwarf oaks as he advanced. There were signs and scents of the pack everywhere. "Suddenly overcome by a desperate loneliness, Courtaud lifted his long muzzle and gave the assembly cry. He wailed it several times and then paused to listen.

There was no answer, yet he felt sure he had been heard. He howled again.

A white form materialized among the rocks. Courtaud could not be sure what it was, so he stopped. The form came closer, moving doubtfully. Then it also stopped. Courtaud half-lifted one of his forelegs and waved it in the recognition signal. The form squealed—a most undignified sound for a wolf to make, but there is no other word to describe it—and rushed forward. It was Silver.

She went half-mad with excitement and Courtaud was almost equally delighted. She nipped his lips, licked him, rolled on her back in delight while he embraced her with his forelegs and, taking her muzzle between his jaws, gently shook it back and forth. Unable to control her ecstasy, Silver left him and tore in great circles around and around the spot, going all out. Courtaud tried to chase her but he was too weak. He was forced to wait until she stopped.

Now the other wolves began to appear. For the last three days, the whole pack had been in mourning for their lost leader and badly shaken by the hunt. They had not eaten and hardly drunk. Now they went from despair to an insane joy. This sudden transition from utter depression to wild delight, from confident aggression to utmost timidity, from anger to contentment, was typical of them. They surrounded their leader, pushed him with their noses, licked his face gently, bit his lips. For once, Courtaud did not stand rigid, accepting these tributes as though he were made of stone. He returned their caresses, hugged them with his forefeet, frolicked with them in the moonlight, and acted more like an overgrown cub than a king.

Black Streak was the last to approach him and the big male was obviously nervous. Courtaud did not treat this possible threat to his position as casually as he had the lesser members of the pack. As Black Streak came up, he struck at him with bared canines but was careful to strike only the heavily furred, thick-skinned shoulder region. Black Streak instantly whined, cringed, and pulled back his lips in what looked to be a snarl but was really a grin of submission. Courtaud took his muzzle between his teeth considerably harder than he had handled the other wolves and at last released him. Black Streak slunk away, relieved to have gotten off so easily.

This happy homecoming was marred by one incident. One of the females came up to Courtaud to express her pleasure at his return, which she did rather more eagerly than had the others. To make matters worse, Courtaud responded to her antics with more than formal acknowledgment. Although she was not in estrus, he went through the motions of mounting her while she moaned with pleasure. Suddenly this play was interrupted by the return of Silver. Without so much as a snarl or warning growl, she went for the other female. In an instant they were fighting, Silver in deadly earnest, the other female trying wildly to defend herself and escape. Silver would have killed her had not Courtaud intervened, and when the dominant males saw him spring on the raging females, they added their weight and broke up the fight. Silver and Courtaud then went off together and spent the rest of the night lying side by side, Silver giving him little love nibbles until he fell into an exhausted sleep.

The next morning, while Courtaud still slept, Silver went looking for the treacherous female. The female had vanished and very wisely never returned. Silver kept a sharp lookout for her during the next few days until convinced that she was gone for good.

The king had departed for his favorite chateau at Mehun-sur-Yèvre, near Bourges, and so knew nothing of Courtaud's mysterious disappearance. When the chief judge learned that the wolf had vanished, he was alarmed but not overly surprised. He had long suspected that Courtaud was a *loup-garou* possessing supernatural powers. He regretted not having sprinkled holy water on the animal's bonds and having forgotten to attach some miraculous relics to the beast's fetters to render him helpless. Next time he would be more careful.

To the Count de Richemont's indignation and Boisselier's delight, Courtaud stopped his man-killing and even ceased to bother the herds of livestock driven into the city. Boisselier was convinced that Courtaud had heeded his warning and was now a reformed character. De Richemont felt that the wolf had betrayed him. As herd after herd was driven in safety to the black sheds of the Marché Palus, it became increasingly hard to convince the angry populace that the high prices charged for meat resulted from the ravages of the wolves. The count was sorry now he had not let Courtaud die on the gallows, for Courtaud had had enough of men—at least for a time.

* * *

Autumn was fighting with summer. The dwarf oaks had turned bronze and the vineyards that cloaked the lower slopes of Montmartre were golden, for the peasants had not dared to strip them as usual for fear of the wolves. The belling of stags sounded on the frosty mornings. It would be a bad winter, from all signs. The swans migrated south early and one morning a white-tailed sea eagle perched on a dead linden by the hill. Sea eagles came south only when the weather was extremely bad in the north.

Courtaud and his band had taken up deer hunting. The deer, especially the fallow deer, were starting to come back, now that the wars made it difficult for the nobles to practice their destructive battues. Fallow deer were a perfect prey for wolves.

The pack set out one night when the birches were silvered by moonlight and the damp mist had slobbered down. In a long line Courtaud led his followers from the hill toward the woods where the deer loved to crop the soft grasses that grew in little glades. So quietly did the pack move and so still was the night that they could hear the drip of water from the leaves in the mist. Always taking care to move into the light breeze, the pack checked several glades without success, until they finally saw the flash of white spots that glimmered like stars against the dark trees.

Cautious as the wolves were, the deer were more cautious. When the crickets stopped chirping, the herd stopped feeding. Then as the pack spread out to surround their quarry, the deer caught their scent. Every deer threw up his head as one, and a visible shudder of fear ran through the herd. The leader snorted and was gone in two great bounds, with the rest streaming after him.

Furious, Courtaud gave chase. The wolves could not equal the speed of the quarry nor could they run them down. That would take hours, and the deer could throw them off by swimming a river or taking to a lake where their scent would be lost. Yet for a while the pack pressed the herd hard.

They saw some of that spring's fawns begin to drop behind. The anxious mothers tried to wait for the offspring, encouraging them to run faster, and the strongest responded, but the weaker continued to lag. Some of the oldest deer were also finding it hard to maintain the pace. Gradually the wolves gained on these, the very young and the very old. The despairing mothers saw it was useless and were forced to save themselves, while none bothered for the old animals. Within a few miles of the glade the pack had killed. all it needed and settled down to feast. Unlike their usual custom with domestic animals, they killed no more than they needed. Chasing deer was too hard work; it was quite different with sheep or cattle.

On their way back, they heard an anxious bleating and Courtaud automatically moved toward the sound. Standing alone, looking about anxiously, was a lamb which somehow or other had gotten separated from its mother and the flock. As soon as it saw Courtaud, it ran toward him hopefully.

The wolf stood quietly and let the lamb approach him. The pack did not dare to move without the leader's permission. The lamb went up to the wolf, baaing, and sniffed at him. Courtaud sniffed the lamb. Finding that Courtaud was not its mother, the lamb went from one to another of the pack, baaing hopefully. None dared to touch it without the baron's consent. At last, the lamb returned to Courtaud and the wolf baron put out one forepaw in a playful manner and touched it. For a while the lamb forgot its hunger and romped with the giant wolf. Then, tiring of the play and remembering that it was alone and lost, it ran off. Courtaud continued on toward Montmartre with the pack after him. The lamb was fortunate that the wolves were well fed, and also lucky that it had run toward them instead of running away. The sight of a fleeing animal always triggered the wolves' hunting instinct, while to have the quarry come to them was confusing.

Not long after this the wolves were driven from their beloved hill, not by man but by an even more formidable enemy.

The deer were not the only wild animals to benefit by the constant war. The wild pigs also profited. Intelligent, highly adaptable scavengers, the pigs, even more than the wolves, had increased enormously in number. Completely omnivorous, they grazed in the fields abandoned by the terrified serfs, ate the fruit from the orchards, devoured whatever livestock was too young or weak to escape them, and, like the wolves, feasted on the bodies of humans and horses after every battle. Highly prolific—one sow might have twenty piglets in one farrow and they occasionally littered twice a year—they might almost be said to have no natural enemies. A bear might attack a sow if he found her. alone, and wolves might manage to steal some of the young pigs, but no wild animal dared to attack a sounder, or herd, of wild pigs, and not even the largest bear cared to engage a full-grown boar. Even men feared them, and to kill an old "solitary," that is, a boar that had grown so old and big that he was expelled from the sounder and lived alone, was considered a greater feat than killing a fully armed knight.

Under natural conditions, the wolf packs and the swine sounders avoided each other by mutual consent. The sounders continued to remain in the forests while the wolves by preference liked the more open country, so they seldom met. Even though both species had increased to unreasonable numbers, they did not conflict. Then nature behaved in a freakish way. For one month there was almost constant rain.

On their well-drained hill, the wolves found the rain only a minor inconvenience, but in the forests, the pigs were seriously incommoded. Their sharp hoofs sank deep into the soggy ground. They were continually drenched by the wet underbrush. Many of their best feeding places were washed out. Migrations on a large scale were common with the sounders. Hunters have a saying, "The wild boar is only a guest," meaning they never stay long in one place. Now the sounders began to move.

Thus it was that Courtaud, returning with his pack from a hunt, became aware of a particularly heavy, musky odor. He had no trouble tracing it to a certain scrub oak. Some three feet up the side of the tree the bark was frayed by a large, powerful animal rubbing against it. There were several wiry black hairs caught in the wood and a patch of black gumlike substance from which the smell was coming.

The entire pack instantly recognized the odor of wild pig and knew this was a rubbing tree where the boar had stropped his massive back, leaving a deposit from his musk gland to mark it as his territory. This was definitely disturbing. Although there was no competition over food between a sounder and a pack, still, having pigs move in was unpleasant. Courtaud wet against the oak to mark the spot as his territory and the other males duplicated his action. Silver and some of the dominant females wet on the ground. The intruders would know that they had a large pack to deal with. Still, pigs were stubborn creatures, and the pack lay down to sleep feeling concerned.

Courtaud awoke at dawn and saw, far below him on the edge of the forest, a number of moving objects. They were too far away for him to see them clearly, but he would be able to tell much from their actions. If they were cattle, they would move solidly on. If they were fallow deer, they would cross the open fields in a mad rush. If they were red deer, they would bound away. These creatures went slowly, halting every few yards with heads up to look for danger. No doubt about it. They were swine.

Courtaud rose with a low growl. Soft as it was, the sound brought every wolf to his feet in an instant. The sounder disappeared in a little grove of willows and now the pack could scent them. As the wolves were much higher than the sounder, the pigs could not scent the pack as yet.

A heavy boar stalked out of the willows and stood looking around. His scent identified him to the wolves as the pig that had marked the oak. He weighed close to four hundred pounds and stood over three feet at the shoulder. His ivory tusks gleamed dully in the morning light; they were, nearly a foot long. He had two tusks in his upper jaw and two much longer ones in his lower. Each time he champed his jaws, the upper and lower tusks honed against each other so they were kept dagger-sharp. These tusks could slay a wolf—or for that matter a man—at a single stroke.

The long-legged boar moved with a slow, lordly walk. He had a silver-gray head, black ears, black legs, and a black muzzle. He held the stump of his tail straight out behind him; most of it had been bitten off in a fight. After him came a group of younger boars two to three years old, called *ragots* by the peasants. These acted as a sort of advance guard for the sounder. Then came the sows and after them the six-month-old pigs, of a reddish color, which the people called *bétes rousses*. At the end were a few sows that had farrowed late and their broods of piglets, known as *marcassins,* still with their baby stripes. It was most unusual for so many age groups and sexes to be together, but the mass migration had upset their usual mode of living.

All the animals were covered with mud from a wallow and now they paused under a stand of oaks and beech trees to eat acorns or beech mast. Their long, flexible noses, driven by their wedge-shaped heads, rooted like animated gimlets in the soft soil, leaving furrows that looked as though they had been made by a plow. Slowly they worked their way up the hill, vanishing among the boulders.

Courtaud decided to investigate these intruders. He slipped down the hill, careful to keep the breeze blowing from the pigs to him. The pack glided after him. It was, in a sense, a fight for territory. If the pigs moved in, they could make it so unpleasant for the wolves that the pack would be forced to move out.

Courtaud had no desire to meet the sounder head on. Instead, he swung around behind them. He came on a pile of fresh pig droppings and rolled on them, rubbing his shoulders in the soft, malodorous dung. For some reason unknown to humans, the smell attracted him and he wanted to take it with him.

There were so many trails here and so much pig-scent that the wolves became confused. They cast around like a pack of hounds at fault until one of the older females, especially noted for her skill at trailing, found the line. Courtaud did not have a particularly good nose and for once he was not at the head of the pack but some distance back, with Silver.

Suddenly ahead of them was an outburst of sound as though the pack had raised the devil himself. Courtaud instantly dashed forward. The leading wolves had come unexpectedly on the rear members of the sounder, the little *marcassins*. The young pigs promptly set up the shrill alarm call that all swine recognize. The anxious mothers rushed to their offsprings' help.

Not only the mothers were coming; the *bétes rousses* and the much more formidable *ragots* were charging back, the roll of their hoofs sounding almost like a cavalry charge. A wolf had grabbed a sow by the ear, but he quickly released her to face one of the boars. The boar charged with open mouth. Unlike the wolves, who fought in silence, the pigs gave their war cry of short, deep grunts that were actually low roars. At the same time, they champed their jaws so that the foam flew, and the gnashing of their tusks gave off an ominous "click! click!" as full of menace as the roars. The wolf fled.

One of the younger wolves unwisely threw himself forward, swerving away from the *ragot* to attack a *béte rousse*. The red boar lowered his triangular head, dove under the wolf, and then jerked upward. The wolf went into the air, turned completely over, and came down on the boar's back upside down. Instantly two other pigs attacked the prostrate wolf. They trampled him with their hoofs until he was dead and then one pig rolled on the flattened corpse.

The old boar had now come up, the bristles on his back standing up so that he looked half again his real size. He pawed the ground like a bull, bit at a fallen branch, and plowed up soil with his tusks, foam from his champing jaws flying left and right. True to his usual technique, Courtaud went for the broad nose, his hindquarters going up as his head went down in typical wolf fashion. His jaws closed on the flexible mass of bristle and he locked his jaws.

The boar gave a shrill scream and instantly several other pigs came to his help. One would have ripped Courtaud from neck to rib cage as the wolf king refused to release his grip on the big boar, had not Silver rushed in and grabbed the attacker's hind leg. Courtaud could barely see what was happening around him, half-blinded as he was by the boar's bristled head and choked by the stifling stench of musk, but the noise was deafening. He was in a maelstrom of grunts, screams, growls, snarls, the click of tusks, the pounding of the pigs' hoofs, and the crash of bodies as a wolf managed to pull down one of the sounder.

Courtaud found he could not make any impression on the

boar's muzzle. It was like chewing leather. He let go and tried slashing the boar's shoulder. He could not have made a worse mistake. The boar's shoulder was protected by a shield of fat and muscle, so thick that the pigs could and often did feed on vipers, the snakes' long fangs useless against this armor. Again the boar charged him, this time not dropping his head to give Courtaud the chance for the nose hold but keeping his head up, trusting to slashing with either his left or right tusk.

Courtaud sprang to one side and the boar tore past him, unable to turn. The boar was so heavy and unwieldy that he had trouble both stopping and turning. Courtaud turned his attention to a smaller pig, a three-year-old *ragot*. Before he could close with it, he saw another wolf spring in and try to get the pig by the throat. He never got past the defending tusks. The boar went under him and with a choked grunt, flung the wolf into the air. A burst of hair flew up and the wolf fell heavily. Instantly the boar was on him, trying to get his tusks under the wolf for another toss. Seeing that the pig was occupied, Courtaud grabbed one of his hind legs and crushed it. The pig screamed, struggling to free himself while Courtaud tried to throw him over on his side. Finding him too heavy and seeing that other pigs were hastening to their comrade's help, he let go and retreated.

All about him the melee was raging. The sows shrieked, the boars roared, the younger animals squealed. Courtaud passed a boar lying so still beside a rock that the wolf did not notice him. Suddenly Courtaud found himself flying into the air. The boar had a broken tusk or the wolf king would have died there. Instead, he managed to land on his feet, and ran. The boar trotted off, looking over his shoulder at the wounded wolf.

The combat was breaking up now. The sows were retreating, the little *marcassins* trailing their mothers by scent like miniature hounds. The wolves also withdrew. After the first hysterical excitement of combat, neither side wanted to prolong the battle. The pigs never had any designs on the wolves; they only wanted to be let alone in the security of a dry, well-drained hill with easy access to the oak and beech groves and plenty of water in the swamp at the foot of the rise. The wolves never willingly engaged any opponents that would stand and fight. They had learned that pigs were the most ferocious opponents they had yet encountered and they wanted no more of them.

Still, the pack was highly reluctant to leave Montmartre. It suited their purposes exactly and they had come to regard it as their home range. For several days, they managed to coexist with the sounder, the pigs avoiding them as they avoided the pigs. But things were no longer the same. The hill slowly became polluted with pig droppings, and their overpowering scent masked all other odors. The wolves hated not being able to scent as much as they hated not being able to see. The local peasants heartily shared the wolves' aversion to the pigs, for the sounder destroyed their vineyards. They begged the nobles in Paris to allow them to kill the pigs or at least drive them away, but the nobles refused. Wild boar were noble game and could be hunted only by the nobility. Unfortunately, the nobles were not willing to hunt the pigs themselves. On the rocky slopes of Montmartre, riding was impossible, and the nobles did not care to go on foot against such adversaries. Boisselier offered to go with a small following and evacuate the sounder, but his offer was refused. It was felt that this English bastard was taking too much on himself.

It was during this strained period that the wolves and pigs met again, quite by accident.

The wolves had come on two red-deer stags fighting. By a most unusual chance, the stags had locked their antlers so they could not separate themselves and were helpless. One stag was already dead and his opponent stood with bowed head, the body of his rival dragging him down. He too would die in a day or so, but the wolves put him out of pain. The pack gorged themselves and were returning to the hill in a contented mood when they happened to stumble on the sounder going around a pile of rocks.

How it happened, neither side knew. There was no breeze, a cold snap had frozen the scent, and both groups were going silently on the mass of dead bracken that muffled all sounds. The first intimation that Courtaud had that the sounder was anywhere around was when the panic-stricken varlet tore past him, going so fast that he nearly knocked the wolf baron over. Before Courtaud could recover himself, there was an explosion of sound. Silver leaped on a boulder to be out of the way and the next instant Courtaud found himself under a mass of screaming, grunting, maddened pigs. The sharp hoofs cut him like knives and only the press of the animals saved him, for in the confusion none was able to use his tusks. Biting and writhing, Courtaud managed to get clear. As he pulled himself out of the tangle he saw a big sow grab a wolf by the leg, lift him clear of the ground with a heave of her massive shoulders, and shake him as he would have shaken a marten. The sounder seemed to have gone mad. The wolves had come upon them while they were rooting for rats among the stones and they felt themselves trapped. Courtaud came on the body of a *louvart* trampled into an unrecognizable mass of bloody flesh and shredded fur, his intestines draped like red ropes over the rocks. Half a dozen boars charged the wolf king and he ducked around the boulder where Silver had taken her stand. In doing so, he ran full into another group of pigs. Using all his speed and agility to avoid them, Courtaud gave a sixteen-foot bound, but a young boar, in striking contrast to the powerful but clumsy old males, spun around on his hind legs, turning within his own length, and gave an even longer leap, knocking the wolf off his feet. Courtaud lay helpless, but Silver leaped down in front of the boar, bit him in his rubbery muzzle, and then raced off with the raging pig after her.

Among the rocks, the wolves had no chance. Their only hope in fighting the pigs was to come from behind and hamstring them or crush the bones in their legs with a quick bite. The pigs knew this, as they had fought both wolves and dogs before, and took up their positions with their backs protected by the boulders. After a few minutes the wolves retired from the field, more than one limping badly or suffering from the knifelike slashes of the tusks.

They left the hill and lay up in the woods that night, licking each other's wounds. They were beaten and they knew it. The hill was in possession of an enemy who could not be dislodged. The next question was, where would they go now?

TEN

Death on Swift Wings

Winter was warring on autumn. The forests had disrobed for winter. The wind blew colder and stronger. There was rime on the wolves' fur in the mornings. They had begun to grow their winter coats, with six-inch guard hairs over deep cream-colored fur and woolly undercoats. Thin white ice lay on the furrows and the pack could smell snow coming.

There were swans swimming in the Seine, stopping on their migration south. Silver amused herself trying to toll them in. She had stumbled on this trick when a cub. In those days, she was well fed by her parents and more interested in playing with the big white birds than killing them, although her hunting instinct was active. It would have been difficult for any wolf pup to know when play stopped and killing began. Their games with each other consisted of growling, practicing grabbing the loins as though crippling prey, seizing muzzles, and trying for the throat hold. These were techniques the pups would later employ when hunting. Still, when little Silver first frolicked down to a pond in the Ardennes, attracted by the sight of the floating birds, she had meant them no harm. She only wanted them to play with her. She had rolled on the bank in her most enticing way, picked up a pebble in her small, white teeth and tossed it in the air, and played with her tail. These were the same motions she would have gone through to induce another wolf pup to romp with her.

The wolf's actions fascinated the swans. They had swum closer and closer. When Silver ran along the shore, they followed, only a few yards from the bank. When Silver—stopped to roll and bat at her brush with her forepaws, the swans were so curious at the sight they swam to within a few feet of her. This temptation was more than Silver could resist. She made a sudden bound and her snapping jaws came within an inch of the nearest swan's outstretched neck. The swans promptly fled, with thrashing wings and wildly beating webbed feet, but Silver had made a discovery that she never forgot. From then on, she made a practice of luring swans within reach by pretending to play. The trick worked only once on each flock, but as she grew more expert, she nearly always caught one bird. Some of the other wolves had also learned this system, either picking it up by accident as cubs, like Silver, or by watching her, but none was as clever at it as the little female. Perhaps her white coat also acted as a lure to the not especially intelligent birds.

It was well that the pack had found a supplementary source of food, even though it was only temporary, for there was every sign of a hard winter. The snow came early that year. At first it was only a pale, shroudlike mist on Montmartre. Then it spread slowly down toward the river, enveloping the city on the way. It began as a white drizzle. Then bigger and bigger flakes began to fall until everything was blotted out. It was soft as foam and the wolves were afraid to go into the low, marshy area between the hill and the city where the snow drifted deep. When snow got to be much more than a foot deep and was soft, they mired down in it. So the pack stayed in the shelter of the goblin-shaped trees twisted by the wind that grew along the lower slopes of Montmartre. Only a few strides away ran the highway from Paris to the northern *pays,* and the wolves could hear and smell the travelers on it. The travelers' horses could also scent the wolves and they nickered and blew as the ominous scent reached them. Sometimes the wolves left their lair to walk along the road, stepping in the horses' footprints, but as long as there was game available, they did not molest the humans or their livestock. Boisselier and his hounds had given them such a bad fright that they avoided any contact with men.

When the storm finally stopped, the world had turned white, and when the sun rose, the glare hurt their eyes. Each pine wore a white gown and each hill had on a white hat. Somewhere the deer were yarded up in the forest, but they were safe from the wolves, for the snow was too deep for the pack to move about.

The ravens soon located the pack and waited patiently for them to provide food. When the wolves did not move, the black birds became indignant. They cawed angrily and when that produced no response, dove at them, occasionally even striking a wolf a blow with their beaks. Finding that there was enough crust on the snow to hold them, a few of the more daring birds lit near the pack and, mincing over the slippery surface, pulled the wolves' tails, squawking with obvious delight when a furious wolf tried to chase them, only to flounder about in the snow. They would deliberately wait until the wolf was only a few feet away before flying off, croaking disdainfully.

Then it turned cruelly cold, so cold that men-at-arms guarding the convoys along the highway found that a sword hilt burned the hand. To the wolves, the cold came as a relief. Insulated by their heavy coats, they did not mind the murderous chill except that it killed the scent. During the day, the sun had melted the surface of the snow enough so when the sudden drop in temperature came, it froze hard and the wolves could walk on it. As soon as they discovered that the drifts would bear their weight, they set out looking for food when darkness came.

Softly as the shadows of clouds, they moved through the white birches, silver in the moonlight. They could make out the ribbon of the road, trampled by hundreds of hoofs and scores of feet. Then they heard, the squealing of a pig.

Instantly the whole pack froze. They stood testing the air and listening. They could smell nothing—the cold was too intense for that—but again came the squealing. Courtaud promptly swung around and made for the sound, the rest following.

It was a very noisy pig indeed. It kept up its squealing and the sound seemed to be moving. It was a domestic pig, not one of the savage wild boars, as the wolves could tell from the sound. Besides, the wild pigs never squealed except when they were tiny babies. Silver moved up until her head touched Courtaud's flank and whimpered a little. A lone pig was so unusual it worried her, but Courtaud kept on.

They saw a sleigh drawn by a single horse trotting along the road. This, too, was unusual, for humans seldom traveled at night. It was from the sleigh that the squealing was coming. Even Courtaud, usually so reckless, hesitated. His experience with the hunting leopard and later in the torture chamber had made him cautious where men were concerned. He was close enough now so that he could smell the pig and also men. There were at least two of them.

In spite of the feeling that there was something wrong here, the smell of food was too tantalizing. It was not only the pig: there was also the horse. Perhaps the men, too. The wolf king led his pack through the trees, moving parallel to the road so he could watch the sleigh for any possible danger. He continually tested the air for any scent of the spotted cat, an animal he had no desire to meet again.

Before long, they were joined by other wolves, including Black Streak and his band. Taking their cue from Courtaud, they also paralleled the road without approaching it. The horse had stopped trotting and was plodding slowly along, the driver slumped over in his seat, asleep. The pig had stopped squealing but his scent was still strong.

Abruptly a wolf broke from among the trees and rushed the sleigh. He was probably the leader of one of the lesser packs that had taken to haunting the city, for he was promptly followed by half a dozen gray shapes. So swiftly and silently did they move that they seemed to float rather than run over the snow, the moonlight making their shadows leap and bound with them. In seconds they had over-taken the slowly moving sleigh and appeared about to leap on it.

From the rear of the sleigh came a sound Courtaud and his pack knew too well: the flat crack of a crossbow. One of the wolves spun around, biting at a quarrel lodged in his shoulder. The rest scattered for the safety of the dark woods. A man rose to his knees from a barrel padded with soft straw where he had been lying in the back of the sleigh. His movement started the pig squealing again. The pig was in a cask with his tail sticking out of the bunghole, where it could be easily twisted whenever the man wanted the little creature to cry out.

The sudden report of the crossbow had an unexpected result. The horse, which had been walking in his sleep, came awake with a shock and started to run. His sleeping driver also awoke and tried to find the reins. Before he could do so, the sleigh had hit a small pine and turned over, spilling both men and the pig into the snow. The horse ran a few yards, dragging the sleigh on its side, before it pulled him to a stop.

The sight was too much for Courtaud. Now he charged with the eager pack behind him. He paid no attention to the horse or the pig but went for the man, who was still clutching his uncocked bow. The arbalister dropped his useless weapon and tried to ward off the wolf with his gloved hands. The great jaws of the wolf champed down and the man screamed. His right hand hung crushed.

The driver was shouting for help. Above his cries came the screams of the horse as it was devoured while still alive and the squeals of the pig, now squealing its last. The arbalister turned to run, futile as such a gesture was. He had not taken two paces when Courtaud gripped him by the leg and he went down. Instantly half a dozen wolves, led by Black Streak, were on him and he died as had the horse. The pack fed well that night.

They retired to the woods to sleep off their gorge and returned the next evening. Men had been there and removed everything except the bones of the horse and the red snow, red from the sunset where it was not red from blood. The wolves were furious. Anything they killed they regarded as their own property, and removing it outraged them, like the digging up of a cache or a territorial violation. They patrolled the road, trying to find out what had happened to the remains of their prey, and in doing so encountered a sleigh drawn by a single horse with a single occupant on his way to Paris. Courtaud held back, remembering the crossbow, but Black Streak and his following charged in. It appeared that they would have an easy victory, for the terrified horse shied so violently when he saw the oncoming gray forms that he nearly turned the sleigh over. The driver kept his head. He shouted to the frightened animal and beat him with the reins until he broke into a gallop. Down the rutted road they went, the horse seeming to fly while the wolves came on behind in a long line. Confident now that there was no danger, Courtaud and his pack joined the chase. The wolves were fast, but inspired by the ghastly fate he knew was hard behind him, the horse was faster. Slowly he managed to pull ahead of his pursuers. The towers of Paris appeared ahead, black against the starry sky, and the driver began shouting for the wardens to open the city gates. He was almost safe now and some of the wolves, seeing the city so close, dropped out of the chase. Black Streak and Courtaud kept on. Now they came to a little rise, the beginnings of the slope of Montmartre. The horse's speed started to slacken as he breasted, the rise. Seeing it, the wolves increased their tireless lope. In a few minutes they were up to the now exhausted animal. Black Streak hamstrung him while Courtaud sprang into the sleigh for the human victim. The wardens heard his cries and the screams of the horse. They dropped the drawbridge and opened the gates, but none was daring enough to venture out. It was not until morning light that they saw what was left of the animal, still in its harness. Of the man, nothing remained except the head, and most of that had been eaten except for the staring eyes.

From that day on, Courtaud and his pack haunted the north road. Even by day, travelers were not safe. Parties that set out were surrounded by armed guards and any attempts to bring livestock into the city by that route were abandoned. A common farewell to anyone taking this accursed way was: "May God protect you from Courtaud!" Starting with the kill made almost at the very gates of Paris itself, there was not a mile of this ill-omened highway that was not marked by one or more of the wolf king's victims. The Count de Richemont was delighted. No one dared to question the price of food, as all knew the dangers involved in bringing it to the city, and the count's *écorcheurs* could set their own prices as guards to wealthy merchants traveling north from Paris. Boisselier did penance by putting a black patch over one eye and swearing he would not remove it until Courtaud was dead. He attributed the disaster to his having dared to question the wisdom of the ecclesiastical judges. Unquestionably, Courtaud was a demon and God had used him to teach the *louvetier* a lesson. However, demon or not, Courtaud could and must be killed.

When the wolves found that they could no longer depend on the road to provide them with food, they were forced to wander wider afield. The situation had grown acute because the packs had so increased in number. Ordinarily, only a few wolf couples raised litters and of these most of the young wolves did not survive their first winter. The wars had changed that. By following the armies and living on the dead, both animal and human, the wolves had found food easy to obtain, and so the packs had increased in proportion to the food supply. Now that supply was being shut off. The wolves were desperate.

Courtaud often went off by himself to search for communities still unravaged or, better yet, isolated cottages such as the one where he had killed the little girl. On a morning of peculiar clearness when the light seemed to be filtered through a giant blue diamond, he came on such a place. A group of hurt were huddled around the stone church, but there were other, separate huts scattered among the fields. One of these especially interested the wolf because the woods came almost to the fence made of osier twigs that surrounded the house. Here was a sheepfold, its sides also of osier twisted between stakes, and a thatched roof to protect the woolly inhabitants from the weather. The top of the osier sides did not reach to the roof, so the wolf could clearly see the sheep within, as well as scent them.

The peasant had taken his pigs to an oak grove a little distance away and was throwing a stick into the trees to knock down what acorns were left for his herd. He would have been easy to kill, but Courtaud wanted nothing to do with pigs, even domestic ones. There was a line of beehives, each with its frosting of snow, bundles of faggots, and a dozen black-and-white magpies picking at grain beside the fold. It had begun to snow again and the wolf could hear the whisper of the sleet on the thatch. From within the cottage came the hum of a spinning wheel.

A group of children came from the village, driving a flock of sheep ahead of them. They paused by the tall, cylindrical dove-cote near the gate and called. After a brief pause a boy of about fourteen in a coat of badger skins came out. He was carrying a crude bayonet made by tying a knife to the end of a stick. He let out the sheep and they joined the others in the flock. Then the children set out to drive the combined flocks to the fields. The wolf noted that they had a dog with them.

Courtaud let the little party get well away from the cottage before he moved. Then he swung around in a long curve to intercept them. He knew that as soon as he struck, the dog and children would set up such a commotion that men would come running speedily to their help, so he wanted them well away from the village and the houses. He was in no hurry. They could not escape him.

The children went on, laughing and talking, while the dog drifted to and fro, herding the sheep. They came to a field where there were several haystacks covered with thatch tops made of the woven hay to protect the stacks from the elements. The peasants must have had a good year indeed, with their barns filled to overflowing, to have left these stacks in the fields. The children began pulling out armsful of hay and scattering it for the sheep, who butted each other in their eagerness to get at the fodder. It was easier to bring the sheep to the hay than the hay to the sheep. The dog, his part done, stood back, watching to see if he would be wanted.

Courtaud had been crouched down, watching intently with his great yellow eyes. Now he gathered his hind legs well under him, gauged the distance, and charged. He flashed across the snow like a crossbow bolt, but the dog saw him. He barked a warning and then leaped in front of the oncoming wolf.

The dog was an exceptionally big animal, as big as Courtaud. The wolf tried to brush him aside, snapping as he hurtled past, and tore off the dog's ear. With almost the same motion, he scored the dog heavily across his shoulder with a slash of his fangs and flung him to one side. This should have settled the matter. By all reason, the dog should have been out of the fight. But this animal was as determined as Courtaud, and as brave. He reeled back and then sprang forward, seizing the wolf by the throat.

For an instant, Courtaud was alarmed. He had not expected such resistance. Fortunately for him, the dog did not have the long, punishing jaws of a wolf and could not penetrate Courtaud's thick winter fur. Dropping his head, Courtaud fastened his jaws on the dog's leg. He heard and felt the bone crack. The wounded animal was forced to let go of the wolf's throat and instantly Courtaud had him by the back of the neck. One crunch and it was over.

The children had stood horrified spectators to the tragedy while the sheep tore away in a compact mass, their bells ringing wildly. One of the girls made the sign of the cross. The others stood motionless, numbed with terror. With the dog out of the way, Courtaud charged the children. He seized the smallest, a little boy, and started to drag him away.

At this hideous sight, the boy in the badger-skin coat made a wild rush at the wolf, stabbing with his feeble weapon. Always far braver when attacking than when being attacked, Courtaud dropped the child and retreated. He circled the little group, who tried to keep behind their champion, and, springing in, seized another child by the arm, this time a girl. He started to drag his captive off, keeping one eye on the boy with the bayonet.

One of the children muttered in terror. "Let him have Jeanne. We must run." The boy with the bayonet replied bravely, "No, I could never face her family if I ran. Besides, he does not dare to face the steel. He is nothing but a big dog." So saying, he ran at Courtaud again. Now several of the other children, ashamed of the coward's suggestion, began shouting and, having no other weapons, pelted Courtaud with snowballs. Missiles of any kind alarmed the wolf. He knew some were deadly and he had no way of gauging their effectiveness. There was a deep dip in the field here full of soft snow, and seeing that the wolf had trouble in the drifts, the children tried to drive him into the dip. They were so successful that Courtaud was forced to drop the fainting child. The older boy lunged with his bayonet, trying to drive the point into one of the wolf's eyes. He missed the eye but struck the head and the knife point grazed on Courtaud's skull. The wolf seized the blade in his teeth and for an instant it seemed as though he would tear it from the boy's grasp. Then the sharp edge cut his lips and Courtaud was forced to let go. He stood back, snarling with frustration and rage, while the boy stood between him and his intended prey. Meanwhile, in the distance, came shouts, and Courtaud could see men hurrying to the rescue. The odds were turning against him. He turned and ran.

Courtaud's defeat was to have far-reaching effects. The fame of the boy who had, virtually single-handed, driven off the *loup-garou* spread through the countryside. A local wise woman had already attended to the children's injuries by putting on poultices made of crushed nettles. The executioner from a nearby town, whose profession made him an expert on the human anatomy, condescended to see the children and rub on their wounds his standard panacea for all ills—the fat of a hanged man. Either the nettles or the fat was effective, for the children recovered, although badly scarred. The little girl would always walk with a limp and the boy bore Courtaud's teeth marks in his shoulder to the grave.

The now-famous children were brought to Paris under special guard and paraded through the streets before cheering crowds to the cathedral of Notre Dame, where they were blessed by the bishop. Several noble families wanted to adopt the young hero who had beaten the famous wolf with his puny bayonet, and it was finally decided that he was to be admitted as page in a wealthy household. True, his peasant manner of speech and behavior caused his benefactors later to change their minds, but he was still allowed to stay with the family and trained to be a man-at-arms. Most important of all, the populace lost much of their superstitious fear of Courtaud. If the wolf could be defeated by a boy armed with nothing but a knife on a stick, the monster was no *loup-garou*. Also, the sight of the two mutilated children enraged public opinion against the man-eater as no tales of his attacks could have done. A large reward was put on Courtaud, and Boisselier was told that either he came back with the wolf's head or his own would be in danger.

Boisselier needed no threats to make him anxious to take Courtaud. Not only was he revolted by the man-eater's crimes; it was a matter of personal pride with him to show that he could capture the famous outlaw. The problem was, he had no idea how to do it. His wonderful hunting leopard was useless in the deep snow. He still had his hounds and they still could track, but he knew it would be impossible for them to drive the wily wolf into an ambush. After much thought, Boisselier decided to mortify his personal pride and let another take the credit for the capture—a man he knew who possessed the only weapon capable of taking the great wolf. By special messengers, he sent word to a fellow huntsman who lived on the edge of the Black Forest in Germany.

There had been another heavy snow. The lower branches of the trees were so laden that they touched the ground. The forests shone silver in the sun. By keeping to the ridges, the pack had managed to get about and were fortunate enough to come on the body of an old hind that had foundered in a drift. They discovered her, not by sight or scent, but by watching the ravens—a reversal of the usual method in which the ravens watched the wolves. They fed up and slept in a patch of ground-growing juniper. The next day they picked the bones. The snow had become hard-packed and they moved about fairly easily.

Shortly after daybreak, they were awakened by the sound of horns blowing the *lancer,* the call to uncouple hounds. They listened without too much interest. The hounds were probably after some other quarry, and if not, they were confident that they could outdistance the dogs. It would have been different if they were surrounded and relays of hounds could be slipped in their faces, but they were on a ridge with an open view of the countryside and could see all about them.

Some of the city wolves raced past them and over the ridge. From the way the hounds were running, Courtaud was quite sure they were on these wolves' trail. That meant they would pass too close for comfort. He rose and shook himself, pausing to bite the ice from between his toes, the rest of the pack imitating him. Then the pitch of the baying changed. From the excited, eager note, the hounds could see their quarry and it was not a wolf. The deep bay of respect mixed with apprehension that they used when trailing a wolf was missing. They had probably jumped a hare.

Dimly, the wolves heard the cracking of whips, the angry shouts of men, and the repeated notes of the horn calling the recheat over and over. Courtaud settled down in the bed he had made for himself among the junipers. After a brief pause, the rest of the pack also relaxed.

For a while they heard nothing. Then the hounds broke into song and at the same time there came the call of the *menée*, meaning that the pack were on the true line. The wolves could not identify the various calls—although in a vague way they knew the difference between the impatient, often repeated recheat and the excited *bien aller*—so they lay listening. Before long, they realized that the hounds were on the trail of the city wolves and coming their way.

Courtaud gave the impression of giving some soundless order to the pack. Whether or not he actually did, the pack rose and went off in a different direction than that taken by the city wolves, Silver pausing to lick her mate's muzzle before she went with the others. Then Courtaud turned and trotted to a position where he would be sure to be seen by the hounds. Boisselier, riding a steady old cob, was watching from a grove of paper birches with a single companion: the German huntsman from the Black Forest. To Boisselier there was no doubt of Courtaud's intentions. He had deliberately chosen to take the hounds off on his own trail to protect the others, especially Silver. Often Boisselier had wondered by what madness he had joined with the Court de Richemont in releasing the wolf king. Now he knew. *Ah, Courtaud,* he thought, *why did you betray me by killing men again? Surely when I freed you, you knew it was not ransom or no ransom, but on your knightly word that you would depart out of this country or at least not kill man. Now you are lost.*

The German spoke. "Is that the man-eater who must be destroyed?"

"It is he."

"I thought as much. He is a very great *Krieger*, yet now his time has come. He will kill no more, eh, my beautiful Brynhild?"

The German spoke affectionately to a great golden eagle gripping a tall perch shaped roughly like the letter T, one end of which rested in a leather socket attached to a belt around the man's waist. The other end, somewhat higher than the man's head, had a crossbar padded with sheepskin, and on this the great bird perched. Her talons were as long as a man's finger, dagger-sharp, and backed with a grip that equaled the force of Courtaud's jaws. The bird turned her head at the sound of the man's voice, but she could not see, for her head was covered with a leather hood, embroidered with gold and silver thread. At the top was the tip of a wolf's brush that stood up like the plume in a knight's helmet.

Her owner was a middle-aged man with a face so hard it looked as though it had worn out three bodies. He wore red hose and turned-down top boots of the finest leather. He had on a close-fitting doublet and a surcoat with undersleeves. On his head was a round cap with upturned brim, embroidered with gold arrows and a crown, for he was of royal blood although a bastard. No one not of the blood royal was allowed to fly an eagle. Boisselier was far more simply dressed, in a belted tunic reaching below his knees and a cloak fastened at his throat with a single button. Behind these two men was a wretched-looking half-grown boy in buskins and a jerkin of tanned deerskin, riding a rincon. The boy was wearing a coat of wolfskin.

The German lifted the perch out of its socket and lowered it sufficiently so he could grasp the leather thongs at the back of the hood with his mouth and free hand. He pulled them so the hood was loose and, taking the wolf brush, slipped it off. At once Brynhild roused, shook herself, and then looked around with her piercing stare. She did not see Courtaud, as he was momentarily hidden by a patch of heather. Instead, she focused her attention for a moment on the hounds. Not that she had any designs on them. She had been raised among hounds ever since she had been taken as a young eyess—a nestling—from her parents' eyrie on the shores of the Baltic. But she could tell from their actions that they were on the scent of some quarry, and she knew that when that quarry emerged, she would be flown at it.

Fastened to the eagle's legs were two leather straps known as jesses and at the ends of the straps were varvels, metal rings. Through the varvels a leash was passed. The falconer pulled the leash free of the varvels and held the bird on the perch by the jesses alone. She was now ready to be released whenever the quarry might appear. The jesses would remain secured to her legs, even when she flew. They were the mark of a trained bird of prey as a collar is the mark of a domestic dog.

Courtaud did not appear as they expected. The wolf allowed himself to be seen by the pack and then turned and headed for the Seine, with the hounds in full cry behind him. He quickly outdistanced them—they were Talbots with good noses but little speed—and ran down to the edge of the water. Then he turned and sped along the bank for a hundred strides or so. Turning, he backtracked and then sprang into the water and started swimming for the far bank.

Both Boisselier and the German laughed in appreciation. They knew what would happen.

The hounds came roaring down the slope to the water's edge. Then they turned and followed Courtaud's line along the bank, still eagerly throwing their voices. When they came to the place where Courtaud had doubled back they kept on a dozen paces, still giving tongue and carried on by their own momentum and the belief that this was only a dead spot in the line, where for some reason the scent had not held. When they finally came to a check and started to cast around, they were far past the place where Courtaud had taken to the water and, as the water carried no scent, they had no means of telling where he had gone. If they had used their eyes as well as their noses they might have seen the swimming wolf, but bloodhounds were so highly specialized that they never raised their heads.

Brynhild had seen the wolf and was bent over, like a racer on his marks, waiting to be cast off. She would not fly without the additional impetus of a toss from the krakel, as the portable perch was called.

Glancing up at his eagle, the German saw that her gaze was locked on the wolf. With a shout, he raised the krakel, and with the full strength of his arm snapped it forward, hurling the eagle into the air and at the same time releasing his hold on the jesses. Even with the force of the throw which catapulted her forward, the huge bird was so heavy that she had to make several slow flaps before she built up enough speed to make herself truly airborne. With each flap she steadily increased her momentum, until she was sweeping along at a speed no land-bound crea-ture could hope to emulate. As she swooped down the hill, she banked sharply to bring herself into position to strike the swimming wolf, the tip of the long flight feathers on her left wing coming so close to the ground that they touched a patch of broom reaching above the snow. Then she leveled off and glided like a skipped stone over the water. On the distant hill, the two men shouted with delight and excitement and even the miser-able boy set up a feeble cheer while wiping his red, wet nose on his ragged sleeve.

Courtaud was totally unconscious of the winged doom rushing down on him. The eagle made no noise and there was no scent. Perhaps even worse, never in his life had he been attacked from the air, so he was completely unaccustomed to the idea. Still, the falconer, for all his experience, had made one serious mistake. It would have been better for him to have held his bird until the wolf reached the far bank. Brynhild had killed many wolves; in fact, her master derived a considerable income from the wolf pelts she provided, yet she had never attacked a wolf in water before. So as she came in, she struck at the wolf's head with her short but very strong hind talons, ripping open the flesh but not inflicting a killing blow. Then, reluctant to bind to the animal under such unusual circumstances, she checked off, turning sideways as she came around to renew the attack.

Courtaud saw the bird wheel and then come for him a second time. Dazed as he was by the blow, he retained enough sense to duck under the water. He did not entirely submerge, but the eagle was going, too fast to grasp the shifting target. Again she shot up, turned on her side, and came in for the third time. Learning from experience, she backed with her eight-foot wings, throwing her talons out in front of her. Courtaud had been forced to come up for breath and she nearly had him, but a sudden tail wind carried her too close to the wolf's head. Brynhild had learned from experience it was not wise to seize a wolf by the head, although she might slash it in passing. She veered off, and now tired, glided ashore and lit on a rock.

Courtaud reached the bank, climbed up, shook himself, and looked around for his foe. Brynhild sat motionless, watching him, getting her breath back. Not seeing her, Courtaud started across the snow-covered fields, making for a distant wood.

Brynhild took off, but without the impetus of the krakel toss she went slowly and ponderously, having considerable trouble picking up speed, especially as she was now flying uphill. As Courtaud could see behind him fairly well, he caught a glimpse of the giant bird toiling along, gaining speed with every wingbeat. Courtaud waited until the eagle was almost on him, then abruptly spun around and, leaping into the air, snapped at her golden-brown breast.

The movement was so unexpected that only by a quick twist did Brynhild manage to avoid the bite. She swung off, made a long circle, beating upward so she could come down in a swift dive, and when she had gained enough height, hung for an instant motionless in midair while with turned head she watched her adversary, planning her stoop. This time there would be no mistake.

At the instant before the eagle began her dive, Courtaud, running through a frozen mass of bracken, put up a hare from its form. The hare bounced away over the hard-packed snow, its broad furry feet acting as snowshoes. The temptation was too much for Brynhild. Hares were smaller than wolves, much easier to catch, and tasted better. She went into her dive but directed it at the hare. As she was about to strike him, the hare dodged, and Brynhild hit the snow. Panting and discouraged, she remained where she was, sitting with half-open wings, ignoring the fast-vanishing wolf.

Boisselier and the German falconer had been delayed finding a means to cross the river. They had finally located a fisherman, who rowed them and the boy over, although it meant leaving their horses behind. They came up on foot in time to see Courtaud vanishing into a pine plantation and located the disgruntled Brynhild, brown and black against the snow. The German said angrily to the boy, "Konrad, lure the bird in."

This was why the unhappy Konrad was taken along on these expeditions. He acted as a human lure to entice the eagle to return. Brynhild hated him. Konrad was a mews boy whose duty it was to clean out the house where the eagle and hawks were kept and carry the birds on his gloved fist to their blocks in the garden during good weather so they could bathe and preen themselves. One day, while he was carrying Brynhild, the eagle in a fit of irritation had struck at the boy's face and torn his cheek with the tip of her beak. Konrad had lost his temper and slapped the bird. Brynhild had an astonishing memory and never forgave him. From then on, the bird's main ambition was to get her talons into Konrad. The falconer soon discovered Brynhild's hatred for the boy and turned it to good advantage. Whenever the eagle failed to make a kill and it was necessary to retrieve her, Konrad was sent out. No matter how exasperated or tired she was, the eagle would attack the boy. Once she had fastened to him, catching her was simple.

Having received his orders, Konrad rubbed his damp nose, gave a sob, and set out on his thankless task. He was plodding through the snow when Brynhild saw him. She knew that if she made a direct attack on the boy, he would run back to the falconer. With an effort, she rose from the snow and flew, not at Konrad, but toward a distant cottage near which the boy was passing. Keeping the cottage between herself and her intended victim, she circled around, dropped low, and then abruptly shot up and over the low building. Before Konrad knew she was anywhere around, she was on him. The boy could only throw himself on the snow, covering his head with a heavy leather hood while the eagle locked her talons in his thick jacket of wolfskin.

Boisselier and the German ran up and the falconer took off the bird, although he had to tear her loose from her captive. Konrad was weeping as he rose and wiped the snow from his. body. One of the eagle's talons had gone through the jacket, inflicting only a slight wound, but the bird's grip had been so powerful he was bruised and sore.

Meanwhile, Boisselier's piqueur had managed to cross the

Seine with ten couples of hounds by means of the fisherman's boat. Boisselier pointed out to him the wood toward which Courtaud had been headed, and he set out with his hounds while the falconer tossed off Brynhild in the direction of a tall oak. The eagle lit on one of the upper branches, bare now in winter except for a few withered leaves, and looked proudly around. From this height, she could control the whole area.

When the hounds hit Courtaud's line, they broke into cry. Courtaud, half-dazed by the blow Brynhild had given him, and for the first time in his life terrified by an attacker, had found some of the city wolves lying up in the cover and dropped exhausted near them. He heard the hounds and knew what the cry meant. He was also convinced that somewhere out there his terrible winged pursuer was awaiting him.

Alas for Boisselier's belief in Courtaud's chivalry having made him show himself to the hounds to lead them away from Silver and the others! If that had indeed been Courtaud's purpose, he had learned the folly of such noble gestures and, besides, these wolves were not members of his pack. He selected the smallest and savagely attacked him. The frightened wolf bolted out of cover, swerved to avoid the oncoming hounds, and began to run.

Brynhild saw him. To her, one wolf was as good as another. Diving headfirst from the branch, she swooped across the field, hardly moving her wings except slightly to alter the angle of the widespread flight feathers to guide herself as she steered with her open tail. Her victim never had a chance. Brynhild swept down on him at the last moment, braking by dropping her bank of secondary feathers so at the moment of impact she was hardly moving, and seized the wolf across the loins with one fearful mailed fist. The wolf turned to snap at her as Brynhild knew he would. She met his open jaws with her other foot, clamping her talons around his muzzle. The tortured animal tried to leap into the air to throw her off, but Brynhild spread her great sails and, bracing herself with them, held him down. She gripped first with one foot and then with the other, kneading her struggling prisoner like dough, and every clench of her foot drove the long talons deeper and deeper into his flesh.

The wolf arched in agony and went rigid. Brynhild released her loin hold and fastened on his chest, crushing it. The wolf became limp. He was dead by the time the hounds had come up. They sniffed at him and then rolled in the bloody snow, ignored by the eagle. She had begun to tear pieces of fur from her kill's body with her hooked beak, and when Boisselier and the falconer arrived, she was gorging herself on the red meat.

Courtaud had not stayed to watch the results of his strategy. He had quietly stolen away and was now deep in the forest with Silver and his pack.

ELEVEN

The Siege of Paris

Not even the oldest could remember such a cruel winter. The weather was enough to make wolves weep and ravens sigh for pity. As the four stars of the Swan rose higher and higher in the bitter heavens, the snow and cold increased. The roads were drifted shut and Paris was shut off from the rest of the world. At first, only the poor really suffered. When communications with Chilly, a town a few miles from Paris noted for its bakeries, were stopped, there was no more white bread on the tables of the rich; only maslin. For the poor, there were no more beans, milk, eggs or cheese. Instead there was bread made of acorns and beech-nuts and not much of that. No crocks of ale with crab apples floating in the hot fluid stood by the ingle. There was weak, stale wine and then nothing except water.

Taxes increased. Every steer sold in the marketplace was taxed four sous. The tax on a pig was eight blancs. A sheep, four blancs. Only the very wealthy could afford any meat, and that seldom. Every house was taxed. If the tax was not paid, the count billeted some of his *écorcheurs* on the premises. Then the tax was paid and paid quickly, especially if there were women there.

Fires had to be kept going night and day or people would be found in the morning dead and frozen rigid. The supply of wood was exhausted and the trees in the parks and gardens were cut down. When that supply gave out, the city reeked with the smell of dried dung burning.

In the early part of the winter, gulls in large numbers had been seen along the Seine, blown inland by the wild storms at sea. Now the gulls were gone. For a while the city had been filled by the rustling flight of starlings. Now they were gone also. People gambled a few handsful of precious grain spread around twigs covered with lime made from mistletoe berries, in hopes of catching some of the pigeons that still found shelter among the gargoyles of Notre Dame. A rat sold for ten sous.

Then came a blizzard that lasted three days. The snow came straight down, each flake as big as a man's hand. When it ceased, there was a rosy glow in the sky but no true light. Landmarks vanished in the white shroud. Drifts the size of hills appeared. The roofs of the city wore shawls of snow and people began to die; first the very old, then the very young.

The wolves were able to endure the weather better than the humans. Their heavy coats rendered them almost impervious to the cold. The wild pigs had deserted Montmartre when the storm came, so the packs moved back there. Some slept together in caves for mutual warmth. Those who could not find a cave slept under the snow, which formed a blanket over them. As long as the snow was soft, they could not travel, but when it froze in the intense cold they were able to go anywhere.

It soon became necessary for the beleaguered city dwellers to bring in food or perish. From the city walls, they could see the gray shapes of the wolves that seemed to drift rather than walk over the snow. The wolves were wary now and stayed just out of bowshot except at night, when they came in to eat the bodies thrown over the wall. No ordinary expedition dared to force its way through those scores of silent sentinels. A man or a horse would be mired in the drifts over which the broad-footed wolves moved easily.

Finally the Count de Richemont sent out a picked band of *écorcheurs,* supported by his best bowmen. The wolves watched them from the hill and made no move to attack. After the menie had passed, they came down to smell the tracks but did not attempt to follow the party. People burned candles thanking the saints, and in Notre Dame a special High Mass was said. Then the city settled down to await the menie's return.

Days passed and still there was no sign of the menie. It was impossible to send messengers. Nothing less than a small army could get past Courtaud and his hordes. Holes were chopped in the ice of the frozen river and people fished through them. One man caught a fish seven feet long. It was regarded as a miracle. Others, risking their lives, slipped out at night to set snares for rabbits along the forest edge or collect what nuts they could find still on the trees. If there were no nuts, they stripped the bark from saplings. One man had an eagle owl he used to decoy birds. He hid in a blind, and when the birds came down to attack the owl, he knocked them over with a long, flexible pole. He was able to do this only twice. The third time he did not return. When his brother went to look for him, he found the feathers of the owl and bloody snow, stamped with Courtaud's great fore. The brother fled back to the city.

In one week, fourteen people were killed and eaten by the wolf packs between Montmartre and the Porte Saint-Antoine. Men prayed before leaving the city as though going into battle. For a while, no one ventured out. Then the wolves disappeared for a time. In desperation, a few of the more daring, or the more hungry, slipped out to search for anything edible. The wolves returned in a wave and killed four women. People standing on the walls could hear their screams as they were torn to pieces and devoured. In spite of this terrible lesson, the next Friday seventeen men made the same attempt, for by now people killed each other over an apple so rotten that the few remaining pigs would not eat it. The men armed themselves with homemade weapons and swore to stay together. Six got back alive. No one tried again.

Then one morning the cathedral bells rang out joyfully. The menie had been sighted and, wonder of wonders, were driving ahead of them a herd of beef cattle. The drawbridge was lowered and the gates opened. Paris was saved.

Then the wolves attacked. They seemed to materialize like evil spirits around the little group of men. Before the archers could notch their arrows or the horsemen draw their swords, the mighty Courtaud had flung himself into the midst of the herd. The herd exploded in all directions, the clumsy beeves floundering in the drifts, bawling with terror. The wolves were everywhere, killing at will. In the confusion the archers' bows were useless and the bowmen drew their knives.

Courtaud, paid no attention to the cattle. He left them for his followers. Instead, he attacked one of the mounted men. The man drew his sword as his horse's hoofs slipped and squelched in the snow, the frightened animal sidling to avoid the wolf's charge. The man struck at the wolf, leaning far from his saddle, and his sword blade struck a snow-covered rock and snapped off. The intense cold had made the steel brittle. Full of battle joy, Courtaud sprang for him, ignoring the horse, but the horse did not ignore Courtaud. Utterly uncontrollable, the animal reared, striking with his forefeet and baring his teeth as he lunged at the gray ghost. His rider slid to the ground and faced Courtaud with his broken sword, the sunlight running like water on the blade. Courtaud, trying to get behind him, tripped, rolled over, and came back on his feet. Black Streak and two other wolves were attacking the horse, one leaping in front of the animal to distract its attention while the others moved in from behind to hamstring. The horse, in its efforts to escape, collided with its master, knocking him down. Courtaud sank his teeth in the man's face, tore part of it away, and sprang back. He had severed the jugular vein, for gouts of blood squirted out. The man struggled to his knees, each of his gasps spraying the snow red. One of his friends came to his help and with a lance forced Courtaud to retreat. A little knot of archers gathered about them and with this protection, the man heard his friend's confession and, for lack of a Host, put a straw he pulled from the padding of his helmet in the dying man's mouth. They did not dare to stay, for the wolves were everywhere, with more coming up every second, drawn by the smell of fresh blood. They were forced to abandon the cattle and even leave the dead man. When one looked back a few minutes later, all that was left of the corpse were the head, intestines, and feet on the trampled, bloody snow.

That was the last time any menie attempted to break Courtaud's siege of Paris.

Boisselier was sent for, but the *louvetier* was as helpless as the rest. He had no more tricks that might serve to outwit Courtaud. Except when the rage of battle was on him, the wolf king had grown cautious. Hunger never made him reckless. He never went twice over the same path. He always studied an area carefully with eyes and nose before leaving cover. When returning to the hill, he always circled around into the wind so he could scent anything there. When possible, he took care to carry off his prey before eating it. So thoroughly did he and his followers invest Paris that a bird could not leave it without their knowledge.

Plague broke out in the starving city. The corpses were thrown over the walls in the hope that the wolves, by eating the bodies, would contract the plague. Eat the bodies the wolves did, and grew fat on them, but they appeared immune to the plague. Courtaud also feasted on the plague victims, yet was always careful to come only at night or to keep out of arrow range.

There was no handsel, the traditional giving of New Year's presents, that year in Paris. At dawn of the first day of the year 1440, when the shivering watchman on the battlements sounded his horn and the bells of Notre Dame rang the matins, there were few who bothered to listen except the waiting wolves.

Yet that was to be a day famous in the history of France. It began simply enough. As usual, the wolves slept until evening when Courtaud awoke, yawned, stretched, and went around waking the other members of the pack. There were many nose-to-nose conferences and much tail-wagging. The younger wolves played tag. Silver came up to Courtaud, waving her tail happily. She was coming into estrus and both of them knew it. Perhaps this year they could mate and raise a litter of wolf pups in a special cave they had found, well hidden in the highest part of Montmartre. Silver wanted again to feel wolflings nursing at her side. None of her first litter still lived.

The pack started down the slope toward the city to see if any food had been thrown out for them. The wind blew a scud of rain in their faces and they were grateful for the cover of the rustling aspens. Once, when a playful raven dove at Courtaud, the wolf king jumped nervously and ducked into the juniper scrub. He still remembered Brynhild. Angry and humiliated, he snarled at the black bird and continued on toward the outer fosse.

The plague had abated and there were no bodies. There had been none for several days. Nor was there any garbage, for the starving people devoured every scrap and boiled the bones for soup. The deer had yarded up deep in the forests where the wolves could not find them, so the packs had become entirely dependent on the city. Furious, Courtaud threw back his head and gave his ghastful cry, in which a few of the others joined. Within the city, people heard him and shivered, thanking God for the safety of the great walls.

It was a miserable night. Squalls blown by an east wind threw the snow in their faces as they circled the city. Whenever the wind blew the snow off a leaden bough, the bough would spring up, making the wolves leap with alarm. The wolves slipped through a patch of elder bushes, floundering on the soft snow, and then found themselves on the firm ice of the frozen Seine. They crossed the Ile Louvier where there were still a few trees, passed the bishop's tenement on the Ile Notre-Dame, and sniffed under the gate of the Porte Saint-Martin. Still they found nothing to eat.

They came to the Hôtel de Nesle, where a tower stood that marked the limits of Paris. They passed several quays, heavy with the smell of fish, and paused to sniff longingly at them. Then they came to the quay of the king's palace, fenced with a heavy iron gate that projected a few feet below water level. They were about to pass it by when Courtaud paused. There was a space under the gate. The intense cold had frozen the sources of the Seine—the Aube, Yonne, Loing, Essonne, and the Marne. So the river level had dropped sharply, leaving the bottom of the gate higher than the ice.

Courtaud investigated. It was dangerous, but from under the gate came all sorts of maddening, alluring odors of food— animal and human. Still, the wolf king hesitated, still sniffing.

What decided him was a watcher on the walls. The guard heard noises below and, thinking they were humans, released an arrow at a venture. It struck behind the wolves and the man cried, "Tell me who thou art. My bow is stretched and I will not miss again."

Feeling that his enemy was behind him, Courtaud took the lesser of two evils and slipped under the gate. Silver was at his tail and the rest of the pack silently followed. A nightmare had become reality. The wolves had breached the walls and were in Paris.

They skulked along streets black as caves, for the swallow-nest balconies that overhung the narrow ways almost met in the middle and cut off all light. Occasionally they encountered chains stretched across the way to trip running thieves. Down the center of each street ran an open drain. The wolves avoided the drains as delicately as cats, although humans often splashed through them. They passed the street of the goldsmiths, the street of the armorers, the street of the cloth workers. None of these interested them. In most of the buildings, the shops were on the first floor while the people lived in the second, so there was no scent of food. In the wealthier section, the air was heavy with the scent of pepper, cinnamon, and cloves, which those who could afford to burned at night to purify the air while they slept. The red light of fires gleamed in the windows.

Silver was moaning softly to herself. She hated anything new and strange. The pack followed the only paved street and suddenly came on two men and a girl returning from their labors in a distant part of the city. Courtaud attacked instantly. The men were armed with staffs and they tried to beat the raging animal off, thinking it was a stray dog. They soon learned differently. With the help of his followers, Courtaud pulled them down. The girl, by a strange freak, managed to escape. She had a scarf draped around her neck and the wolf attacking her grabbed the scarf. She tore it off and ran, screaming, while the pack concentrated on the men.

The noise awakened the street although most people were afraid to open their doors. The first man out was a man-at-arms, one of the city guards, who had just come off watch and had been on the point of retiring, his gambeson undershirt showing the rusty stains of his armor. He had a torch in one hand and a drawn sword in the other as he came shouting, "Out, harrow, what mischief is this?"

The wolves gave back before him. At first, the man-at-arms also thought that they were dogs, but the loping gait and lower tails told him the truth. "By Saint Richier, the wolves have come to Paris!" the man shouted. "Stay back, you devils, or I'll put a cold wind in your guts!"

At the cry, the guard's partner rushed out, brandishing a spiked mace known as a "holy water sprinkler." He went at Courtaud, who ran before him until, finding himself in a cul-de-sac, the wolf king turned. There was a cresset set in an iron sconce on the wall, and by its light the guard saw the reddish-gray form with the white chest and the short tail. For the first time he realized what he had been chasing. He dropped the club and fled back to the house, half fainting from terror.

Lights were springing up in house after house as the wolves tore great gobs of flesh from their two victims, bolting the mouthfuls without bothering to chew, while keeping an eye and ear on the rising excitement around them. They ran, some still carrying pieces of flesh in their jaws. The street led into the Parvis, the great open square before the cathedral. There had been a mass at Notre Dame to pray for the city's deliverance and the congregation was just leaving the great building. The wolves attacked with great bounds. One of their first victims was a butcher, perhaps because he smelled of blood; Courtaud tore the arm off a child in spite of the parents' efforts. One man happened to have an axe, for he had been chopping a little wood that remained, and he put his back against the stone arcade of the church and held off his assailants.

Several people were scalped as the wolves tore at their heads. Many escaped but forty were killed and partly eaten. No one dared to challenge the pack even when dawn came and the wolves were still at their feast. Silver, alone, remembered the way back to the water gate. Once she had eaten her fill she had been trying to induce the others to throw off their blood glut and leave the city. Now, with daylight, they recovered their customary caution and followed her to safety.

This raid was the wolves' greatest triumph. They had penetrated into the heart of Paris, killed at will, and escaped unscathed. The people were close to panic.

The king had returned to Paris and he sent for Boisselier. The *louvetier* found the monarch on the ground floor of his palace, as the king had a phobia that upper floors would collapse under him. One once had and he had never gotten over it. Two men-at-arms stood on either side of the throne, both as stiff as their halberds. Boisselier knelt, already knowing what his orders would be.

The king rubbed his big nose and stared at the kneeling blond giant with the patch over his eye.

"*Louvetier,* this beast is an enemy of God, pity, and mercy. What think you, is he possessed of the devil that he can defy my hunters and soldiers and even the walls of my city and 'scape away alive?"

"My lord, he is only a beast and I have no more respect for him than I have for Mohammed. Make me high constable of the city and I swear to you that within a month either he or I will be dead without remedy."

The king pulled his heavy lower lip.

"It is said that a white wolf is always at his side. Think you that he is a witch and the other is his familiar?"

"Nay, sire, the white wolf is his mate. Wolves join for life and are always together, never being unfaithful to each other."

"You seek to deceive me, bastard. Is it not a saying, 'No wolf knows his own father,' for they couple like dogs? And do not men say of a bastard, 'He is like a wolf, for he knows not his father'?"

"These sayings are lies, my lord. Every wolf knows his parents, who together raise and nurture him. He owes them obedience and through them he serves the pack, dying if need be that the pack may survive."

"My noble cousin, the Duke of Burgundy, has three wives, twenty-four mistresses, and sixteen bastards. Do you tell me to my teeth that a wolf is nobler than a duke?"

"The duke is a Christian, my lord, and can hence receive absolution for his acts, if he has not been given an indulgence beforehand. Wolves could not survive if they behaved like humans, for a pair must stand together against the world and in defense of their offspring."

The king considered this. "Is it true that every wolf in the pack must obey his king?"

"It is, my lord. Otherwise, they would be lost, for their strength is only in him, for he provides them with food."

"I would that my nobles had as much loyalty as wolves and also as much intelligence, for now each man thinks only of himself and can defy me at will." The king sat musing for a time. "It may be, Boisselier, that if the English are ever to be driven from this land, it will be by an army of men-at-arms composed not of nobles but of any man who is willing to make a living by fighting and knowing how to use arms. That will be the end of the feudal levies that come and go as their various lords wish. When that day comes, the king will be greater than any duke, or even greater than all the dukes together, and this whole land will be known as France rather than only the small *pays* about Paris."

"If Your Majesty can see that so clearly, then Courtaud is not a demon but has been sent to you by God."

"It may be. The church says that Joan, the Maid, was a witch, but she won me my throne. Perhaps this wolf will win me France if I but follow his lead. There is one other matter. We must find a weapon stronger than the English longbows. It may be we have it in the new bombards, or as they are being called, cannon. There is now even a light bombard that can be held to the shoulder, called a gonne. The English despise them and retain their bows, much as our chivalry refused to change their way of fighting even after Crécy, Poitiers, and Agincourt, and continued to charge English bowmen standing in their accursed 'herce' formation."

"They would have thought it cowardice to do otherwise."

"Yes, yes, they were willing to die to the last man—but they died. I have been thinking of these wolves and how they hold my whole city of Paris at naught. What think you of a menie made of men who depend on the king and the king alone for their bounty, who think of war not as a game or a means of gaining ransom, but as a way of life, and are armed with bombards and gonnes?"

"Once in derision Your Majesty was called 'the King of Bourges' for that was your only domain. If you can bring about such a plan, I say you will be known as 'Charles the Victorious.'"

The king smiled. "It may be, it may be. Yet here I am shut up in Paris like a bird in a cage, and at this rate few of us will see the spring. Can you destroy this beast?"

"May I never know God's forgiveness if within a month he ever feels heat or cold again."

"Then for one month you are my high constable. Give what orders you will."

Boisselier's first order was to seal the river gate by which the wolves had entered the city. His next was that no one, man, woman or child, was to leave the city for any purpose whatsoever. His third was that nothing was to be thrown over the walls.

Two weeks the *louvetier* waited. Meanwhile, the packs grew increasingly desperate. For the first time, if a wolf became too weak to defend itself, the others would tear it to pieces. This showed that the packs were starving indeed, for it was their custom to bring food to an injured comrade and do all they could to help one in trouble. The watchers on the walls observed this and told each other that wolves were ruthless even to their own kind, forgetting that cannibalism was not infrequent in the starving city.

From the walls, the Count de Richemont and Boisselier stood watching the gray forms. Courtaud was easily distinguished by his great size and short tail. As usual, Silver was with him.

"He has made many orphans," remarked the count. "Many an entrail has been strewn and many a brain scattered by him."

"The same is true of you and your *écorcheurs*," remarked Boisselier.

"True. But what would you? If God Himself were a man-at-arms, He would be a cutthroat. But old Short-Tail has gone too far. How shall we get rid of the wolves, *louvetier*? Tell me the secret and I will give you whatever you wish."

"Stop the wars."

The count laughed. "I would enrich you, not spoil my honor," and he walked away.

At the end of two weeks, Boisselier ordered a number of the few remaining beeves in Paris to be brought to the Parvis and there butchered. The entrails were left in the square and all streets were blocked except the one leading to the water gate. The gate was raised a few feet that evening.

No wolves came that night nor the second. On the third, the smell of the meat was too much for them. A few crept in, fed, and then stole out again. Boisselier let them go. The next night there were more, and still more on the fifth night.

Now Boisselier ordered twenty beeves slaughtered in the Parvis. Even humans could smell the strong odor of blood and fresh meat. That night, scores of wolves passed under the lifted gate and feasted on the carcasses. There still remained the question, was Courtaud among them? In the dark, no one could tell.

Boisselier gave the order to lower the water gate. He, himself made sure all streets leading into the Parvis were blocked. There were twenty-one churches overlooking the square as well as the Hôtel Dieu. Boisselier stationed archers in all of them. He took up his own position in the Hôtel.

When dawn came, the Parvis was packed with the slinking gray forms. People watching from rooftops chattered like magpies. As usual, when the wolves found themselves trapped, they lost all spirit. A child could have killed them.

Boisselier saw Silver first. The female's white pelt made her stand out. She was crouched by a fountain with a broad basin supported by four pillars. Looking more carefully, the *louvetier* saw the wolf king squatting under the basin.

When it was fully light, Boisselier turned to his piqueur and said, "Sound '*Aux alviers*.'"

The piqueur raised his horn and blew the signal, which meant to man the ramparts. The archers bent their bows and the arrow storm poured down on the helpless animals. Many ran for a long time before bleeding to death from the broadheads that sliced through veins and arteries. When Silver was struck, she refused to run and died beside Courtaud.

The wolf king was safe from arrows, shielded by the basin. When there were no more wolves left alive in the Parvis, Boisselier drew his Poitevin dagger and told the piqueur, "I am going down to him."

"Nay, my lord, loose the alaunts on him or at the least, if go you must, go in armor. Better yet, remain here and let the men-at-arms finish him."

"Few of my calling die in bed. I would hold myself a coward to stay here."

"Then guard your gullet, my lord."

Boisselier descended the stairs and the door was opened for him. Slowly he walked across the Parvis, now littered with the carcasses of the slain beeves and the dead wolves. Courtaud watched him but did not move.

"Come, wolf king, you who know so well how to kill should also know how to die," Boisselier told him. Still Courtaud did not move. "Beast, you will kill no more." The *louvetier* approached the quiet animal, his dagger held point foremost before him.

The wolf king had been lying with eyes wide open, a sure sign of fear. Boisselier was confident he would make no resistance to the steel. A pure-bred wolf probably would not have done so, but Courtaud was part alaunt. Abruptly, Boisselier saw the eyes narrow to slits and the tail stiffen and rise. He knew what that meant, but before he could recover himself Courtaud was on him. For the last time, Courtaud was able to clamp on his famous head grip. As his jaws locked, Boisselier stabbed him. Man and beast fell dead together, the black patch over the *louvetier*'s eye slipping off. After all, there was no further need for it: Boisselier's oath had been fulfilled.

The siege of Paris was over.

From the cathedral, the choir set up a Te Deum.

An enterprising bourgeois had two men hoist Courtaud's heavy body into a barrow, propped open the mouth to make him look more terrible, and took the corpse through the streets of the city, charging ten francs to anyone who wished to touch the famous monster. Silver was flayed and her rich, white pelt sold to a wealthy lady for a large sum.

Boisselier would not have approved of that had he still been alive. He would have wanted them to be buried together.

ABOUT THE AUTHOR

Daniel P. Mannix was an award-winning American author and journalist, as well as a magician and filmmaker. Mannix's magazine articles about his experiences in the carnival, where he performed under the stage name "The Great Zadma," became popular in the mid-1940s and were compiled with the assistance of his wife in the book *Step Right Up!* His dozens of books and extensive essays range in subject from children's animal stories, environmental issues, and hunting accounts to historical examinations of the Hellfire Club, the Atlantic slave trade, and the Roman gladiatorial games. Mannix was particularly interested in the Wizard of Oz canon and composed a biography of L. Frank Baum for *American Heritage* magazine in the 1960s.

DANIEL P. MANNIX

FROM OPEN ROAD MEDIA

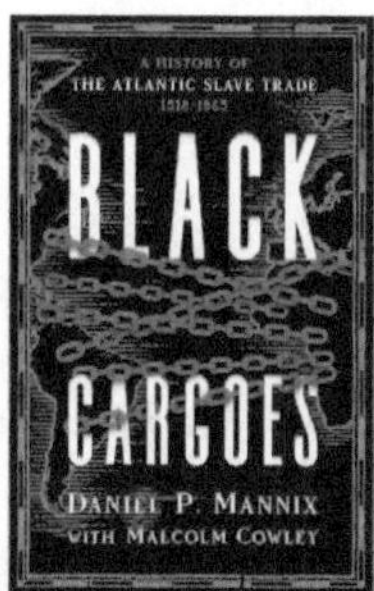

EARLY BIRD BOOKS
FRESH DEALS, DELIVERED DAILY